FOLLOW YOUR HEART

Wars of the Roses Brides Book 2

RUTH KAUFMAN

FOLLOW YOUR HEART

Cover Art by The Killion Group, Inc.
Interior Formatting by Author E M S

Contact: www.ruthkaufman.com

Published in the United States of America.

For Romance Writers of America® and Chicago-North RWA:
Thank you for all of the craft and industry knowledge and amazing
colleagues and friends.

England 1460: Joanna Peyntor has two uses for a man: to pose for a stained glass window design or to commission her skills. But when her brother conspires to ruin her reputation, she concedes to a third: a husband to help save her glass-painting workshop.

On a quest to redeem his family name and lands, Sir Adrian Bedford must marry without delay. But what woman he'd accept would wed an impoverished former nobleman who insists on an unusual stricture in their marriage contract? Joanna, a woman striving to succeed in a man's world, agrees that discussions of a personal nature are prohibited.

When irresistible attraction makes their marriage of convenience inconvenient, will his dangerous secrets keep them from following their hearts?

Praise for Ruth Kaufman's *At His Command* Wars of the Roses Brides Book 1

A wonderful debut sure to please lovers of romance!
   – *NYT* & *USA Today* bestselling author Madeline Hunter

With a bold knight and a strong-willed lady, Kaufman's story is positively medieval.
   – *NYT* & *USA Today* bestselling author Tracy Anne Warren

If a book lingers in my mind for more than two weeks, then I say the author has certainly deserved to be put on my keeper shelf.
   – Bookworm2bookworm

PROLOGUE

York, England 1442

The old woman's unearthly wails carried over the sibilant whispers of the crowd.

"Save me. Someone save me!"

Chills coursed through twelve-year-old Adrian Bedford. He looked around the large courtyard, watching each spectator make the sign of the cross. Some seemed fearful, others angry. His mother was grief-stricken; his father clutched her tightly so she would not fall. His twin Andrew looked as confused as Adrian felt.

For in the center of the yard, bound to a splintery stake, stood their grandmother. Three men held torches to the kindling piled high beneath her bare feet. To burn her as a witch.

"Use green wood instead! Make her suffer longer!" someone yelled. A few others took up the cry, stamping their feet in the dirt.

"Don't look too close, she's got the evil eye!" a woman shrieked.

The public display sickened Adrian. What had his grandmother done wrong? Why was it so terrible to know things before they happened? She'd helped many people by warning them before disaster struck. His father and the vicar told him that Grandmother came from the devil. That good Christians did not see the future, hear voices in their heads or dream such dreams. Yet Grandmother had always been kinder and more interested in him than his own parents. She had told him he was destined for greatness. Why would she lie?

But if she were a good woman, why would the vicar and his parents allow this to happen? Why would they let her burn?

He looked away.

The vicar took Adrian's head between his bony hands, forcing him to watch as the hungry flames licked ever higher. The old woman's tattered gown caught in a rush of blazing orange. Bile rose in Adrian's throat. He almost disgraced himself by vomiting. He slid his fingers into the pouch attached to his belt, seeking the scarf Grandmother had given him only a few days ago. The silky fabric comforted him.

Then Grandmother spoke. No fear lingered in her face, now suffused with mystical calm. Her voice, normally soft and soothing, projected harsh and compelling.

"Hear me! 'Tis the truth I speak. You will soon see it is so!"

Grandmother's words seeped into him, easing his nerves and giving him strength. Her withered face bore no sign of strain, no indication of the pain she must be feeling as the flames surrounded her, climbing relentlessly. Her gray hair floated up eerily in the wind from the blaze. If any had thought her innocent before, now all were convinced she was a witch. Otherwise how could she be talking? Shouldn't she be screaming?

All eyes were on her, every ear straining to listen against the crackling and snapping fire. For a witch's last words would be passed on for years to come.

Her head turned against the pole and she looked straight at Adrian. Her gaze bored into him, branding him in a way he could not describe.

No, he thought. *Leave me alone or they'll know that I'm like you. I'm afraid!*

Grandmother looked away with a slight nod as though she heeded his warning. "Evil cannot be burned. Be ever vigilant. Only then can you escape the prison of a troubled mind. Who is worthy of your trust? Follow your heart."

She exhaled, a small sigh barely audible above the popping, burning wood. Her head drooped, chin meeting chest. The blindingly bright wall of flames encompassed her with a whoosh.

"I love you...." Adrian whispered, suppressing tears as his mother sobbed beside him.

Grandmother's final words echoed in his mind. Were they a special message for him or the meaningless ramblings of an old woman? They would haunt him until he knew the answer. As would the horrors of this day. The unforgettable sights and odors of burning flesh, of his grandmother.

The person he loved most in all the world.

CHAPTER 1

York, England – November, 1460

Redemption. It was the only thing that mattered to Sir Adrian Bedford. He'd do anything to redeem his family's position, no matter how low he himself had to sink or how degrading the task.

Until the bony, sour-smelling dowager sprawled across his lap as he sat in Bedford Manor's great hall.

He had to pay redemption's steep price by playing the paramour.

This deed tested his principles, but what he stood to gain outweighed his hatred of the means. So he smiled at the one woman who could help him serve his country and restore his family's losses.

Open to the waist, Lady Anne Uffington's velvet gown exposed her small breasts to the harsh light of morning. Sunlight filtered through the tall stained glass windows, turning her sallow complexion into a mosaic of brilliant reds and blues. The glowing colors couldn't alleviate her distasteful assault on his senses. Nor could they dispel the rank odor of one who rarely bathed. He'd seen her tub. Why didn't she use it?

"Touch me," she said, placing his hand on her waist.

Adrian held his breath. He could do this. He had to, though vines of shame snared his heart and aversion besieged the rest of him.

Her high voice quavered. "Hold me. I want your strong arms around me." She ran her gnarled fingers over his biceps, across his chest, then between his thighs. "Do you want me?"

"Yes," he said, hating the lie as much as the untenable position he was in.

"You're lying."

"What did you expect? This was your idea."

"You get what you want, I get what I want." Her fingers tightened around him once again.

"Then content yourself with that." Adrian regretted speaking. He should've mollified her, not snapped.

Disgust surged in his gut. But he'd accepted this devil's bargain. Every man had to make sacrifices to achieve his goals.

"You agreed to visit me, yet you cannot even try to enjoy being here?" she asked.

Adrian looked away to avoid the obvious desire in her gaze.

After a few more moments of Lady Anne's fumbling and his carefully placed caresses, he satisfied her. The lady covered herself with the rich but faded velvet, a smile lifting her thin lips.

He dressed, ready to drink the requisite cup of wine. Staying after that would only prolong his misery.

"Next week, come to me at night instead of the morning."

"Night trysts were not part of our arrangement," Adrian said, biting back harsher words.

He'd not spend the night with her, nor sleep in her bed. The thought of being that close to her for that long on her musty, stained sheets was the least of it. Just as he wouldn't comment about her appalling odor, he couldn't discuss his other reasons for preferring daylight meetings. And the more time he spent with her, the more opportunity for her to uncover elements of his personality he didn't wish to reveal. He could never allow that.

He was close, so close. This dalliance with Lady Anne would shorten his path to restoring the family name his father destroyed. Adrian had spent decades trying to right his father's wrongs, starting with accusing Grandmother. Succeeding was the only way he could make his life worthwhile.

He gulped the last of his wine, anxious to leave. At least it was good wine, not the cheap swill he could afford.

He heard a knock at the door.

"Enter!" Lady Anne called.

The arched door opened with a high-pitched creak. A stooped servant announced a visitor.

"Ah, yes. The glazenwright. Send her in."

Excellent timing. Adrian could use the visitor's arrival as an excuse to depart.

"Until next week, then." She clasped his hand between hers. He subdued the urge to pull free. "Please go out the back door."

"The back door?" Lady Anne had never asked this. And usually he offered at least two farewells before she stopped asking him to stay. Yet he couldn't stop wondering what business Lady Anne had with a glass-painter. "Why are you so eager for me to leave?"

"I am not sure you should meet…"

Too late. The glazenwright entered the hall as Lady Anne reached around his neck to bring him down for a farewell kiss.

Avoiding her mouth, his lips met her parchment-dry cheek. He caught sight of the glazenwright. A woman glass-painter? Chagrin filled him as she stopped short, taking in the scene before her. She put a roll of documents on the table and pushed back the hood of her cloak.

Adrian straightened, his desire to leave evaporating despite the awkward situation. The glazenwright was beautiful, with a delicate oval face, high cheekbones and a small, straight nose. He knew he was staring, but didn't want to stop. There was something compelling about this woman aside from her lovely face, which was all he could see. Her heavy, serviceable black cloak and headdress concealed the rest.

Her expression captured him. Not the simpering moue of court women, nor the lustful gleam of barmaids or the respectful, downcast eyes of servants. She radiated a quiet confidence he found enticing.

Their gazes met and locked. Hers conveyed curiosity and mayhap a challenge. He couldn't tell if she recognized him or what she'd gleaned of his relationship with Lady Anne. Surely she'd be appalled if she knew. After a long moment, she looked away.

"My pardon, Lady Anne. Your servant bid me enter. I can wait or return another time," she said.

Accustomed to Lady Anne's shrill waver, Adrian absorbed the pleasant, soothing tone of the guest's voice.

"No, no, now is fine," Lady Anne replied, her hand sliding possessively down Adrian's arm.

He stepped back abruptly to detach the clinging fingers. Lady Anne should know better. The servants might suspect something, but no one else needed to know. That wasn't part of their arrangement.

Distancing himself from Lady Anne allowed him to return his attention to the glazenwright. She was staring at him again. If only he could see her hair…was it the same shade of red as her delicately curved eyebrows? He cursed the fashionable concealing headdresses of the day.

Her skin was fair and smooth, her lips delectable, a tempting rosy red. Her large eyes were green. Bright green. They pierced him with a keen alertness that made him wonder if she could see into his soul.

She must be intrepid as well as ambitious: a woman working as a glass-painter. He wanted to know more about her.

He wanted her.

If only he was like other men. But he couldn't risk getting close to anyone. Because a secret encumbered him, so unfathomable it could destroy him and possibly anyone he cared for.

What would being free feel like? Being loved by a woman like her? Alas, he'd never know.

Redemption, not love, would be his salvation. Soon he'd earn his freedom from the miseries of his past. His approach might be convoluted and unconventional, but given his situation ordinary means wouldn't serve. Once he completed his mission, his twin Andrew could wed and continue the family line, while Adrian would live alone with his dogs and the satisfaction of achieving his goal. Given his perilous affliction, he couldn't ask for more.

"Your mutual absorption has gone on long enough," Lady Anne said. "Let us get to business." She tugged at Adrian's sleeve. "Are you staying, then?"

He moved too far away for her to touch him again. Every man had his limits. "Perhaps."

He appreciated Lady Anne's discretion in not introducing

him to her guest. Still, the stretching silence made him uncomfortable. Lady Anne poured herself more wine, the sloshing loud in the quiet.

The glazenwright made her way around the rectangular room, studying the elaborate windows that reached up three of the walls. Sunbeams turned blue, green and red by the stained glass danced upon her face as she moved, turning her into an unearthly being. The jewel tones highlighted and enhanced the loveliness of this glazenwright, transforming her into a woman of mystery and enticing possibilities.

Adrian forced his thoughts from her to the magnificent windows. Each wall told the story of a different saint, replete with symbols of heraldry and detailed borders. They were old, like many things in the manor house, but they didn't seem to be in disrepair or in need of a glazenwright's services. He could find no reason to make any changes in this home.

This home, which was once his.

🐝🐝

After studying the glorious windows, Joanna Peyntor turned her attention to Lady Anne's visitor, an exceptionally handsome man. Had he truly kissed her patron?

As her artist's gaze skimmed over his striking features and the elegant cut of his black tunic, a strange tingling raced through her. His unfashionably long hair was thick, slightly wavy and the blackest black, like the arnement she painted on her glass.

There were two uses for a man in her world: a face to be used for a design or a source of gold to commission her services. He looked as though he could fulfill either role.

Had she ever seen such a perfect chin? Joanna noted his broad shoulders, though like his imposing height they were less important than the sculpted angles of his face. She pictured him draped in velvet. Red velvet. He'd be perfect for the window of St. George and the Dragon she had planned. She had to get him to pose for her. But how? One didn't just say, "I need your chin, please let me draw you." Not everyone shared her artistic fervor.

Immersed in admiring him, Joanna realized she was staring. She turned away to view the many windows again. She felt his gaze on her, following her. Almost as if he touched her. The strange tingling returned and intensified. Joanna was glad her back was to him. Certainly a blush brightened her cheeks.

Lady Anne asked, "Did you bring the designs?"

So there were to be none of the customary niceties. Why didn't Lady Anne think her worthy of an introduction? Because she was a woman involved in trade? What was this handsome, finely dressed man, likely of noble descent, to the lady?

"Of course," she answered.

As Joanna unrolled her drawings, Lady Anne turned to him. "I've decided to replace some of the windows in the hall. Perhaps the chapel, too." She sounded as if she taunted him.

The man stiffened, his lips tightening. The lowering of his dark brows was impressive. Perhaps he could represent a more sinister character. Some day she might need a fiend or devil.

He sat heavily on a carved chair and glared at Joanna with eyes the brilliant blue of the glass jewels she often used. She refused to cower, though he seemed to blame her for something. Why should he care what Lady Anne did to her windows?

Lady Anne sipped her wine. "Bedford Castle. It isn't even a castle, but a lovely manor house. Perhaps I should rename it. What think you of Uffington Manor?"

The man took a deep breath and clamped his lips together.

"Of course this house has such a history, I could never think of doing such a thing." Lady Anne waved her goblet in the air, the wine surging to the rim and threatening to spill. She laughed, a scratchy sound that reminded Joanna of metal scraping glass.

Joanna sat beside her at the broad, highly polished table.

"There is no need for you to remain," Lady Anne told the man. "I must speak with Mistress Peyntor. I look forward to next week."

He stood, towering above them, his expression unreadable. Without a word, he grabbed his cloak and left.

Joanna closed her eyes briefly, committing his features to memory so she could sketch them. It wasn't likely their paths would cross again.

❧ ❧

Two hours later, Joanna's booted feet crunched the snow as she walked, clutching her designs and huddling into her cloak to hide her face from the wind. She spared no attention to the houses and shops she passed as she made her way back from Walmgate. The faster she walked, the sooner she'd reach her workshop with its cozy fire and could get back to work. The sooner she could focus on finding a solution to her troubles with her brother.

Lady Anne's wavering presented a new problem. She'd requested more major changes and hadn't approved the final version of a single window. Joanna stood to earn a sizeable profit once Lady Anne made up her mind. Because of this, only for Lady Anne did she draw on costly paper. For other clients, she sketched each design right onto her worktable.

Though frequent alterations took more time and work, Joanna didn't complain because Lady Anne paid her deposits, and on time. She couldn't afford to anger a good client by letting impatience get the best of her.

Joanna desperately needed Lady Anne's coin in her coffers.

She was about to cross Foss Bridge when a deep voice called, "Mistress Peyntor!"

Joanna turned, knowing before she saw the speaker who she'd see.

Him.

The exquisite man from Lady Anne's looked even more attractive in the full light of day. His eyes, so incredibly blue, so clear, met hers. Latent power in his gaze sent a shiver through her. His hair glistened in the sun. Astride a huge brown horse, his cloak swirling about in the wind, he intrigued her as no other man had.

Had he waited in the cold the entire time she was ensconced with Lady Anne? Her heart fluttered. What could he want with her? She dared not hope he felt the same unsettling sense of fascination she did. The same desire to learn more.

"I am Lord Fitzhugh. Might I have a few moments of your time?"

A noble, as she'd suspected. He certainly had the bearing of one. Too bad noblemen and craftsmen didn't often mix, except to conduct business. Just as well, she knew, but she couldn't dispel a sensation of regret.

"What can I do for you, my lord?" she asked.

He dismounted gracefully. "To hear that Lady Anne is removing some of Bedford Castle's windows saddened me. I have oft admired them." His breath wafted in white clouds. "Did you recommend that they be changed?"

She'd clung to a shred of hope that something about her had called to him the way something about him connected with her. But why should he find her interesting? She was a struggling, hard-working glass-painter with calluses on her fingers, not one of the fine, pampered ladies he must know. Or perhaps was already married to.

"No. Removing them was Lady Anne's idea," she answered. "I merely recommended that their frames and some of the armature—the framework—be repaired. They could be restored for far less than new windows will cost."

"To destroy such beauty seems a waste. Can any be salvaged and reinstalled elsewhere?" He stroked his horse's neck.

What would those long fingers feel like on her skin? Her mouth went dry. Never before had she longed for a man to touch her. She shook her head to dispel her strong reaction to this man.

"Perhaps Lady Anne would give the windows to you, if you asked," she said, burning to know the nature of his relationship with her.

Lord Fitzhugh looked at the ground before answering, his hair falling over his face, then lifting in the wind. "I'd rather she not know I want them. I'll pay for them, of course."

What was he hiding? The windows meant enough to him that he asked her join him in keeping a secret from her client. If she agreed, Lord Fitzhugh would be in her debt.

How could she use this to her advantage?

"'Tis not an easy task you've set me to," she said. "The windows are large, and almost a hundred years old. Removing them could weaken the leading."

"I assume you can repair any damage."

His respect for her skills made her smile. "I paint, design and cut the glass. I know of others who could do the repair work. I'll agree if you'd do me a favor in return."

His straight black eyebrows shot up. "What might that be?"

"I need someone to pose for my next window. You would suit."

How dare she be so bold? But as her father always said, what was life for if she didn't try to attain the things she desired? Joanna held her breath. Please say yes, she prayed silently. She wanted to spend more time studying Lord Fitzhugh.

And not only for the windows.

Only recently, and with great reluctance, had she pondered a third use for a man. From what she'd seen of Lord Fitzhugh, he might be a perfect fit for this, too. A noble who exuded power to protect her from her brother William's schemes to wrest control of her workshop.

Over the course of several drawing sessions she might be able to persuade him to help her, if he was equally as chivalrous as he looked.

Joanna believed in destiny. As the sun shone brighter, illuminating him from behind with a mystical glow, she prayed that her destiny was this man.

⁂

Two surprises in one day, Adrian thought. First Lady Anne's pronouncement, which she knew would infuriate him, about changing windows that had decorated his family home for centuries. Now an unusual woman presented a strange request.

She reminded him of a Van Eyck painting he'd once seen of a Madonna, pale and pure, yet with an inner core of steel. The wind tugged a curling red tendril from her headdress. It tossed in the gusts and dangled near her mouth. Enticing. His groin tightened.

He wished he hadn't had to lie to her by making up a name when he introduced himself. Though certain tales of his family's history were well known, he'd worked hard to maintain some privacy, especially about his arrangement with Lady Anne. He was fortunate that the glazenwright hadn't recognized him. Who knew who her other customers were?

He'd hoped the false title would make her aware of the differences in their stations and prevent her from asking too many questions. How could he take the lie back now? How many more lies would he have to tell her? He pushed aside a wave of remorse.

Joanna drew her cloak about her against the wind, looking at him with alert expectation. The cold tinged her cheeks crimson. He wanted to take her in his arms and keep her warm.

But he knew better than to get involved.

"Will you sit for me?" she asked.

This was going too far. Adrian had hoped to conclude their business quickly, with any future contact in writing. He'd not intended to see her again after today, despite the fact that her beauty and demeanor had captivated him from the moment she walked into the hall.

Sitting for a window was no worse than things he'd already done in the name of redemption. But the more people caught up in his life, the more danger he might bring to them and to himself. The more likely that Andrew would learn who Adrian worked for.

Adrian had to keep these secrets from his proper, religious twin, whose disapproval could lead to Adrian's downfall. The Lady Anne arrangement alone would bring on a fit of righteousness. If Andrew also learned who employed his twin, he could send the carefully built scaffold of Adrian's life tumbling to the ground. Bad enough Andrew knew he was like their Grandmother.

Adrian reminded himself of his goal. Visualizing himself at home in Bedford washed away any lingering doubts. He would sit for Mistress Peyntor. He wanted those windows, even though he'd have to relinquish some of his hard-earned gold and precious time to salvage them.

Another setback on the long road to recovery.

"How long will this take?"

"That depends on your patience, but three sessions should suffice. A small price to pay for such lovely windows," she said, with a small, knowing smile.

Aha. He'd seen that look on many women. Maybe she was like the others, always conniving, plotting to acquire men, coin or jewels. Maybe she wasn't as unique as she seemed or as he hoped.

Her character shouldn't matter. Only her ability to preserve his windows.

"My workshop is on Stonegate," she said. "I have another commission I must finish this week. Shall we say Monday next?"

Three afternoons, as she said a small price to pay for such valuable windows. For a part of his heritage. Even so, intuition warned him that spending time with her would not be wise. Her mere presence aroused him. Her beauty, her manner interested him too much already. He could not, ever, care for a woman. It would be his undoing.

Suddenly his heart skipped a few beats. Dizziness washed over him. Reality faded as the beginnings of a vision swirled before him.

Not now!

Adrian squeezed his eyes shut and held his breath. Slowly, the signs of an imminent vision faded. He'd managed to stave off an unwanted glimpse of the future.

His breath came out in a rush. He was safe, for the moment.

You see, he silently admonished himself, *you see how dangerous this could be?*

He opened his eyes and saw Joanna. The eager expression on her face swayed him against his better judgment.

"Shall we say early afternoon?" he asked.

And prayed he wasn't making a mistake.

CHAPTER 2

top making demands of me," Joanna's half-sister Margery complained as she tucked her fair hair into a headdress. "I hate when you do that."

"I'll not work while you preen. Besides, how can you snare a husband if all you do is stare in your mirror?" Annoyed by Margery's reluctance to contribute, Joanna snatched a ribbon Margery had left on the floor of their bed chamber and tossed it to her.

Margery, who sat before a small table, dropped the ribbon amidst a heap of jars, pots and combs. "How can I make a suitable match while selling your designs like a common merchant?"

"You *are* a merchant." She made sure her tone hid her frustration. Margery responded better to reason than nagging. "If only you'd accept the truth, we'd both be happier. Some merchants are as wealthy as the nobility."

Joanna crossed the short distance to the room that served as kitchen, eating and living area. She wet a cloth in a pitcher of water and wiped crumbs from their morning meal from the narrow wood table.

"I won't go to Lady Anne's today," Margery said.

Joanna squeezed the damp crumbs in her fist. How she wanted to throw them at her sister. But she'd only have to clean them up again. Instead she dropped the crumbs into the slop bucket.

"If I discuss final revisions I won't have time to finish Henry de Mamesfield's window, which is behind schedule. And someone is coming to pose for another window this afternoon," she replied.

"Why? Designs can be reused. If a single cartoon can become twelve of the saints in York Minster's choir, you can use yours again." Margery adjusted her headdress as Joanna rejoined her in the bedroom. "Let William take on some responsibility. He and John Twygge could run the workshop. You'd paint and design, for John's thick fingers are good for nothing except lead work. And he hasn't a creative thought in his ugly head."

Joanna cringed. She wouldn't let Margery's suggestion unsettle her. "You know how hard I've worked. How much Father wanted me to be in charge."

"Think on it," Margery suggested. "You'd have far less to worry about and more time to create. You inherited the talent. All I got was father's lovely golden hair." Margery turned to study her reflection. "I might add that those dark circles under your eyes won't help you find a husband."

"I've had other things on my mind." Joanna smoothed her skirts, noting their practical but plain wool. Unlike Margery, she wouldn't waste her coin on things she didn't need. "Marriage would hinder my work. A husband would want to control me or not want me to work with glass at all."

Joanna refused to admit Margery had made a few good points. Did she look tired? She forced herself not to peek in the mirror, but couldn't seem to stop her fingers from feeling for bags under her eyes.

"If I go to Lady Anne's I'll miss the chance to play merrills with Lady Elizabeth." Margery sighed as if she'd never recover from such a lost opportunity.

"Stop being selfish. I may be the best painter, but you're better at dealing with the customers," Joanna said. "I lack patience. Sometimes I want to scream when they dawdle over their choices. I thought you enjoyed writing up the commissions."

"I'm sure there are worse occupations," Margery allowed as she pinched her cheeks.

Joanna had tried to protect Margery from the severity of their financial woes. But she had to reveal the latest reason why giving control to their brother would be a bad idea. Margery might understand at last.

"Stop your pinching and pay attention," she said. "I don't know how much longer I can work with John. He asked me to marry him last week. And William wishes it."

Joanna shuddered at the thought. And shuddered again, because her brother's support of such an unseemly plan showed how little he cared for her.

Margery tilted her head and frowned. "That can't be true. You're making up a tale so I'll go to Lady Anne's."

Like the scrape of a stick removing paint from glass, her half-sister's tone abraded Joanna's nerves. She'd hoped to find solace by confiding in her.

"Your expression says you aren't making it up. Oh, Joanna." Margery took Joanna's hands in hers. "How could William choose such a husband for you? Our brother used to display better judgment. John's never in a good mood, nor is he kind. And he's ugly."

"He'd make a horrible husband," Joanna agreed.

"Then we must each find a better man to wed. I'm so tired of working, of living on our own."

Joanna clenched her fingers to keep from shaking her sister. "For one moment, Margery, just one, try to understand the pressure of wanting to accomplish something. Of being a woman trying to succeed amongst men, in their world."

Margery looked at her blankly.

Joanna sighed. No matter how hard she tried to explain, Margery would never understand her quest to achieve success in her chosen craft.

As a young girl, she'd sat beside her father's table, watching him draw and cut glass, admiring his skill and yearning for the day when she'd be of an age to design and create objects of such beauty and meaning. Fortunately Father recognized and appreciated her talent, allowing her to train to be one of the few women glazenwrights. But being a woman alone in a man's world was a constant challenge.

She already had enough trouble with mere months left, according to the terms of her father's will, to turn a sizeable profit.

Failure lurked outside her door.

Every moment she'd spent drawing lately had been tainted by anxiety. Anxiety now bordering on desperation.

She wouldn't fail. William and John would not win. No matter what.

Could she advance Margery's ambition and her own?

"Mayhap a client will have a son or friend for you to marry," she said. "Lady Anne had a most handsome visitor last week. He might be there again."

Joanna wished she could suck those words back in. Strange, but she thought of Lord Fitzhugh as hers. She didn't want to share her time with him, especially with her lovely half noble half-sister.

Though she and Lord Fitzhugh had shared only a brief conversation, something powerful had passed between them. Joanna had sensed the curious connection at Bedford Castle, along with that constant awareness of his presence even when her back was turned.

Today he'd pose for her. She couldn't bring herself to tell Margery that an attractive, noble and possibly available man would be in her shop. If he saw her half-sister, for certes he'd prefer her perfect face and golden hair, which would complement his dark looks so well.

What Lord Fitzhugh thought should make no difference. She'd seen him touch Lady Anne, a memory that made her stomach curdle. Perhaps he was Lady Anne's lover. Or perhaps some fortunate woman's husband.

Joanna had no time for romance, even if a noble deigned to court her. Work consumed all of her energy. As it must, despite Margery's words of warning, to keep the workshop out of William's clutches.

But thoughts of Lord Fitzhugh kept interfering. No man had affected her so. A shared moment, an undercurrent of interest was all it took for this man to wend his way into her mind. Perhaps she'd read more into their talk than she should.

She had to focus on her windows. Already she'd wasted time reliving her meeting with Lord Fitzhugh and anticipating today's sitting instead of applying herself to the tasks at hand.

"I'm going to work." Joanna descended the steep flight of stairs leading to her studio.

Satisfaction filled her as she opened the door. She'd come so far, salvaging the remnants of her father's workshop after his death. He'd been ill for so long, barely able to work near the end. Yet Joanna hadn't refused his feeble attempts to contribute, for she knew how useless he felt as his abilities dwindled.

Margery followed her down, went outside to open the shutters, then settled at a table layered with pieces of parchment.

Joanna analyzed the design she'd drawn on her whitewashed glazing table. The Madonna and Child under an ornamented canopy were carefully detailed with the aid of a compass and ruler, with all of the colors she'd use designated by letters and symbols.

She'd already cut pieces from glass sheets of various colors by splitting the sheets with a hot iron. After using a grozing iron to trim the edges, she'd placed the pieces on the appropriate areas of the design. Her favorite glass was flashed-ruby, white glass with a thin coat of red blown onto only one side.

Now she needed to paint several pieces with arnement, special black paint. For this window, she'd need a quill in addition to a squirrel hair brush, so she could pick out the intricate shading she envisioned for the Madonna's robes.

Engrossed in painting a fine line around the Madonna's eye, Joanna jumped when a knock sounded at the front door. A client, or her handsome noble, arriving early?

Margery walked to the door as Joanna set her brush aside. Her heart sank. What if Lord Fitzhugh was smitten by Margery at first sight? No matter. Joanna had no room in her life for flirtation.

John Twygge, a mammoth of a man with stringy hair and a misshapen nose, stormed into her studio. "I want to talk to you, Joanna. Now." He turned to Margery. "Get out."

His pockmarked face flushed red, the veins on his thick neck stood out as he pointed toward the door.

Though her eyes were round with shock, Margery stood her ground. "No. You can't make me leave."

John stomped toward her, fist raised. "Can't I? I said, get out!"

With a fleeting look of sympathy mingled with fear, Margery

grabbed her cloak off its peg and ran out. John slammed the heavy portal behind her.

Joanna managed a pleasant expression though her knees trembled and her heart raced. John clearly wanted her to be afraid. She wouldn't give him that power. He hadn't actually hit Margery, she reassured herself. Threats resulted in fear only if you let them.

"You have no hold over me," she said, keeping her voice low and calm. "*You* work for *me*."

"I'm through yielding to you. Starting now." He stalked toward her.

Joanna refused to back away. She swallowed, then took a deep breath. "I'll not tolerate your hostile behavior. Cease now, or lose your position."

John moved closer, leering at her, trapping her against her design table with his bulky arms. He smelled of ale and stale sweat. She felt the pressure of her cut out glass pieces through her gown as he pushed her onto the table.

"Mistress Peyntor." He sneered and leaned closer. "The woman glass-painter. Thinks she's better than the rest of us. I'll show you. It'll be so easy to ruin you."

Anger penetrated fear. How dare he treat her this way? His sour breath invaded her nostrils as she fought to move.

"How many clients have taken their orders elsewhere since your father died, because you are a female? Because your work isn't as good as your father's. Like All Saints Church—"

"Let me up," she demanded. "That's not true. Why are you doing this? You know how hard I've worked and how far the workshop has come." She struggled for air under John's suffocating weight. "And you know even while my father was alive, I did much of the designing and painting. I've been a master in my own right for years." She shoved ineffectively at his barrel chest. "Let me go."

"You have worked hard, hard as a *female* can," John admitted. "Not enough. With a man to manage things while you keep to the painting, we can do much more." He loomed over her, his beard-stubbled face inches from her own. "You're slipping, Joanna. What of the window you ruined…the commission for Edward of Wykeham?"

The painful memory slashed through her, as real as when the disaster occurred. "I don't know how that window broke."

"I do," he said with a self-satisfied smirk. "You've taken to drinking. Out of despair that you might lose the shop to William if you don't earn enough coin in time." He laughed. "Everyone at the guild knows what was in your father's will."

Joanna gasped. "'Twas you. You destroyed that window! It doesn't matter. No one will believe such lies about me."

"Lies, are they? By the time I'm through, they'll be truths. If you don't do as I say, I'll destroy you, piece by piece."

John reached behind her. He held up a section of white glass, the Madonna's head, and threw it to the ground.

She flinched as the glass shattered.

"Just like that."

Again she tried to free herself. John bore down. Her back ached from being crushed against the table. Fear slithered through her veins. Her employee, whom she'd trusted, had been plotting against her. How could she repair the damage he'd done?

"Whatever you say, it'll be your word against mine. Most of my clients don't know you well. They'd never trust you instead of me," she said.

"You are smart, for a woman. But I'm smarter. I've a way to get to your clients. I've already begun," he warned, a smug expression on his face. "Look there—take it."

He nodded toward his waist, keeping Joanna pinned between his arms. She couldn't break free, but she could grasp the rolled parchment protruding from his wide leather belt. Her fingers trembled as she examined the document.

"No...." she breathed, tears forming as she read the notice of cancellation. "How can this be? I'm behind schedule on Sir Reginald's window, but he said a short delay wouldn't be a problem...."

"Remember yesterday at the Mermaid Tavern? Sir Reginald was there. He saw you drinking. Didn't take much to make him think you're spending more time with a pitcher of ale in your hand than a paint brush of late."

"I had half a cup of ale! You had at least three."

"That's what you say. Now that Sir Reginald believes you've

become a drunkard, he'll serve as a reference to warn others of your unreliable ways. Such a shame." John shook his head with false concern.

Joanna forced herself to remain calm, but her mind raced. Margery might've gone to get help. Just who she'd find, Joanna didn't know. Again she wished she had a man to protect her from her brother. John would never have dared act this way if she had a husband.

She had to get away. With a mighty tug, she freed her left hand. Her fingers scrabbled across her table. Charcoal. *No.* Piece of glass. *Not sharp enough.* A closing nail....

She couldn't reach it. Tamping down frustration, Joanna tried another approach.

"What do you want from me?"

He leaned closer, pressing her still harder against the table. "You know. I want you to marry me." He stroked her hair, the gentle motions a contrast to his hostile attitude. "Now you'll have no choice but to be my bride. I get what I want. There's no one to help you. William's on my side, Margery's just another woman. You have no one else. No one cares what happens to you."

His words hurt because they were true. No one did care.

"Perhaps there's some truth in what you say. I'll need a week or two to consider your proposal." She forced the words out with effort enough to wring a wet gown dry. "For the moment, we must get back to work. Let me up."

John's hands on her hair made her feel as though dozens of ants crawled on her scalp. She shook her head, but his fingers tightened. Squeezed.

"No work until you say yes."

His breath, his furrowed brow, his tone, everything about him repulsed her. But to free herself, to have time to plan and seek aid, she had to tell him what he wanted to hear. She'd say "Yes," though the lie would curdle on her tongue.

"I don't want to marry you!" Joanna spat instead, instantly regretting her outburst. She was supposed to be mollifying John, not antagonizing him. "If you drive away clients there'll be no workshop to run, whether I marry you or not."

Had she been too engrossed in her work to see what was

happening around her? Could she have prevented his rebellion?

"Easily fixed," he said with smug satisfaction. "I'll say with my guidance you're much recovered and returned to your industrious self. Even I can't find fault with your talent. I could never create the windows you do."

The reasoning for this mad plan came to her in a flash. "If I lose the workshop to William, you'll be nothing but his employee. If I maintain control and you marry me, everything I own will be yours, too."

She couldn't go on, she was that sickened. Like the master glazier who once offered for her, John wanted to marry her only to control her and everything she stood for. Theirs would be a marriage of sheer domination, without a single pleasant aspect. Without a single benefit to her.

No matter her problems, she wouldn't be coerced into a travesty of marriage with John.

"You'd try to force me to do things your way. I won't. I will fight for my workshop until I take my last breath," she vowed. "If I die, then where will you be?"

"You're not listening, Joanna. Pay attention." He grabbed her face with a meaty hand and squeezed her cheeks hard. "You will marry me. As soon as possible."

John bent lower, his face inches from hers. His body pressed against her, crushing her. "You will marry me because I won't let you out of my sight until you do."

CHAPTER 3

Three afternoons alone with Mistress Peyntor. A perfect amount of time for a pleasant flirtation with only slight risk, Adrian decided. Opportunities to converse with women, especially interesting and intelligent ones, came all too rarely. He'd make the most of this, then savor the memories. That would be that.

He walked down the paved street in search of her workshop. The red-tiled roof crowded close together with its neighbors, with the upper story hanging over the lower, seeming to reach for the house across the narrow street.

Adrian knocked. No answer. He opened the door slowly, then poked his head in. A man had Joanna bent backward over a large white table and was kissing her greedily.

She deserved a passionate husband or lover. Yet the sight of her in another man's embrace irked him. Why did he care? Joanna meant nothing to him.

He should leave. But he couldn't help but admire Joanna's unbound hair. An unusual vivid red, it spilled about her in dozens of curls. Her companion clutched a thick handful. Adrian itched to feel the softness. With an inward sigh of longing for what could never be, he backed away. This was none of his business.

Joanna cried out. She wriggled and shoved. The man stood abruptly, grabbing his lip.

"Bitch!" he hissed. He shook her, sending her curls bouncing in all directions.

"John, stop!" Joanna screamed.

Joanna wasn't enjoying a lover's embrace. She was in trouble.

The need to protect her surged through Adrian's veins. He rushed forward.

"You bit me!" John smacked her in the face.

Too late.

Joanna flew off the table, sweeping pieces of colored glass with her, and knocked over a smaller table crowded with pots of paint. She collapsed to the floor with a crash, black paint splattering and glass shattering all over her and against the wall. She didn't move.

Catching sight of Adrian, John roared, "Who the hell are you?"

"Who the hell are you?" Adrian yelled back. He wanted to see to Joanna, but had to get past his opponent first. John, though not quite as tall, was far broader.

"I am her betrothed. What goes on here is none of your business," John said.

Betrothed? Joanna didn't belong with a lout like this. The thought of her with a man who hit her made him ill, but he couldn't justify intervening. Betrothal was almost as good as being married. If a man beat his woman, there was little even a concerned relative could do to help.

An anguished moan from Joanna sent them both hurrying toward her. She sat up, her hand touching her cheek, which bled from a small cut. A smear of black paint mingled with blood on her pale skin. She looked up at John, green eyes huge with fear. Then she saw Adrian. A deep sigh evidenced her relief and the worry lines faded from her forehead.

Ignoring the larger man, she turned to Adrian. "I'm glad you were early."

"Who the hell *are* you?" John demanded.

"A friend," Adrian answered, keeping his gaze on Joanna.

He extended his hand to help her to her feet. Hers felt small and fragile in his. Though anger at John's treatment of Joanna seethed, he matched her calm tone. "I'm never late, nor am I fond of those who are."

Glass fragments dropped from Joanna's skirts onto the wood floor. She trembled as she stood. He fought the desire to comfort her. She walked to the counter, crunching bits of glass beneath her feet, then picked up a jar filled with brushes. As if ignoring the facts that she'd been swatted like an insect and her cheek was bleeding. How could she be so at ease? She must be furious.

Adrian wanted to clobber John.

"She doesn't need you. Get out," John demanded.

Adrian stepped between them. "Or?"

"Or this!"

John took a swing at him. Though Adrian raised his arm in defense and deflected the brunt of the blow, John's massive fist connected with his eye.

The pain infuriated him. He swung back, hitting John in the stomach.

"Ooof." John doubled over.

Adrian smiled.

"Shall we get started?" Joanna asked from behind him. She walked behind her counter and gathered parchment and brushes.

He couldn't comprehend her composure. Most women he knew would've fainted or would be in hysterics by now. Maybe she acted as though men fighting in her workshop was a common occurrence because she didn't want John to know he'd upset her.

That he understood. Never let the enemy see your fear.

"Aren't you going to introduce me to your betrothed?" he asked.

An unladylike snort was his answer. "Is that what he said? John is not my betrothed, nor does he work for me any longer." She came around the counter, regarding John with as much disdain as a duchess might use to stare down an underling. "You're dismissed, effective immediately. I'll send any wages owed."

Adrian heard a slight quiver in her voice. He could almost see the effort she used to control her emotions. Almost see panic in her eyes. How could he alleviate her distress?

Clutching his belly, John stepped toward Joanna. Adrian tensed, ready to spring if he attempted to touch her.

"We're not finished. William and I will see to that," John said.

He turned to Adrian. "As to you, hero, if I see you again you'll regret it."

John shot a glare at Joanna, then stomped out and slammed the heavy door.

The minute he was gone, Joanna heaved a sigh and slid down the wall to the floor. At last she revealed her fear.

Adrian bent down to her. He smelled paint and rose water. "How can I help?"

"I'm fine." She took his proffered hand. "A bit shaken, but fine. John has never behaved like that. I...."

She shook her head, sending her curls tumbling over his fingers. So silky, so sweet-smelling...exactly as he'd imagined. He clamped down the urge to caress them.

She let him pull her to her feet, then freed her hand.

"Your cheek is bleeding," he said, concerned. He picked up a clean cloth from her counter, then dipped it in a pitcher of water. "May I?"

When she nodded, he moved closer. The odd mix of paint and roses washed over him again. He sensed her studying him as he gently dabbed the cloth against her cheek and wiped away the blood. The curve of her jaw, the fullness of her lips tempted him to abandon the cloth so he could touch her skin.

She reached up, her fingers grazing the back of his hand. The slight, unintentional contact sparked desire.

"My face. Do you think it will scar?"

"No. The cut is small, and not very deep. Does it hurt?"

"Not as much as John's betrayal," she answered. She caught her breath, as though she'd revealed too much. "Lord Fitzhugh. You arrived at a most opportune time. I don't know what I'd have done without you. I'm so sorry you were hurt on my behalf."

"My timing was a bit off," he replied. Had he moved seconds sooner, he could've stopped John from hitting Joanna.

"Your turn. I'll get a cool cloth for that eye."

Adrian had had worse injuries, but didn't want to pass up the opportunity to have her tend to him.

She wet another cloth in the pitcher, then perched on the tall stool beside him. "Closer."

He leaned down as she lifted the cloth to his face. The

coolness soothed his eye but her nearness warmed the rest of him. He closed his good eye against the sudden urge to kiss her. Did she have any idea how attractive she was to him? That he wanted her?

"Hold that," she said.

He held the cloth while she used another to wipe the worst of the black paint from her hands. "Are you sure you're all right?"

"Yes. I don't know how to thank you. My sister should return soon, and then I'll be fine."

Adrian doubted that. Curiosity urged him to try to find out who William was and what John was really after. With his uninjured eye he watched her every move. He admired her efforts to be independent and brave, but could see she needed comforting.

He had to erase this need to hold her and protect her. Though he wanted to help Joanna, her problems weren't his.

Yet he asked, "What if John returns?"

"If John returns...." She shuddered. After a long moment, she turned to look at him, a strange expression on her face. "Are you married?"

Adrian dropped the cloth.

"Are you married?" she repeated.

"No."

"Would you like to be?"

How could he answer that? Yes, he would. *Could* he be? Unlikely. How could he live with someone the way he was?

To stall for time, he looked around the small studio, taking in whitewashed walls, sheets of glass stacked in bins, the table with what remained of her work in progress and various tools he couldn't identify arranged neatly on a counter.

What should he tell Joanna? She didn't even know his real name. Normally, he was a good liar. He'd had to be to survive. Yet he couldn't bring himself to lie again to this beautiful woman, who just by being in the same room stirred a strange yearning within him.

"My name isn't Lord Fitzhugh."

Her expression told him it was her turn to be taken aback. "Oh?"

He pulled another stool closer to her and sat. He picked up the damp cloth and wiped his hands. "I am Sir Adrian Bedford."

Nothing could be heard but their breathing.

Her remarkable green eyes widened. "Sir Adrian Bedford."

Hearing his true name on her lips pleased him.

Joanna nodded. "I see now why you used another name when we first spoke."

So she'd heard the stories about his family, which still circulated after all these years. He'd expected that, one reason he'd concealed his true identity. But what did she believe, truth or rumors?

She tossed a dirty cloth into a small bin. Then her mouth formed an O. His heart sank. Would she understand?

"The stained glass windows. Bedford Castle was your home. Of course I'll do my best to preserve them for you."

Relief washed through him like a cleansing rain. There was no disdain, no fear, no revulsion in her face. Just acceptance. Maybe even understanding.

"What have you heard?" His voice came out a whisper.

It was important to him that she not believe the rumors. He could almost see the vapor of dread hovering above him, awaiting her answer before it blossomed into an enveloping cloud that would spoil their fledgling friendship.

"A sadly romantic tale. That your mother died and your father couldn't tolerate life without her. He gambled away everything, even Bedford Castle. And borrowed from his friends, debts he couldn't repay," she said. "Is that true?"

"Yes. But I'm working to earn everything back."

Enough truth. Joanna's opinion of him would worsen if she knew what he had to do to regain his home. Her acceptance of his explanation for giving her a false name and her sympathy for his plight meant more to him than he could say.

"Then why would she make changes, especially if she knows you wouldn't approve?" she asked.

"I was too angry last week to ask," he admitted. She must want to hurt him in some way, for not caring about her or some such womanly grief.

Joanna thought for a moment. "I also remember hearing that your grandmother had a part to play. What happened to her?"

The urge to unburden himself, to share at least some of his past, was overwhelming. For the first time in years, he wanted someone to know more. No, he wanted *Joanna* to know more. He could acknowledge now the fragile tie that bound them from the instant they met. Adrian wanted to strengthen that intangible connection despite the price he might have to pay.

Then again, telling her would make him vulnerable, which no man wanted to be.

"My father thought my mother's mother was a witch because she had the Sight and had visions of the future. In his eyes, her death was the only way to protect the family from her taint," he explained. "When I was twelve, he turned her in to the authorities. I saw her burned at the stake." Truth won out. Vulnerability was as unpleasant as he'd thought, though tempered by a sense of freedom. "How horrible! Such a sad tale," Joanna said. "How could he betray her?"

Were those tears glinting in her eyes?

Adrian wouldn't let her sympathy affect him. "He believed his actions were for the best. That he was protecting the rest of us."

Thank God his father never learned Adrian too had uncontrollable visions of the future. Or he'd have sizzled along with his grandmother.

Joanna swiped her cheek. "Wait. You said 'Sir' when you told me your true name. Why not 'Lord?' Didn't you inherit your father's title?"

She noticed too much. He didn't want to go into that, having said too much already. "Perhaps another time."

What had he been thinking? His father's demise was common gossip at court, as was the tale of his grandmother's death. Joanna couldn't know the truth of his affliction. No one did, except his twin. His dire need to have someone understand what could not be understood had made him jump to hasty conclusions.

Joanna sat up straighter and squared her shoulders. "Do you want children?"

He started. This had to be the most unusual conversation he'd ever had. And how had he wound up revealing so much of himself when what he wanted was to learn more about her?

"I would like an heir of my body, as most men do." A truthful, but not a complete answer.

He hated the way the secrets he had to keep interfered with daily life. Only one reason he often kept to himself.

"Of course you would," she replied with a nod.

She leaned forward, her curls covering her injured cheek, tempting him to touch. He could see flecks of gold in her eyes. Her gaze was so intense, he couldn't break away. Not that he wanted to.

Heat pooled in his groin. He had to kiss her. Now. He leaned toward her.

"What I'm about to ask is most irregular and seems quite sudden, but I don't know where else to turn." She swallowed. And swallowed again. "Sir Adrian, would you marry me?"

He almost fell off his stool. He had no idea that this was where she was going with her questions.

"Will I marry you?" he parroted, stunned.

"I wanted to be independent," she said, her gaze steady. "And to believe that a woman alone could succeed. Maybe some can. But recently I've had…difficulties with my brother William and John, as you've seen." She looked down, as though what she was about to say embarrassed her. "I don't know how far they're willing to go to get what they want. After what happened today, I must accept that a man's protection would be valuable. My shop must thrive or—"

"Or what?"

Her expression was unfathomable. "Or I'll lose it. My father left me the studio and his supplies in his will, but if I don't earn enough profit by a certain date all goes to William. He's promised John more responsibility and money if I fail." Joanna took a deep breath, as though she fought back tears. "John has been undermining my work by lying to clients. He destroyed a window I'd almost finished and blamed me.

"With a husband like you, I'd have enough power to keep them at bay. I wouldn't have to fear them."

"But—"

"Please, let me finish." She focused her complete attention on him. He could feel her trying to persuade him. "I wish I didn't, but I need a man like you. You may not be noble now, but you're still a knight. You have connections to people with money, people who might commission a window.

His surprise faded as he absorbed her explanation.

"Equally important, you don't work with glass," she continued. "After my father died, a master glazier offered for me. He hoped to combine our shops. Of course I couldn't take the proposal seriously. For he only wanted one thing."

"To marry a beautiful woman?" Adrian dunked the damp cloth in the water pitcher and replaced it on his aching eye.

She flashed him a look saying she hadn't expected him to understand. "He was interested only in my painting and designs, and wanted to own my talent and have me under his control. The advice of a mentor is one thing, to be ordered about like a servant is another. I refuse to be a mere employee serving a master. I'll be an equal partner, nothing less."

Joanna looked away, perhaps disconcerted by exposing her innermost thoughts. She walked to the corner, picked up the broom and clenched the handle. "I realize this is unexpected. And that, whatever happened to your title, you come from nobility while I don't," she continued over the tinkling sound of broken glass as she swept. "I believe we can reach an amicable arrangement. Unless you hope to marry for money. Though I imagine rich heiresses are in relatively short supply these days, what with the problems between the king and the Yorkists."

Her unforeseen offer intrigued one part of him and appalled the rest. What was he to make of her dismissive attitude toward such a serious subject? Nobles and tradesmen... tradeswomen...rarely wed.

"Most marriages are transactions arranged for financial reasons or political gain by parents or relatives. Not the spouses themselves," he said, setting the now-warm cloth on the counter.

"I have no parents and don't trust my brother. We're both far older than most when they marry," she replied. "People like us, people with goals, must take matters into our own hands. We must look to the most practicable way to achieve our dreams."

"You don't harbor romantic visions of marrying for love?"

"Once I did. As a girl hopes and dreams. But few women,

even the most highly-ranked, can choose whom they'll wed. Pleasure is fleeting. It doesn't merge great holdings or pay for sheets of glass or food. I can't afford to waste time trying to find someone whose kisses make me sigh, however pleasant that might be. Can you?"

"I suppose not," he agreed. For more reasons than he dared reveal. "But you don't even know me."

"Many marriages are made without the spouses knowing each other well. And I do know you. You are kind, determined, and very strong," she said. "You'll be wealthy again, for I know you'll accomplish your goals. I assume you have all of your teeth. What more can a woman ask of a spouse?"

Her implicit faith overwhelmed him. No one, even his own brother, had ever offered him such trust. Everyone else insisted on proof first. Even then people were wary of his next venture until it too succeeded.

"You might not want to bind yourself to a craftsman—"

Adrian cut her off. "It's not that. You can't know what you are asking."

He bit his tongue to keep from telling her why he couldn't marry her, though he wanted her with him and beneath him.

She continued, "I'll provide your heirs, and as much gold as I can. You'll support me in my glass-painting as needed. I warn you: my work comes first." She rested the broom against the wall and sat across from him. "Cooking and sewing have no place in my repertoire. Is that understood? Perhaps we should write the terms into a contract. And attach our seals, so we know exactly where we stand."

"Joanna...." Adrian didn't know what to say.

He reluctantly acknowledged her idea had some merit. An impersonal marriage might be the solution to his problems, too. As the older twin by five minutes, he'd once dreamed of continuing the family line after restoring his estates, but feared marriage was too great a chance for him to take. She was right that if he could marry, his bride should be noble, to enhance his family's standing in society. On the other hand, until he recovered his estates and title, he'd have little chance of finding a noble bride. He'd never considered marrying a merchant or other commoner. It wasn't often done.

And what about Andrew? He'd be furious if Adrian had children, for he expected to remain Adrian's heir, assuming there'd be something to inherit. His twin had suffered too, and had kept his foremost secret. Thus far. Would Andrew remain silent if Adrian accepted Joanna's proposal?

He noted the expectant look on Joanna's face. She was industrious and determined. She was lovely and he desired her. Most important, she trusted him. But it was too soon for him to trust her no matter how much he wanted her or how sincere she seemed.

Too well he knew the temptations of betrayal. His own father had succumbed. What could hurt more than betrayal by those closest to you, those with the power to cause the most pain? Nothing could crush trust more than losing faith in someone you loved.

Who knew when a friend might become an enemy?

Joanna waited, idly twisting a curl around her finger. A small smile hovered on her lips.

Adrian wanted to kiss her. Many times. He needed to know how she'd taste, how her body would feel in his arms. He hardened at the thought of her pressed against him.

"Well?" she asked. "Perhaps you need some time to consider."

If only he were like other men... "I cannot."

Her face fell, sending a bolt of sorrow through him. Though he hadn't meant to hurt her, he hadn't anticipated he'd care if he did. *She doesn't know me. She can't know what she's asking.*

"Thank you for giving my proposal such serious consideration," Joanna said, her voice harsh with sarcasm. "I'm sure I'll find another solution. However, I find I am no longer in a creative vein today. When can you return to sit for me?"

She looked down her slender nose at him, any remaining disappointment hidden behind her controlled expression. Her eyes looked hard as marble as she squared her shoulders.

Never was the answer that might best serve them both. He couldn't deny his attraction to Joanna, the desire that ignited when she was near. Her intelligence, talent and determination had snared his interest.

Though her plea touched his heart, he couldn't solve her

problems without sacrificing his own goals. On the other hand, he needed to rescue his priceless stained glass windows and preserve his family home.

But more time spent with her meant more chance of a vision overtaking him in her presence.

Dare he take the risk?

CHAPTER 4

"Your sister is a bitch!" John exclaimed as he stormed into William's chamber. He slammed the door, then pounded his fist against it, denting the decaying wood. "She refused me. Then she bit me."

William concealed his fury by jumping off his narrow cot and attempting to brush wrinkles from his well-worn garb. He snatched up a slightly wilted apple and scraped the peel with his eating knife. If John weren't careful, he'd take the knife to his thick neck.

"What am I going to do now?" he demanded. "You promised you'd succeed. Try again."

"She won't have me. Maybe before. Not now," John said. "She's got a man looking out for her."

His heart sank. Joanna had a protector? How did that happen? "What? Who?"

"Don't know, but he's almost as tall as me and he can hit. Talks like a lord."

"A lord? Maybe he's a new client. Damn," William muttered. The knife bit into the fruit deeper than he intended, sending juice dribbling down his fingers and onto the floor along with his plans. "Didn't you woo her with sweet words as I told you? Tell her how pretty she is?"

"Not exactly." John scuffed the dirty floor like a frustrated boy. "All should still be well. Most of her clients believed the lies I told."

William slapped his knife onto the cracked wooden table

beside him, then bit into the apple. "Why did I trust you? I've wasted too much time. Now I'll have to deal with her myself."

"*You* can't marry her," John scoffed. "What else can you do? Kill her?"

At that moment, he sorely wished he could. Fury at his own ineptitude replaced dread. William paced the small chamber, sending puffs of dust into the air. He took another bite, only to uncover a rotten spot. He spit the mouthful onto the floor and tossed the core after it.

"If you've raised enough doubts about her as you said, I won't have to resort to violence. Her clients will cancel their orders. With no coin coming in, she'll have to give the studio over to me to keep a roof over her head," William said through clenched teeth. "Then I'll give her to you. If you serve me well." John needed incentive to follow through, after all. "Can you picture that, John? Joanna in your bed?"

"I just told you she refuses to marry me," John said.

William tightened his lips to keep from snapping at his sole henchman. "She's lost the chance to be your bride. Now she'll merely be your mistress. And you can still marry someone else."

"Joanna deserves whatever befalls her. She should have let me take care of her. That's her duty as a woman."

How William would enjoy having his proud sister at his mercy. Just like the apple, they were. She was the sweet fruit and he the rotten, smushed spot. Deep in his core, a small seed of guilt sprouted for what he'd already done and would soon do to his only sibling. But he was in far too much trouble to worry about her.

John leaned against the wall and folded his arms. "When do you have to pay up?"

The change of subject made his gut churn. As did the smug expression on John's face. "Leave. I've plans to make."

"I know what I know. When do you have to pay?" John towered over him.

William stood his ground. He flexed his fingers over the hilt of his knife, yearning to use it. "Any day now they'll be back to collect. I'd better have their gold this time. But I've nary a groat to my name."

William hid his left hand behind his back, as though he could conceal the still-painful evidence of his creditors' brutality. With the glove he wore, no one else could tell that the bastards had cut off his little finger. He'd rather die than suffer the indignity and pain of losing another part of his anatomy.

"What happened to the coin you won dicing?"

"I lost it all back," William confessed. "If I'd had enough to place one more bet, surely I'd have triumphed."

"Hazard is a dangerous pastime, my mother always said."

Fury ensnared him. "Out. Out!"

With a snide chuckle, John left. William threw his knife. The blade sank into the closed door with a satisfying thud.

What to do? William rubbed his elbow on his tiny window to remove some of the grime. All would be clear, in time. He smiled as he looked through the wavy glass out onto the bustling street. Though he couldn't trust John, he could trust himself. He'd prevail and the glass-painting studio would be his at last. Then John would work for him and Joanna would be under his thumb, where she belonged.

Assuming by then he still had a thumb left.

🐚 🐚

Nervous anticipation clung to Joanna like dust from the glass she'd ground as she gathered the materials necessary for Adrian's sitting. She hoped he wouldn't mention her impulsive marriage proposal. She'd act as though the embarrassing incident never took place. Just like a good window design required planning before execution, she should've developed her reasons and laid out her strategy before discussing marriage with him.

Uncertain whether she'd prefer charcoal or ink for her drawing, she set out both on a small table near the window. She had all prepared more than a quarter hour before he was scheduled to arrive, yet kept checking to be sure all was in order.

Her spontaneous suggestion that he sit for her still surprised her. What about him made her act and speak without thinking? Any excuse to look at him for long periods of time suited her.

She could see his features clearly in her mind, but wouldn't tell him so. He'd promised her three sittings and she'd enjoy every minute of them.

She dried her damp palms on her skirts. She was making too much of this visit. He wasn't coming to see her, merely fulfilling his obligation in return for her saving his stained glass windows. That was all.

At last Joanna heard a knock. She ran to the door, taking a deep breath to compose herself before she opened it.

Her memory hadn't done Adrian justice. He was far more attractive in the flesh. Talented as she was, could she capture his high cheekbones, square chin, perfect nose and well-shaped face on parchment? His flowing, slightly wavy hair with its intriguing white streak would be easy to represent. His most compelling feature, his bluest of blue eyes, would be her biggest challenge. They shone with intelligence and fascinating mystery. A large purplish bruise marred one eye, remnants of John's hostility.

"Shall I enter?" he asked.

"Oh, yes, of course." Embarrassment washed over her, for she'd been staring unabashedly. And the session hadn't even started yet. "Sit here, if you will."

She'd arranged the chairs so he'd face the window and catch the best light.

Adrian turned briefly, broad shoulders stretching the fabric of his tunic. Then he sat, his long legs crossed at the ankle. He seemed at ease, while nerves teased her skin at his mere presence.

"Your eye, does it hurt?" she asked.

"No, now that the swelling has gone down. Your cheek looks much improved."

Joanna moved her chair and table a little closer. In contrast with her chilled fingers, a strange heat formed deep within. She rubbed her hands to warm them, hoping her fingers wouldn't tremble as she drew.

"What shall I do?" Adrian asked.

"Remain still and sit. Try not to move."

"Just sit?" He shifted, as if already uncomfortable with inactivity. Or having her study him.

"Yes. It's harder than it sounds." She sat in her chair. "Please turn a little more to the right."

Lord, he was beautiful.

Joanna couldn't wait to begin.

❧ ❧

Adrian complied, feeling ill at ease as she scrutinized him.

"A bit more...stop! That's perfect."

She had a writing desk on her lap. On the small table next to her waited a pen, ink and charcoal. She selected the pen, dipped it into the ink, then paused over her parchment as she considered him.

This had to be the strangest thing he'd ever done with a woman. He'd slept with several, seen their naked flesh and touched them in their most private places. Yet this meeting felt more intimate, though they were fully clothed. Though they merely sat close together, not speaking. Or doing anything besides watching each other intently.

Joanna tilted her head slightly to the side, then concentrated on the lines she sketched. As she worked, with the only sound the scratch of her pen, he had time to notice more about her than he'd ever noticed about anyone. He'd never paid much attention to what people wore or how they looked, or wanted to, until now. Everything about Joanna intrigued him.

If he hadn't thought to look for the cut on her cheek, he wouldn't have known it was there. Her red-gold hair was down, the way he liked it. She'd pulled the front portions back and secured them with a ribbon. The rest tumbled down her back past her waist. As she bent forward to outline his head, a few curls fell over her shoulder. The way the sunlight made her hair shimmer enchanted him. Each curl seemed highlighted with liquid gold. God, he wanted to touch that hair.

Clenching his fists, he looked out the window.

"Is something wrong?" she asked.

"No, why?"

"You tensed and changed position," she said.

"Oh." He returned to his original pose. "You were right. Sitting still is more difficult than it seems."

She dipped her pen in the ink. "Glass-painters often reuse their drawings. My father left his book of drawings to me in his will. But I grow tired of seeing the same face in every window I make. More so than I'm bothered by the same canopy or design element. So I thought I'd try to capture some interesting faces for new designs. Like yours." She stared at him for a moment, then returned to her drawing.

Joanna's hand moved swiftly over the parchment, then dipped pen into ink and returned to draw. When he'd arrived, he'd sensed nervousness in the way she glanced at him then away, how she picked up and put down her supplies for no apparent reason. Now each movement revealed confidence and faith in her skills.

No one had ever spent so much time looking at him, or studied him so intently. He felt her gaze, could tell when she examined his eyes or his cheeks. His skin began to tingle. A hot flush raced from his face to his groin. He resisted the urge to move.

What was wrong with him? This wasn't meant to be an erotic experience. Two fully dressed people staring at each other, that was all.

He concentrated on her clothing. She wore an undergown of deep red wool with an overgown of dark blue. The gown had a scooped front that clung to her full breasts. Her breasts. No, he couldn't think on those, their sweet curves or how they would feel filling his hands. How he wanted to make her moan with pleasure—

Move on to something else. But he couldn't see her shoes, she wore no jewelry. Help. He was running out of safe things to look at.

She ran her tongue over her lips. It was sweetly pink, and the way her moistened lips....

How would he ever survive two more sittings when all he wanted to do was touch her?

❧ ❧

"Not a word is true. How can I make you believe me?" Joanna's knees gave way. She dropped onto a stool in her workshop. Sweat beaded on her upper lip despite the slight chill. Her hands were fisted in her skirts.

"Mistress Joanna, I am sorry," said John Petty, head of York's Glazier's Guild. He pointed to several documents he'd placed between them. "The evidence goes against you. I have received complaints from both Edward of Wykeham and All Saints Church. And I've heard several tales of your drinking."

A tall man whose costly robes hung loosely on his frame, John Petty had supported Joanna from the beginning of her career. Which is why his doubt hurt so much now.

"Master Petty, John Twygge made all of this 'evidence' up. He told me as much when he…"

"Do you have a signed confession from him?"

Joanna shook her head.

"Have you witnesses, as he does?"

"No, not at this time." Her thoughts raced, but failed to latch onto a solution. Adrian had witnessed John hitting her, but hadn't heard their conversation. Would anyone support her, or would they too believe John's lies?

"I'm sorely disappointed in you, Joanna. I was warned that you might blame your mistakes on another. You know the rules." He rose from his stool and paced the few steps to the front window: her father's creation of a glazier at work, once a reminder of all she hoped to achieve. A sign that her father was still with her. Now the window represented all that was at stake.

Joanna's heart sank. Her former mentor couldn't meet her gaze, he was that ashamed. Her father would've been, also, because she let the situation get so out of hand by being too trusting. A flaw she couldn't seem to fix. But she couldn't melt herself down like an imperfect piece of glass. She'd have to mold herself into a wiser, more capable woman.

"What is the fine?"

Not that she thought she should pay, or could afford to. She had few spare coins to her name. All she'd earned was invested in her supplies.

"Payment of a mark or two won't compensate for your behavior." He turned toward her, his face full of disdain. The number of times he'd looked at her with warmth made his coldness all the more painful. "I regret to inform you that I must revoke your guild membership. Effective immediately. As the rules say, 'Whomsoever is found untrue of his tongue is to be avoided from the said craft unto the time that he find sufficient surety of his truth and good bearing.'"

Joanna jumped to her feet. "Master Petty, finding proof of my innocence in the face of these lies will take time. If I'm no longer part of the guild, I can't sell to my clients. I'll be forced to let them down and make matters worse." She couldn't bear doing so.

"It seems you already have." He walked to her table and examined her work in progress, a window for a musician that incorporated his viol and lines of notes. He shook his head. "Your talents will be sorely missed."

"I have outstanding obligations to fulfill. You were my father's friend, you know how hard we've worked to make this workshop thrive," Joanna said, failing to keep a pleading tone from her voice.

Master Petty frowned.

If personal reasons wouldn't sway him, perhaps her experience would.

"I completed my apprenticeship years ago and submitted my master-piece to prove my skills. I've paid my admission fees. My work has passed the searchers' inspections time and time again," she said. "And I'm in the Freeman's Register."

"Despite your skill, your experience, your achievements, we have standards to uphold. You've violated guild rules," Master Petty replied. He pushed a piece of glass into its place on her design, then looked at Joanna. "Your father would be most disheartened to see his hard-earned reputation destroyed by a fickle woman."

Joanna gasped. "Is that it? You're building a case to reject me because I'm a woman?"

"We don't want members who fail to meet their deadlines, nor do we want those who produce inferior work. Such behavior reflects poorly on us all." Master Petty closed his eyes briefly and folded his hands. "I've had no reason to distrust you before. So I'll give you the benefit of the doubt. If you can disprove these claims within a week, I'll see what I can do to reinstate you."

Her nails bit into her palms but she needed the pressure to keep from crying. "I appreciate your kindness, but one week…"

"...is more than I should allow," he said. "You had best get to work, Mistress Joanna. Farewell."

Two visits in two days from two men who were destroying her. Joanna rubbed at the small line of stinging marks her nails had made. The frying pan or the fire, that's what her life had come to. Only a week to defend herself from carefully and deeply plotted false accusations.

Would she have to marry John just to stop him from ruining her career?

She couldn't keep back tears that threatened. They dripped down her cheeks, draining her like a squeezed sponge.

The familiar stacks of white and colored glass, pots of paint, dozens of tools and brushes, her design table and her small furnace for firing the pigment onto the glass pieces. The implements of her success, now useless to her. If they could speak, they'd laugh, mocking her weaknesses. Her failures. She swiped the tears away.

Margery rushed in, closing the door against the crisp air. "Have you been crying?"

Joanna ran her hands through her hair, working her way through the tangles. If only she could unsnarl her life as easily. "What was I thinking, trying to make my way in a world that men control? Shouldn't I be happy, as so many other women seem to be, running my household with a husband and children?"

She shouldn't want more. What was she trying to prove?

"But Joanna, you're not like other women. I mean that as a compliment," Margery said as she removed her cloak.

Before Master Petty arrived, Joanna had been using the tip of her brush handle to pick out an inscription. She couldn't concentrate on fine details just now. And why bother? She couldn't legally deliver the piece even if she finished it. "Maybe you were right. It would be easier to give William all responsibility so I could paint for pleasure alone. If his views on the way the studio should be run differ from mine, so be it."

"Joanna, what's happened? This isn't like you. William would never have the discipline to manage the myriad details you deal with every day. And worse, he'd gamble away any profits," Margery warned. She moved to Joanna's table and looked over her shoulder. "That's coming along nicely. Martin's fingers on the viol strings look so real."

"My thanks." But what did her skills matter now? "All I've ever wanted was to work with Father. I promised him again and again that I'd carry on in his stead."

She'd begun her apprenticeship at the age of seven, needing even at that early age to create, to perpetuate beauty. Back then, she'd spent hours staring at the vast, elaborately detailed stained glass windows in York Minster. She knew she was the luckiest girl alive because her father made windows and soon she would, too. To fulfill the promise she made to her father on his deathbed, she couldn't give up. No matter the obstacles she faced.

"Did I pass Master Petty on my way here?" Margery asked.

Joanna filled Margery in on the details of Master Petty's visit.

"Oh, Joanna. I'm so sorry." Margery gave her a quick hug, which brought fresh tears to Joanna's eyes. "I've never been fond of John, but didn't know he could be so cruel."

"Before my world collapsed, I spent most of the afternoon drawing a model." The thought of Adrian warmed her. "I'll use his face in some future projects, but I shouldn't have dallied. I have important deadlines. Now, one even more important: a mere week to find proof of my innocence to salvage my guild membership."

"A model? How did you find one? Is he handsome? Unwed?"

"I first saw him at Lady Anne's. And he is handsome. And unwed." The memory of her impetuous proposal stung. She'd allowed her fascination with Sir Adrian and his physical perfection to distract her. Capturing his likeness on parchment hadn't satisfied her interest the way she'd hoped. He hadn't spoken much, which heightened her need to learn more. A couple of times his intense gaze made her think he saw her as a woman, not merely a means to an end. She couldn't stop herself from wishing he was attracted to her. Unsettling, because this was the first time she'd had such thoughts about a man.

As much as she wanted to spend more time with him, she'd have to postpone, maybe even cancel, their remaining sittings.

How could she afford to enjoy herself when she was forbidden to sell her wares? When she stood to lose everything she'd worked so hard for?

"What are you going to do?" Margery asked.

"If I fail, move away from York, somewhere the guild lacks jurisdiction. No, I don't mean that." Joanna needed the prestige and security of guild membership to secure clients. "The only solution I can think of is to visit clients John hasn't swayed and garner their support. And call upon the clients who have complained to convince them John has been lying. Perhaps then they will retract their complaints. Will you come with me?"

Unfortunately, her chance of success would be much greater with a husband standing beside her. A man to champion her would impress clients far more than another woman. A nobleman would impress even more. If only Sir Adrian had accepted her offer of marriage.

Her brother and John had put her in an untenable position. The additional consequence of their slander was that instead of making progress on promised windows, she'd have to spend the majority of her time defending her position, thus putting her farther behind.

Could she salvage her ruined reputation in a week?

CHAPTER 5

Adrian's nerves were on edge as he entered the meager quarters he shared with his twin. He'd left Joanna's workshop with a promise to return later in the week to sit for her again. Though they hadn't mentioned their peculiar conversation about marriage, it felt unresolved. He wanted to help her, yet how could he?

Though he wanted her.

He girded himself for another confrontation with his sanctimonious twin. Andrew awaited with the dour expression that reflected how he'd changed over the years from the laughing child everyone once doted on to a judge always ready to pronounce a dire sentence. As a boy, Adrian had often been jealous of the attention his outgoing twin received. Especially every time he had to hide when he suspected a vision was forthcoming while Andrew remained in pleasant company.

Andrew sat in his high-backed chair facing the door, slowly tapping each of his long fingers on the carved arms. The detailed carvings of birds made the chair quite uncomfortable, yet Andrew sat in it for hours.

A chair. All they possessed from their once-vast estate. A chair and two pieces of jewelry: their father's gold signet ring and a ring of braided gold with a dark amethyst in the center. Adrian wore the signet ring on his right hand as his father had done; Andrew had placed their mother's ring on a thin strip of leather he wore around his neck.

Deprivation and fear had diverse effects on people. Adrian

knew his childhood suffering made him even more ambitious. More determined to prove to the world and himself that he could accomplish whatever goals he set. Then his worth would be obvious to all.

Andrew had become increasingly morose, with religion his consolation. If not for his brother's seemingly incessant need for pleasures of the flesh, Adrian was certain Andrew would've become a monk or a priest. The kind who wore hair shirts and believed self-flagellation proved penitence and faith. When Andrew wasn't in his chair, he was on his knees, praying.

But he was the only family Adrian had left.

Adrian's greyhounds, Beowulf and Chaucer, bounded over to him. He bent to greet them, smiling at their boisterous play.

"Where were you? Why did you miss morning Mass?" Andrew demanded.

Andrew's need to know his whereabouts was just one quirk Adrian found annoying. "I'm sitting as a model for a glass-painter in exchange for some rare windows."

"How enterprising. We need so many windows here," Andrew said, a wave of his hand indicating their plaster walls.

Andrew's way of offering a compliment and a criticism at the same time grated on Adrian's nerves. "The windows are for Bedford Castle."

"Do you know something you haven't shared? You act as though it will be ours again any day now." Andrew leaned forward. "How can you be so certain?"

"Because I will make it so." Adrian bit his tongue to prevent himself from telling Andrew about his relations with Lady Anne. Even though the end result was what they both wanted, his behavior would never justify the means to Andrew.

"God sees to our needs. You of all people should know that and pray for your soul as I do. For the burden of concealing your true nature continues to weigh on mine."

Adrian gritted his teeth. Would he ever get used to Andrew's babble? He'd learned to keep his mouth shut. A verbal battle with Andrew inevitably left him the loser.

Though his patience was short, Adrian tried to be understanding with the one person who really knew him and accepted him as he was. He owed his brother much for keeping the secret that could mean his death should anyone else learn of it.

"How much coin was dispensed on the fine garments you wear?"

Self-consciously, Adrian smoothed the front of his new tunic, the only one he owned that wasn't frayed or out of fashion.

"It's plain, lacking embroidery or jewels." Adrian couldn't stop himself from sounding defensive. "I need to look the part when I go to court. A downtrodden appearance won't aid our cause."

Andrew's criticism was getting out of hand. But at present, he had no solution to curb it.

❦ ❦

Andrew sneered as he watched his brother romp with his mangy dogs. Adrian rarely listened to him anymore. Had he ever really been in charge of Adrian, or had Adrian's silence oft made it seem as though Andrew had some control?

He'd allowed Adrian to make many important decisions in their lives, including the means by which they would regain their family's estates. After all, Adrian was the elder, which would've made him the next baron. Andrew was merely the second son, forced by ancient laws of primogeniture to fend for himself or rely on his brother's charity. His faith helped him conceal resentment over happenstance, the way a few minutes regulated his entire existence.

God must have a plan for him. He must, or what was all of his suffering for?

Look where his misplaced reliance on Adrian had gotten them. Did they live in Bedford Castle? No. "Because I will make it so," Adrian said. But he hadn't. All they had to show for themselves were three tiny, sparsely furnished rooms in an inconsequential area of York.

Andrew had been patient. Now he had to think about himself. Years had passed, but Adrian's affliction hadn't lessened. Andrew owed it to his soul to make certain Adrian didn't drag him down any further.

As their father had done with their grandmother. He'd done the right thing by turning in the witch to save the rest.

Now it was his turn.

"Adrian. Do you remember the tale of Eleanor Cobham, Duchess of Gloucester?"

"How could I forget? What happened to her and her cohorts is what led Father to accuse Grandmother," Adrian replied, patting one of his dogs.

"Precisely. Eleanor was accused of consulting with sorcerers and trying to communicate with the dead in order to predict the future. She wanted to know when King Henry would die, because her husband was in line to become king."

"Her accusers wanted to discredit her husband through her. So he'd lose political power," Adrian countered.

"But Eleanor admitted to several of the charges. Her compatriot Margery Jourdemain was known to be a witch. Both were found guilty," Andrew recalled.

"What does that matter now?" Adrian asked.

"What matters is that those close to Eleanor were tainted by her evil and sentenced along with her. Four others were accused, and one a clergyman! Margery was burned for high treason and witchcraft. A scholar in Eleanor's employ was hanged, beheaded and quartered. She was sentenced to public penance and imprisonment for the rest of her life. What matters—"

Adrian cut him off with a wave that infuriated Andrew. "Those in power wanted to be rid of Eleanor because she was ambitious and could've become queen. Which they didn't want."

"What matters is that the time comes when the righteous must point out and destroy evil in their midst lest they be consumed by it. Whatever the consequences. You've tried to convince me you aren't evil, are not from the Devil. Yet evidence to the contrary is clear. You see the future. You have visions just as Grandmother did. And what did the authorities do to her when they found out? They burned her. As they should have done." He held up his hands to stop Adrian from offering excuses. "Don't tell me you have a gift. Nor remind me of the time you saved Old Randall because you knew his horses would bolt and run him over. Or times you helped others without letting them know you knew about their impending peril. Because if you told them, they'd question how you knew what would happen. They'd come after you. All of that was the Devil trying to trick me, to make me less sure of my path."

He stood and paced their confining quarters with slow, methodical steps. Adrian continued to stroke one of his dogs. Perhaps the dog was Adrian's assistant from the Devil. Hadn't the rebel Jack Cade been accused of harboring the Devil in the form of a black dog?

"My soul is heavy with untold truths. I've struggled for some time and prayed for the answer. For my salvation and yours." Andrew met his brother's gaze. "Adrian, with God's help I have made the most difficult decision of my life. I must turn you in."

※Ə Ə※

Adrian felt as though he had been stabbed in the gut. The walls of their dark rooms closed in, making it as hard to breathe as if he were about to have another vision.

With those damning sentences, his life's work transfigured from an admirable plan into a mockery. His twin, ready to betray him. Just as his father had done to his grandmother. Did loyalty exist in his cursed family?

"Andrew, I've spent years trying to regain our family's properties, for *you*," he said. "You are my heir."

Adrian's stomach rebelled. The relationship with Lady Anne that still tormented his conscience…all for nothing. His entire life, all thirty-one years of it, was a waste.

He dropped onto a stool because his legs would no longer support him. The blow Andrew had dealt was worse than any he'd experienced in battle. It was a blow to the heart.

Andrew sighed. "Adrian, you never asked me what *I* wanted. You simply assumed we shared goals. The only honor that matters to me is my own." He folded his hands. "I plan to sell Bedford Castle when it becomes mine. Despite your Sight, you've never been able to see that all I want is to get as far away as possible from any reminders of the past."

Adrian gasped for breath as pain washed over him anew, wave after wave battering a sinking ship. Restoring his brother to the life they should've had was his only goal. Because he was like their grandmother, Adrian knew a normal life wasn't possible for him. He'd hoped to accomplish something by enabling Andrew to marry well and continue their line.

What did he have to live for now?

Adrian forced himself to look at his brother. "What makes you think they won't arrest you as well?" His voice was hoarse. He swallowed to ease his constricted throat. "As you just reminded us they did with Eleanor Cobham's cohorts? You're not merely an associate. You are my brother. My twin. They'll assume you are like me. What proof do you have to the contrary?"

"I admit that very issue has troubled me for some time. But they didn't arrest Eleanor's husband, did they? Prayer has shown me I must have faith. Whatever the Lord wills, I must accept. Even if I go down with you, at least my soul will be at peace. I'll not burn in Hell, like you." Andrew bowed his head. "To ensure that I'm making the right decision, I plan to travel to Rome, to pray at shrines far holier than those in England. The power of the relics there will guide me toward the right path."

"Why don't you just apply for an indulgence?"

Andrew's head snapped up. "Sarcasm doesn't become you. I'd do anything to shorten my time in Purgatory. But indulgences are expensive. And you know how little coin I have. Why is it, I wonder, that your *gift* didn't alert you to my plans?"

Adrian gripped his knees to keep himself from wringing his brother's neck. "You know I can't control what I see, or when. I can't ask questions and have them answered. I've never had a vision about you or myself. They come and go as they will."

"As the Devil sends them, you mean."

Adrian crossed the short distance to his brother. "Why now? How could you let me work so hard, come so close, just to destroy me?"

He stared at his brother, at the face so like his own. Were his own eyes as troubled, as full of indecision as his twin's?

"My recently-discovered calling compels me to act, not the desire for worldly goods. You must believe it pains me to take such action. We've only had each other for years." A tear dropped onto Andrew's cheek. He wiped his face with the edge of his sleeve. "Don't you see? I don't want to, yet I must. I've grappled with my obligation just as you have toiled to earn gold. I cannot bear it any longer. The conflict is tearing me apart. God will show me the true way on my pilgrimage. When I return, your time as a free man will very likely be up. I suggest you use it wisely."

Adrian couldn't believe what he was hearing. "Why are you telling me this? To give me time to run?"

"Ah, Adrian, where could you go?" Andrew placed a hand on Adrian's shoulder.

Adrian pulled away, sickened by his brother's behavior. By Andrew's use of religious devotion to destroy the little that was left of their family and any chance to continue the line.

"Redeeming our family home and status means everything to you," Andrew said with a shake of his head. "If you ran, the Lord would lead me to you. There's nowhere you can hide."

Andrew pursued Adrian and grabbed his hands. Andrew's were cold and clammy.

"My brother, I do this, to give you one last chance to free yourself from the Devil and walk in the way of God. The only way to restore our family's name is by rejecting the evil burning within you."

Adrian snatched his hands away. "What make you so certain it's God, not the Devil, who shows *you* the way? What makes my visions evil and your gleanings from prayer holy? Because scenes of what will be come to me, without my asking to know…without hours of praying on my knees for guidance? Because priests have decreed that praying to an unseen God is acceptable, yet knowing the future from an unseen source is not?"

Andrew crossed himself. "You speak heresy."

"Why shouldn't I be revered as wise, considered fortunate? People are so afraid of what they can't understand." Adrian sighed. "Instead, I must bear the guilt of knowing what will happen, often unable to aid those in danger. Why? For fear of discovery. For fear the power of rumor will discredit me, then lead to my death. Yet others will die or suffer grave injury if I don't speak of what I see, while I remain safe. That weighs on my conscience." He turned away, not wanting Andrew to see his pain. "I avoid people if I suspect a vision is coming. I hate being reminded of all I must do without…a wife, a family of my own.

I'm as much a prisoner to the sights and sounds in my mind as a man lashed to the wall in Newgate is to the guard's flogging. Why am I destined to live my life longing to be normal?" Adrian stalked to Andrew. "Is that what God wants?"

Andrew backed away as he again made the sign of the cross, his face pale as if he'd seen a ghost. "Your seemingly logical arguments are more deceiving blasphemy from Satan. You haven't tried hard enough to free yourself of your curse. For that is what it is, a curse on our family. You're lucky Father never knew you were like Grandmother, or you too might have burned that day. The guilt I feel for helping you keep your secret torments me now."

He fell to his knees and began to pray aloud in Latin, raising his face and hands to the heavens.

Adrian recoiled in horror at the strange glow in Andrew's eyes. Was his brother a fanatic? Lunatic?

Many people went on pilgrimages to pray for cures or to try to save souls. Even kings and nobility participated in such journeys. Adrian himself had been in the Duke of Norfolk's party when he visited the shrine of the Blessed Virgin in Walsingham several years ago. But a pilgrimage to validate a decision, when the decision dealt with sending one's brother and possibly one's self to an almost certain death.... How long would Andrew's pilgrimage take?

Adrian's heart began to race. He had to do something, fast.

CHAPTER 6

Sonorous church bells informed Joanna that another hour had passed. Three in the morning. Time moved too swiftly. She hadn't succeeded in finding a witness or someone to vouch for her, despite spending most of the day searching. Hours of work remained on this small window of the Holy Trinity promised for delivery later in the week. She had to believe she'd be readmitted into the guild and so needed to complete her work. Setting her brush down, she flexed her fingers, then straightened and rubbed her back.

Her thoughts wandered to Sir Adrian as they often had since she'd met him. She wished she had their next session to look forward to, but with the pressures of her commissions and securing proof for the guild, she'd have to cancel. She didn't know where he lived, so when he arrived, she'd tell him she had no time to spare. At least she'd see him again, however briefly.

The ease with which he handled John and his determination to achieve his own goals convinced her that he could solve her problems too. His handsome face and powerful build only enhanced his suitability. That she had confided so much to him surprised her. That Adrian had seemed interested surprised her even more.

She'd thank him again for coming to her rescue. If not for Adrian's fortuitous arrival, John might have beaten her or kept to his lunatic threat not to let her out of his sight until she agreed to marry him. The fear, the helplessness she'd felt lying beneath

John still haunted her. She couldn't imagine how terrible being his wife would be. Much less having to share his bed.

But who would be there for her if John tried to manipulate her again?

The moment Adrian raised her from the floor glowed in her memory. The touch of his warm, strong hand on hers had sent a frisson through her arm, so unexpected that she'd pulled away when she really wanted was to prolong the contact. How could a simple touch elicit so much feeling? His grip had been solid and reassuring, making her feel as though nothing could harm her while he was near.

She'd experienced something else, too, undefinable yet urgent. She wouldn't admit to herself it might be the beginnings of desire. And the pleasure of the quiet, uniquely intimate moments spent drawing him—

Joanna Peyntor, stop thinking about him and get back to work. Stop letting him distract you.

She was putting the final touches on the face of the Holy Ghost when furious pounding on her door sent her squirrel-hair brush slipping off of the glass, leaving a thin black streak on her drawing.

Joanna set down the brush to blot the mistake but made the mess worse in her hasty frustration. Who'd be out at this hour? Her heart thudded. Not John trying to force her to marry him....

"Who's there?"

"Adrian. I need to talk to you."

Joanna's fear became anticipation. What was he doing at her door in the middle of the night? She didn't care. He was here, nothing else mattered. The smeared face on her window forgotten, Joanna hurried to let him in.

He rushed past her, then turned to face her. The fresh scent and chill of a winter night followed him into the room. His eyes held anger and a strange emptiness; a man seeking somewhere to hide from a reality he didn't want to face. She waited, breathless, appreciating the way intense emotion heightened his attractiveness.

Adrian paced restlessly. His heavy steps made her sheets of glass rattle in their bins. His mood was a fog swirling about her studio. Joanna wasn't afraid, only concerned. She sensed he'd never hurt her like John Twygge, no matter how upset or angry he became.

Adrian's circuitous pacing brought him to face her. He stopped by her table and scowled down, his sapphire-blue eyes glinting in the candlelight, his hair draping over his shoulders. The shadow of a beard made him look a bit wild. His body heat encompassed her.

"Sir Adrian, what is it? Why are you here?"

"Circumstances have changed. I must marry."

Joanna gasped.

"Does your offer still stand?" He pinned her in place with his unwavering gaze.

She stared back. He *must* marry? What changed his mind? "Does your offer still stand" wasn't the most romantic offer of marriage, but could suffice. Part of her hoped romance would come later. He interested her more than any other man, and she believed he felt something for her, too.

Yet she knew how dangerous love could be, had watched it destroy her father. She needed a protector and supporter, not a lover. Adrian already offered more than John ever could. The comfort she felt in his presence alone was a gift.

With his five words, her life became uncertain yet secure. Her workshop could be saved, but what would happen to her heart? *Yes* hovered on her lips even as a shred of doubt held her answer back. As much as she needed a man's backing, marriage was a huge step. Could she make such a decision so quickly? She turned away. She couldn't think clearly while looking at him looking at her.

"Well?" he demanded.

"I need a moment to decide."

🕸 🕸

Adrian couldn't stand still. The walls of Joanna's studio confined him. What was she thinking? He felt trapped. Yet he knew this was what he had to do. Andrew was no longer a suitable heir. Adrian didn't have time to seek another bride willing to accept him without his estate or title, much less one with as many wonderful qualities as Joanna possessed.

She busied herself with a jar of brushes, her back to him, making him feel oddly abandoned. Her glorious hair flowed down her back in myriad ringlets. He clasped his hands to keep himself from burying them in her curls.

Her silence and his need to touch her frustrated him. "Changed your mind so fast?"

"What happened to change *your* mind so fast?" she asked, turning to face him.

"I need an heir. As soon as possible." He wanted to tell her the rest, but couldn't reveal so much. Soon, if he completed his assignment, his overlord would restore his family's fortune and petition the king to award his father's former title.

In either case, he needed another heir before Andrew returned from his pilgrimage. Adrian was so close to regaining all his father had lost. He couldn't give up his quest. If he married Joanna, he'd change his will so that any land, property or other wealth went to her and any children they should have. *And I shall pray fervently that my children don't share my affliction. That if I'm found out and turned over to the authorities, my family will be spared.* A family that might soon include Joanna and their child.

How could he tell Joanna about the risks he took? The dangers she and their child might face? Was it hubris or some greater sin to imperil those closest to him?

She needed him, he needed her.

"Is your answer yes or no?" Adrian demanded.

He winced as Joanna did at his harsh tone, but he couldn't be courteous at the moment. His conversation with Andrew still troubled him. Too much was at stake.

Joanna remained silent.

He couldn't bear the waiting. He had to have her answer.

Adrian walked to Joanna, meeting her gaze. Her green eyes flecked with gold revealed fear of the unknown, uncertainty, determination, and underlying all, the beginnings of desire. He didn't want to know her so intimately, but he couldn't look away.

God help him, he felt those things too. He wasn't prepared for the impact of her beauty combined with the pleasure of shared emotions. Nor had he anticipated the way the unexpected bond they shared drew him to her against his will. His hands smoothed over her shoulders and enticed her near until their bodies almost touched. Her intriguing scent of roses wove around him. Her face was mere inches from his, her soft lips enticing. Anticipation tugged at his groin as her breath caressed his neck. But he held back, needing her answer first.

"Well?"

"Yes," she breathed softly.

'Yes' to his kiss or to marriage? No matter, for he'd have both. Adrian bent toward her, his mouth hovering above hers. Her lips parted slightly, revealing the tip of her tempting tongue. Desire unfurled inside him.

No. If he kissed her now, acted as though he cared for her, she might expect a closer relationship than he could afford to give. Adrian clamped down the longing to taste her.

"Good." He released Joanna. She turned away, leaving him feeling strangely empty. "We shall marry, but only if you agree to my conditions."

She inclined her head gracefully, sending shimmering ringlets cascading over her shoulders. *You'll get to touch them once you marry her.*

He'd touch every damn one of them. Often.

"I expected no less," she said, her expression annoyingly blank. "You've heard mine."

This impersonal discussion about such an important relationship grated on his nerves. Did it bother her, too? He wouldn't care what she thought, or what she wanted. Not at all.

"Yes. I remember your stipulations: you'll provide children and gold when possible.

A pained expression crossed her face. "That gold might take longer to earn than I'd thought." She explained what had happened with the guild.

Guilt hit him. She'd confided in him. He didn't dare reciprocate. What were the chances she'd accept him? Even if she did, she'd be more likely to join him at the stake if she had knowledge of his Sight. He was weaving a web stickier than a spider's, but he couldn't think of a better plan.

"I'll support you in your craft as needed. Starting tomorrow, we'll figure out how restore your guild membership," he said. They had more in common than he'd thought…both needing to reclaim what was most important. "We'll write down every word and sign our agreement. So neither of us forgets his or her obligations," he said. "Here are my conditions. One: we agree that this marriage is a business, like your glass-painting or any other. We'll conduct ourselves accordingly. Conversations of a personal nature will be kept to a minimum.

"Two: aside from agreed upon commitments, no additional time together will be required or requested." Adrian swallowed. Laying out the restrictions he'd decided upon was harder than he'd thought. "Three: we'll keep separate rooms. I will visit yours when I wish."

Adrian watched closely for her reactions to his demands. The first two passed by without even a flicker of an eyebrow. At the third, she dropped her hands in her lap and looked down at them. Was she saddened or gladdened? He'd heard that some women despised physical intimacy. Was she one of them, or would she wish to share a bed with her husband? With him?

Adrian wished he hadn't had to add that dictatorial condition. Just speaking the words made his stomach roil. But he couldn't allow her to spend too much time with him. Her glass-painting needs and his need for children would put him at enough risk. He had to have some means of controlling any other contact.

Or they'd both suffer the consequences.

Joanna stared at her paint-stained hands, keeping her expressive eyes from his view. "I agree. Write the terms down."

Her voice sounded flat, as though he'd beaten the life out of it. Is this what marrying him would do to her?

She gathered parchment, pen and ink and handed them over without looking up. He sat on a stool next to her well-polished counter and started to write.

❧❧ ❧❧

As Joanna watched Adrian draw up their agreement, their marriage contract, an unsettling mixture of joy and frustration filled her. Though a bit more warmth from Adrian would be appreciated, she had no right to expect it. She was enormously curious about the reasons behind his haste and his conditions, far more stringent than she'd planned when she first brought up the idea.

Yet far better this way, she reassured herself. An impersonal marriage would prove best for her too. She'd get exactly what she wanted: a strong man who'd work with her but wouldn't try to control her or her plans for the studio. So why had she felt a rush of dismay when he demanded separate rooms? All she needed was a husband's security, the presence of a man to uphold and protect her craft. His love wasn't required.

She knew what happened to people in love.

If she allowed herself to care too much for Adrian, she'd think of him, what he was doing and if he was safe, and be unable concentrate on her windows. She'd want to be with him. All these things had happened when she'd been infatuated with Henry, the eldest son of one of her father's best clients. Weeks had passed while she fantasized about marrying him, with barely a design completed. But he married someone else. And her heart smashed into painful shards, like broken glass.

Wasn't it bad enough that she was attracted to Adrian? That her thoughts already strayed to him far too often? *I could watch him for hours.* She admired his distinctive profile. His hair fell forward as he wrote. The pen scratched its way across the page, revealing his strong script.

She'd been honest with him, but sensed Adrian kept much from her. She wanted to know him, to unearth the truths he didn't wish to share. There'd be time for that once they were wed, despite his unpleasant conditions. He couldn't keep his secrets forever.

"'Tis done." Adrian pushed the completed document across the counter and held out the pen. "Sign."

Joanna took the contract and reviewed his words, praying that her face didn't reveal her thoughts. She would have her marriage, but if they followed the precepts of their agreement, it would be a cold and lifeless one.

She read the last sentence out loud. "Should either person violate this agreement, the other has the right to end the marriage."

The statement hung in the air. At least she had just as much right to get out as he. The fact that most of the conditions applied to both of them boded well for a fair and equal marriage, didn't it? She glanced up at Adrian for reassurance, but his face was cold and hard. The quill felt heavy in her hand.

Yes, she needed to marry Adrian. She wanted to, for no man intrigued her the way he did. Yet how could she sign this restrictive document and relegate herself to such an impersonal existence? Though preferable to the servitude she'd have suffered had she married a fellow glazier, and far better than the misery John Twygge would've brought her, part of her knew all that Adrian offered was still not enough.

Why should she settle? She'd hoped they could at least be friends, with the possibility of closeness developing over time. Spouses didn't have to be in love to be close. The forbidding terms of this contract relegated their relationship to working partners.

With another man, such bland fare might suffice. Adrian could offer a more sumptuous feast, if only he would. Just moments ago, she'd been sure he was going to kiss her. But even as she lifted her lips to his, as she savored standing so close with the warmth of his hands on her shoulders, he'd turned away. He left her wanting more.

Is that how she'd spend the rest of her days if she married him?

Maybe she could use his need to marry as leverage with which to lessen the severity of his provisions. Would he make a few changes if she asked him to? She and Margery often negotiated with clients. Joanna opened her mouth, but before she could say one word, he pounded his fist on the table, making her jump.

"No. Do not even think it," he bit out. "Not one word will be altered. Accept what is before you or I will burn the page and we will be as we were. No marriage."

He looked harsh with his thick black brows drawn together and lines of determination marking either side of his mouth. A vein pulsed on his neck. Underneath his stern expression she thought she detected a hint of desperation. He needed this as much as she did.

Joanna stared at the document. The quill hovered above the page for what seemed like an eternity, ink drying on the tip. She slowly dipped it in the inkpot. The room was so quiet she could hear each beat of her heart.

Was she consigning herself to another form of misery, subjecting herself to Adrian's whims? What would she do if she didn't sign? She couldn't leave herself exposed to John Twygge, who with her brother would ruin everything she had worked for, the workshop that had meant so much to her father and to her. What would her life be without her guild membership? How could she bear losing the studio to her brother?

All that mattered was her safety, her reputation and the peaceful, profitable continuation of her glass-painting. She couldn't afford to be concerned with feelings or emotions.

They were not for her.

Joanna signed.

ఠ❧ ❧ఠ

Later that morning, Joanna broached the news to Margery as they broke their fast.

Margery froze, a morsel of brown bread smeared with jam halfway to her mouth. "What? Surely I didn't hear you aright."

"I'm getting married," she repeated. "As soon as the banns can be read."

"Ha. You don't know anyone worth marrying." Margery popped the bread into her mouth and reached for more.

"I do so. I met him last week."

Even to her own ears her words sounded silly, and she felt childish having to defend herself. She didn't need Margery's approval. She had made the right decision.

"The model?"

She couldn't bring herself to tell Margery the whole truth, so she limited her tale about Adrian to the basic facts.

When she finished, Margery's mouth hung open. "You agreed to marry a man after two conversations? Just because he saved you from John? Or was it love at first sight? I don't believe you."

She bit off more bread. Joanna watched Margery eat, but she had no appetite.

"Our marriage will be better than an arranged one where the parents choose the spouse and the bride and groom don't have a say in who they wed. We have agreed to marry."

Ours. We. For the instant it took her to say the words, she imagined they were a couple. But they weren't. At least they would be a team.

"You're truly going to marry this man." Margery stood, abandoning her food. "Joanna, what are you thinking? I know you want to be free of John Twygge and his threats, but you act too hastily!"

"Thank you for your felicitations." Joanna hid her disappointment. She'd counted on Margery's support.

"Where will you live?"

"His quarters are nearby."

"You've seen them already?"

Joanna wouldn't tell Margery about his rooms, for even she had found them small and unappealing when Adrian had shown them to her after they signed their agreement.

Margery would be appalled at the thought of living in such conditions: worn furniture topped with threadbare pillows, only a single wall hanging to brighten the space and keep out the chill. No kitchen. Two rooms contained a narrow bed and not much else. Her curiosity almost forced her to ask if anyone else had shared his quarters, but she wouldn't violate the terms of their agreement. She would believe that as their marriage progressed, so would their fortunes. And their bond.

"How am I to afford our rooms by myself?" Margery demanded.

Joanna sighed. "I'll have to keep my workshop here. So I'll continue to pay my share of the rent."

"You work all hours of the day, whenever the mood strikes. You can't be wandering the streets alone to come here when you can't sleep or have a deadline." Margery tilted her head and looked shrewdly at Joanna.

"We'll work something out. This is for the best, Margery. It has to be. Can you think of any other way for me to keep William and John from ruining me?"

Margery thought for a moment. "No. I wish I could, but I can't. What is Adrian like? I want to meet him."

"He's very handsome, strong, and serious. That's what I've gleaned thus far."

"To think you found someone to marry before I did. A knight, too. Joanna, I hope your marriage turns out to be everything you want," Margery said. "But just in case, I'll keep fresh linens on your bed."

❧❧ ❧❧

When he arrived at Joanna's studio the next morning, the strain in Joanna's face and the weariness around her eyes attested to her dismay. "I'm not looking forward to trying to convince my clients I'm not the drunk incompetent John made me out to be."

Could her reputation be restored in such a short time? He'd toiled for years to restore the status of his family name and still hadn't succeeded. If not for the allegiance of his overlord, the Duke of Warwick, who knew where he'd be. To help Joanna, as required under their agreement, he'd have to set his cause aside for the short term.

Another uncustomary urge to help her nagged at him. He'd focused on his own problems for so long he hadn't thought much about anyone but himself and Andrew. Even though he was having trouble resolving his problems, he might be able to help someone else. The beautiful someone who would soon be his wife. That felt good.

"Where do we start?" he asked. He wanted to hold her, comfort her, but he didn't want to set a precedent of intimacy.

Listlessly she moved about the workshop, tidying the already tidy space. She probably didn't even realize she picked up each tool and brush and put it back in the same place. "I need every single day to complete outstanding commissions and sell new ones in order to earn enough money by the deadline in Father's will. The irony is that I could accomplish this with an apprentice, but I can't afford to hire one. So I need to take advantage of our agreement already."

Her faith in him was humbling. By the stars, she was beautiful. That hair tumbling about, her clear green eyes combined with an enticing smile. He couldn't help but imagine her awaiting him in their bed, awaiting the pleasure he'd give her. The pleasure they'd share.

On the surface they made a good pair. But he feared she had

far more to offer than he. He hoped she wouldn't think she got the poor end of their bargain.

"I need you to visit a few clients with me, as a witness to persuade them the rumors are untrue. And convince them the lies were fabricated by my brother and his henchman, who want to control me." She ran a dry brush back and forth across her palm. "It's strange," she said with a wry grin, "I wanted to be independent and do things on my own. Maybe I've been a bit stubborn. Now I see that achieving independence can require assistance."

Adrian braced his hands on the counter. Was that why he'd had so much trouble reaching his goals? Joanna admitted she needed support and asked for help, though she wasn't happy about it. Until recently, he'd been too proud to accept he too might need help. If he'd done so as a youth, if he hadn't been so determined that he alone had to do all the work, would he have succeeded by now?

His betrothed was beautiful, but already displayed an annoying tendency to make him think about unpleasant, albeit provoking, issues. Issues he'd avoided dealing with to spare himself pain.

Perhaps that was one benefit to being alone. With no one else to compare yourself to, it was easy to convince yourself you were doing the best you could. You didn't care what anyone else thought because you only had to live up to your own expectations, not meet someone else's.

He wondered how high Joanna's expectations were.

CHAPTER 7

"Are you sure you want to speak with your brother before visiting clients?" Adrian asked as they crossed the bridge over the River Ouse, passing houses, shops and the chapel of St. William. She held her nose against the foul odor of the bridge's privies.

His hair blew in the wind, reminding Joanna of the day they first met. Every time she saw him he seemed more handsome than the last. He looked so concerned Joanna could almost believe he cared about her. But she knew he performed under the terms of their agreement and for no other reason. It was too soon to hope he even considered her a friend. She'd like for them to be friends at least, since they couldn't be anything more.

"Yes. Who knows what he might do if he found out after the fact? Besides, I want him to meet you and see that you'll brook no resistance." She clutched her cloak tighter to ward off the damp chill.

He held her elbow to keep her from slipping on icy patches. She appreciated his courtesies, even if he offered them out of instinct. Her hands were cold, making her wonder what having someone's warm hand to hold would be like. Never before when she'd seen couples strolling hand in hand had she had wistful thoughts about having such affection for herself.

What would Adrian do if she took his hand?

"Do you owe him even this effort?" he asked.

"He's still my brother."

With the ink barely dry, she hadn't had time to adjust to their pact. Relying on Adrian and asking him for help felt like her shoes were too tight. Pinched. She didn't like owing anyone. But she feared facing William alone when revealing the news of her impending marriage, especially if John Twygge was with him. William might be her brother, but she no longer trusted him.

"I am here for you, as you will be for me. When the time comes."

Joanna sought the hidden meaning his reassuring words seemed to conceal. Did she imagine the strange tone in his voice? Except for his secrets, thus far Adrian was exactly what she would've wished for in a husband.

But there was so much she wanted to know about him. What had happened to his father's title? What did he need to hide that was so important he had to make her agree in writing to avoid personal conversations? She shook her head. She had to stop analyzing everything Adrian said and accept what he offered without wanting more.

They reached William's apartment. She knocked. "William, it's Joanna."

❦❧

William's heart surged with joy as he rushed to the door, tossing a blanket over the pile of dirty clothing in the corner. A rat scurried out from beneath the clothes and dashed under the bed.

No matter, Joanna had forgiven him. He'd been up all night wracking his brain for nothing. The solution had come to him.

A genuine smile on his face, he opened the door. "Jo—"

His face fell as he caught sight of the man behind her. Though he couldn't make out the man's hair color or features in the dim light of the tiny entranceway, he could see the outline of his large shape.

And knew this was the man John had spoken of.

Shocked, William stepped back, allowing them to enter. The intruder was tall and sturdy, with a face women would consider handsome. His stern expression said, "Don't test me."

William hated him already.

The man scanned the room as if seeking sources of potential danger. He moved to the far side and leaned against the back wall, crossing his arms. What was he, Joanna's personal guard?

"Joanna?" William squeaked. Why couldn't he control his voice? He'd sounded like the rat.

"William, this is Sir Adrian Bedford. Sir Adrian Bedford, my brother, William Peyntor."

William appreciated the fact that Joanna introduced him first, instead of the higher-ranked Adrian. He clung to a thread of hope. "A new client?"

Joanna and Adrian exchanged a glance. How well did she know this man that they could communicate with a mere look? William's hatred exploded. This Sir Adrian connected with Joanna in a way he, her own brother, never had.

"Adrian is my betrothed."

"What!" William was glad his legs continued to support him. He forced out a chuckle. "I never knew you to have a sense of humor, sister."

"There's nothing humorous about this. We plan to wed as soon as we can. I thought you should know."

He didn't know what to say.

Sir Adrian came to stand beside her, but, William noted, didn't put his arm around her or take her hand. Joanna stood, awaiting his response. She stood because he had nothing for her to sit upon but the unmade bed.

Sudden hope surged through him. Joanna was marrying a knight.

"I'll be sorry to lose your talent, Joanna, but will come to enjoy the challenges of running the studio on my own," he said. "Felicitations to you both."

"I'm not here to tell you I'm handing over the workshop. My marriage has nothing to do with my glass-painting," Joanna said.

William glanced at Adrian. The man looked as though he wanted to skewer him.

"Certainly your husband will want you to cease your labors," he said. "Won't you be off to some castle?"

"No, we shall remain in York. And I'll continue my work. On

my own," she said firmly. "I also wanted you to know that."

Crushed. Like nuts under a mallet. That was how he felt. If there was no glass-painting for him, there'd be no money.

No more fingers.

What was that strange feeling, that nauseating twisting in his gut? Envy. Joanna had done quite well for herself. Sir Adrian wasn't scrawny or fat or old like many of the gentry he had seen, but a knight who exuded power. The mixture of confidence and obvious strength made him a formidable opponent.

Under other circumstances William might be happy for his sister. But Adrian's very existence would make his own life a living hell. The chances of him getting control of the glass-painting studio were disappearing faster than his coin on a bad dicing gambit. He'd never have Joanna's talent under his leadership. Never be able to prove his own worth. His hand burned, reminding him of the agony and humiliation awaiting him when his creditors came to collect.

Jealousy, yet another sin, lurked within as well. Joanna, who never relied on her own brother, so easily trusted this stranger. How could she give herself to a man she barely knew? She'd live in luxury while he suffered.

Unless....

No man was perfect. There had to be some unsavory fact he could uncover about this man. Perhaps he kept a mistress. Or drank to excess, or gambled. Something, anything, to discredit Adrian in Joanna's eyes and put him, William, back in her good graces. In gratitude for his saving her from a horrible fate, Joanna might make his dreams come true after all.

He wiggled his fingers in anticipation of victory. All nine of them.

᪣᪣ ᪣᪣

Joanna's heart sped as she and Adrian waited in Sir Reginald Langland's expansive oak-paneled hall. Her design depicting Sir Reginald, his wife and his coat of arms, replete with glass jewels, would replace one of the bay windows overlooking the courtyard. She focused on not crushing the rolled cartoon in her hands. Did Adrian's presence spark her uncustomary nerves, or were her palms moist because Sir Reginald would be the first client she faced since John and William spread their lies?

"Joanna. You're pacing. Sit beside me. All will be well." He stood and pulled a chair out for her.

His deep voice and courtesy were surprisingly reassuring.

Sir Reginald, a tall, thin man with greying brown hair entered before she could sit.

Her courage faded in the face of her glowering client. The damage John and William had done to her business hurt her, too. She hated that because of them she needed a man to vouch for her, but wouldn't let them win. Nor would she let the fact that she wanted to impress Adrian add to her stress.

Adrian stood as she made the introductions.

Sir Reginald sat and crossed his arms. "Only on Master Petty's suggestion did I agree to give you another chance and consider reinstating our contract. We shall see if having him and Sir Adrian on your side sways me to it. Or if I should return to a male glazenwright. Proceed."

"Thank you for meeting with me. Us." Joanna maintained a pleasant smile as she rolled out the cartoon on the table and used candlesticks to hold the corners down. "Though this isn't required in our contract, I wanted to show you the design and colors I've chosen."

She hoped she appeared calm on the outside. Because inside she was a molten mass of worry.

🐝🐝

"I can't thank you enough, Adrian. I'd never have been able to accomplish this so quickly without you. Nor did I realize you could be so persuasive. You made the impossible possible," his soon-to-be-wife said three days later.

Their meeting.

They stood outside her studio door, bathed in light from the winter sun. People hurried past, carrying various implements of their trades. Church bells rang out the hour. But all he noticed was how the sun illuminated her eyes. How she looked up at him with admiration.

God had truly smiled upon him, to make her his.

"Nobility, even tarnished as mine, has advantages," he said. He wasn't used to receiving praise. Yet it warmed him so he didn't even feel the cold.

"Your eloquence persuaded Sir Reginald, Edward of Wykeham and All Saints Church to reinstate their orders. Which made Master Petty agree to let me stay in the guild," she said, smiling.

Her smiles did peculiar things to his insides. He had to stop making her happy.

"I never could've done all of that on my own, not within a week's time for certes," she finished.

"That's why we signed the agreement, to help each other," he reminded her.

He should thank *her*. He'd been focused on his own problems for so long he hadn't realized how good it felt to help someone else. He also enjoyed the sense of accomplishment, instead of putting forth effort without succeeding.

"Perhaps you'll allow me to return the favor," she said. "But for now, we have more work to do. I need to find a replacement for John Twygge. If you have the time, I'd like you to stay while I interview the candidates."

The memory of Joanna bent backward over her table when John slapped her flashed through his mind.

"I'll make the time," he replied.

☙ ❧

Joanna unlocked the door and they went inside. Removing her cloak, she said, "The first candidate should be here any minute."

Adrian nodded and sat on a stool.

She was glad he'd agreed to stay. Not that she needed his help choosing her assistant, but she was afraid John Twygge might return. If he'd heard of her betrothal to Adrian, he could be desperate.

For the first time in weeks, she felt a glimmer of happiness. As she'd hoped, Adrian had helped her restore her clients' trust. Now she could concentrate on her work. On moving forward instead of dealing with problems.

She wanted to concentrate on Adrian. She'd had the urge to throw her arms around him to celebrate their success. But the terms of their agreement prevented her from doing that, and from telling him how good it felt to have someone on her side. A few of the things she'd said bordered on personal. Would she have to weigh every word she uttered for the rest of her life?

Moments later, a knock sounded. Joanna opened the door.

The man who entered was so tall he had to duck under the arched door. To Joanna, Adrian was far more handsome in his dark, sensuous way. But this man's light brown hair, bright aquamarine eyes, and patrician profile seemed the epitome of elegance. Sparks would surely fly if Margery met him. Perhaps that could be arranged.

"Mistress Peyntor, I am Thomas Osbert."

"This is Sir Adrian Bedford, my betrothed. Master Osbert, I've heard kind words about you from your present workshop in Norwich."

"I'd be happy to remain there, but I want to live closer to my family. My mother isn't faring well."

"I'm sorry to hear that."

"Here are my letters of reference," he said.

She took them and read through the glowing missives. "Let me show you some of my designs."

As Thomas reviewed the cartoons she piled on a table, she asked, "What do you think of working for a woman?"

"Your work shows you are as good or better than your father. I'd be honored to learn from someone with your skill."

As they talked, Joanna noticed that Adrian's frown grew deeper and deeper. Was he seeing a flaw in Master Osbert that had escaped her?

After a few minutes, Joanna had the information she needed about her potential glass worker. "Thank you, Thomas. I have several more men to talk to, then I'll make my decision."

"I await your reply. Again, it would be an honor to work with you."

The door had scarcely closed behind Thomas before Adrian said, "Absolutely not." He crossed his arms to punctuate his decision.

"Why? I'm interested in your opinion. However, I'll make the decision as to which man to hire." She started toward him, wanting to be close to him, then realized what she was doing. Without even trying, he drew her.

Marriage is our profession, she reminded herself as she walked to her work table instead.

"He is too...soft. He doesn't look sturdy enough to work for you. Who's the next applicant?" Adrian scanned several pieces of parchment on the counter, as though seeking a list of names.

"Thomas's credentials are above reproach. He has a pleasant demeanor, unlike John, and seems amenable to taking direction. He didn't balk at the wages I offered. What more could I ask?"

She turned around to find that he had moved closer to her. Were they like magnets, if one pulled away the other had to follow?

"I will withhold final judgment until we see the others," he said.

"How gracious of you."

"There's no need for sarcasm."

The next man was bulky and harsh, though he came with a good recommendation. She kept the interview short.

"Too much like John," Joanna decided.

"Agreed."

The third was older, with a touch of gray at his temples. His experience, however, didn't match either of the other two.

"I'm not sure any of them is right for you," Adrian commented as he perused their letters of recommendation.

"If I had more time, I might continue the search. But Thomas can start immediately and meets my other requirements."

"There's something about him." He stretched slowly, almost as if to show off his excellent form.

"If I didn't know better, I'd think you were jealous. He is a very attractive man, after all."

Their conversation bordered on the personal, yet remained directly related to her work.

"You prefer fair-haired men, then? And those overly tall." A rare smile followed that comment.

A smile that made Joanna want to melt like glass left too long in the kiln. She couldn't help smiling in return. Until today, she wouldn't have been able to detail what she wanted in a marriage. But this was exactly what she hoped for: companionable conversation, working together, enjoying each other's company. Maybe theirs could become more than a working arrangement after all. Each day she spent with Adrian she found herself wanting a true relationship more and more.

"It's not a question of preference, merely an appreciation of various kinds of beauty. My half-sister Margery would likely drool over Thomas. Perhaps I should introduce them."

He idly toyed with one of her curls. She liked that. Was he was finally going to kiss her? How she wanted him to breach his firm mien and—

"Joanna, I have to talk to you." William burst into the studio, destroying the moment. The door slammed against the wall and made her sheets of glass rattle. He stopped short when he noticed Adrian, then glared. "Alone."

"I'm sorry, but I don't trust you anymore, William. You're lucky I'm willing to talk to you after you and John conspired to destroy me. If you seek a bit of privacy, we can talk in the corner," Joanna said.

After a glance over her shoulder at Adrian, she moved to the corner. Adrian took his stool to the opposite side of the studio. He sat, then folded his arms across his chest as if he had nothing better to do than wait for them to complete their conversation.

"If you insist." William removed his threadbare cloak and dropped it on a stool. "I thought you didn't want to be controlled," he began softly when he joined Joanna. "But you've got this Sir Adrian following you everywhere as though you can't complete a single task without his advice and approval. You didn't want me, your own brother, to tell you what to do. Why him?"

"What I do or don't do with Sir Adrian is none of your affair," she whispered back.

"You'll lose the studio to me no matter what," William said in a falsely soothing tone. "I asked around, and learned that your Sir Adrian is no wealthier than we. Why make this sacrifice and bind yourself forever to a man you've barely met? How do you know he can be trusted?" He shook his head and sighed. "You look exhausted. Why struggle so hard, when with your beauty you can surely find a well-off man to wed and have children with? You shouldn't be a craftsman. You should be like other women, content with hearth and home."

Joanna tamped down fury. She'd said everything she needed to in William's rooms, and had hoped their lives could proceed peacefully and separately. Instead, she'd opened the door to more of his complaining. At least Adrian was there to prevent William from doing anything else…making threats, or worse.

William stood, his black-gloved fists clenched by his sides. He resembled a belligerent child who hadn't gotten his way. But in his tirade a good point or two surfaced, hitting on some of Joanna's own concerns.

"How dare you tell me I'm making a mistake?" she hissed. "Or try to undermine Adrian? I know full well 'twas you and John who lied to my clients and put my guild membership at risk.

"Why would I take your advice? Every time it looks as though I'll comply with the terms of Father's will, you try to stop me."

She didn't bother to whisper. She wanted Adrian to hear. Because of their agreement, he wouldn't learn much about her through their conversations. How could you come to care about someone you didn't know? If he happened to overhear some information about her, his interest in her as a person might grow.

Adrian hadn't moved. Why had he insisted upon not discussing topics of a personal nature…because he feared they might become more than friends or business associates? What could be wrong with that?

"I'm your brother, and if not for Father's will I'd be responsible for your welfare. I want what's best for you. When you refuse to accept that, what choice have I but to take action? I do it all for you!" His voice got louder with each sentence, as though he'd forgotten that he was the one who'd wanted privacy.

"You gamble and drink for me, throwing your coin away on sinful pursuits?" Joanna replied. "You have no talent for, nor even an interest in glass painting. Worse, you only want the workshop because you think that, as eldest and male, you should've been the heir. You made so little effort to learn about the craft. How could Father leave his life's work to a man who'd rather drink and wench than earn an honest living? Than follow in his footsteps?" Anger's acid burned her stomach. "Father gave me this opportunity to prove myself because I worked hard while you didn't, even when given many chances."

"If he was so convinced you should have it, he wouldn't have added the part in his will saying the workshop would go to me if you can't earn enough coin within the year," William reminded her.

"He wanted you to want it so badly that he opened a small window for you. But he knew I would succeed."

"This is not over, Joanna, I promise you." William left in a huff.

Joanna prayed he wouldn't stir up more trouble.

Adrian walked over to her. He put his finger under her chin. "Is the workshop worth it? I actually agree with William on one point," he said softly. "You do work extremely hard."

Joanna relished the concern in his voice and gaze. Perhaps he'd come to regret their strict agreement.

"Sometimes I wonder if glass-painting is worth giving so much of myself to. But seeing my beautiful windows in their new homes never fails to reassure me. It's as if the light streaming through them shines on me to provide courage and strength," she explained. "So I can't give up. I won't abandon the studio, no matter what."

❧ ❧

At that moment, Joanna glowed. Her eyes, her expression, her words captivated him. Adrian could no longer resist her allure. In an instant he drew her into his embrace.

He kissed her, hard and hot.

Joanna opened her mouth against the urging of his. She tasted better than his favorite cherry pottage. Adrian plunged his hands into her hair. The thick, curling masses he'd so longed to touch felt as soft and smelled as pleasing as he'd imagined.

She leaned into him, her breasts against his chest, the softness of her thighs flush against his hardening groin. He clutched her closer, awash in yearning.

Adrian pulled away, struggling to catch his breath. "Joanna. We— I—"

Stunned by the force of his desire for her, he couldn't speak.

Couldn't bring himself to discuss what they'd just done. Doing so would breach their recently signed agreement.

So he left without another word. And cursed himself for acting the coward.

❧ ❧

Two days later, he returned to Joanna's studio.

"Who's there?" she asked when he knocked.

Good. She was being careful about who gained admittance.

"Adrian," he said.

The door remained closed. Wasn't she going to let him in? He was just about to call her name when the door opened.

Her face was still and composed, not warm and welcoming. "Yes?"

"I apologize for my abrupt departure the other day."

She didn't step aside so he could enter.

"All I can say is this business of getting married is unfamiliar. I'm here to confirm the time of our wedding."

She let him in. "Very well."

Warmth from the studio filled him and the sight of her chipped at the barrier he'd erected.

He lingered after they finalized the details, not wanting to leave her just yet. Against his will he found himself interested in her current project, a depiction of St. Edward the Confessor with a flowered border. The quality of her work, of course, is what he cared about. Not the slight blush in her cheek. Not the way she moved, not the expectant look in her eyes.

Did she think constantly of being in his arms, as he thought of holding her again?

He wouldn't revisit the welcome feel of her body or imagine the wonders he knew her clothing concealed. He was bound to support her glass-painting. That had to be why he wanted to stay. He admitted he also wanted to know more about his betrothed. But he'd restricted their relationship. At least her work was an acceptable topic to discuss. He could learn about her through her daily tasks.

What if she wanted to know more about him? She couldn't ask. Her part of the bargain, her safe topic, was providing an heir. Most unlikely she'd want to talk about that. What else did that leave, the weather? Food?

"What's the tool you're using? It looks dangerous," he said.

"This is a dividing iron. You're right, it could be dangerous. I heat the tip to crack the glass." She held up a different tool with a hook at each end. "And this is a grozing iron, which helps me chip the glass into the shape I want."

"What makes glass different colors?"

"Ash and sand are the main ingredients for what we call white glass, which is actually clear. But if there's iron oxide in the mix, you can get a green tinge. Some glass is colored by oxides in the materials and how long they're heated. Oxides are added. As you might expect, cobalt makes blue glass. English glass isn't the best, but glass made elsewhere is more expensive."

When his estates were restored, he'd buy her whatever kind of glass she wanted.

"After I draw the design, called a cartoon, I can use colored glass or add color by painting each piece, sometimes on both sides."

"Where do you buy paint?"

"I mix my own. Then I fire the pieces in my furnace."

Impressive. He made his way around her studio, looking at her tools and bins of glass. Thinking of her touching them and changing them into something beautiful.

The swish of skirts told him Joanna followed. A hint of rose told him she was near. Near enough to kiss again if he turned and took her in his—

"I hope you'll help me delineate the limits of our agreement, which I've memorized," she said. "One condition reads, 'conversations of a personal nature will be kept to a minimum.' But I've noticed that you favor your left wrist and would like to know how you injured it. Is that too personal?"

So the agreement filled her mind as much as it did his. He'd made that restriction to avoid inquiries he didn't wish to answer...why he'd disappear for random periods, maybe even run from the room. Fortunately, recent visions had come upon him when he was alone. He couldn't involve her.

He wasn't sure he liked that Joanna tested the limits so soon. Or that he'd had to establish them in the first place.

Adrian rubbed his wrist. This he could talk about. "It grows stronger, but hasn't returned to normal despite nearly five months of healing. I broke it in July, at Northampton."

"The battle the Yorkists won...where King Henry was taken prisoner?" Joanna asked, her attention on St. Edward.

He nodded.

"Which side were you on?"

"I fight under Warwick's banner."

She looked up at him. "Against the king?"

He couldn't tell if she disapproved or was merely curious. Surely living in York, she too supported the Yorkists in their quest for reform. Not only had Henry VI proved a weak king, many believed the Duke of York was the rightful heir to the throne.

"*For* my overlord," he answered. "His family and mine have been allies for generations. Warwick tried to negotiate before the fighting at Northampton. But the king's commander, the Duke of Buckingham, said Warwick would die if he came into the king's presence. We might have lost if one of the king's men hadn't betrayed the king to help us. Since then, King Henry and the Duke of York have reconciled."

"Again. That I heard...leading to the Act of Accord saying York will be King Henry's heir. But what about Henry's young son? There can only be one king, the anointed one...Henry. Thus, Edward, the prince, should be the next king."

So his betrothed supported King Henry, despite living in York's own city. He never considered that their political views would differ. And didn't like that they did. "Unless you believe the king has usurped York's rightful place, as I do. Our country is as divided on the issue as are we."

He completed his short tour of her workspace and leaned against her counter. She perched on a stool.

After an awkward silence, Joanna said, "We were talking about your wrist. How did you break it?"

He was glad she'd returned to a less volatile subject. "The ground was slick from incessant rain. The poor weather helped us because it prevented the king from using his artillery. But the mud hindered us. I slipped while climbing into the king's camp."

He flexed his hand. If he'd been fortunate enough to have

had a vision about himself, he might've avoided injury. Fortunately, he'd had no visions of that battle. One of the few he could fight as a normal man, without knowing the outcome and who would live or die. Without agonizing over whether he could or should share his knowledge and worry about what might happen if he did and his fellow soldiers wanted to know how he knew.

His head ached with memories of that day and other battles he'd fought in service of his country. Every time it looked as though peace might thrive between the Yorkists and the king, something pulled them apart. Because Warwick was one of York's main supporters, Adrian was often in the thick of things. Part of his duty, but another distraction from his own goals.

"Do you think there will be more fighting?" she asked.

"Yes," he said. *I know so. And soon.*

Joanna was surprisingly quiet again. No more questions, no commentary on the war. Her skin was paler than he'd seen it, her eyes huge and green as the glass on her table.

"Joanna, what troubles you?"

"You'll leave if there is more fighting."

"That depends," he began.

He realized what was bothering her. She depended on him to protect her and feared what might happen while he was away. Her reliance made him feel more powerful than victory in battle.

"Already I see a flaw in our agreement. There's no provision for absences. How do we uphold it if you're not here? If you die in battle?"

He couldn't tell her why it was unlikely he'd be joining Warwick for any fighting in the near future.

"Let's not worry about that until we come to it," he said, disheartened.

She nodded and returned to her work, but he sensed her unease. Already his secrets came between them.

CHAPTER 8

A wedding should be a special day, with feasting and revelry. But so far, Joanna's was nothing like the weddings she'd been to or heard about.

There'd been no procession to the church, because there weren't enough witnesses. Only Margery and a few favored clients were in attendance. Adrian hadn't invited anyone and wouldn't explain why, which irked her. Of course she couldn't ask.

She lacked coin for new finery, though she stood in the church next to Adrian in her best gown, which Margery had hastily embellished with a few ribbons. He looked so handsome in the black tunic he'd worn when they first met.

Three saints in a window her father had designed seemed to mock her. If he'd been alive, none of this would've come to pass. Well, it had, and she should start making the best of it.

"Are there any known impediments to this marriage?" asked the priest.

"No," she and Adrian answered.

They shared a smile, which eased her fears.

At the priest's prompting, Adrian said in his deep voice she could listen to for hours, "I take thee Joanna to my wedded wife, to have and to hold, from this day forward, for better or worse, for richer for poorer, in sickness and in health, 'til death do us part, if Holy Church it will ordain, and thereto I plight thee my troth."

Joanna's consent was similar, though she also had to say she'd be meek and obedient. Yet another advantage given to men. Her voice sounded clear and confident despite her racing heart.

The priest blessed a gold band Adrian handed to him, then placed it on her right hand. Though thin, it felt out of place on her finger.

Now for the kiss. Adrian leaned forward for a brief meeting of lips, nothing more. Disappointing. Maybe he was saving his kisses for later. When they were alone.

Afterward came not a wedding banquet, but a small supper of mutton tart, almond pudding and fresh ale at her favorite inn, The Swan. Amidst laughing patrons, Joanna felt numb.

"And I'm very much looking forward to visiting my friend Lady Isobel next week," Margery said. "She has the most adorable dog who just had even more adorable puppies. They're so tiny, with such sweet little tongues and paws. I wish I could have one, but of course we don't have a garden...."

For once Joanna was glad her half-sister had so much to say as they enjoyed the meal. Being a wife was too new, too unsettling.

When her half-sister finally paused to take a sip of ale, Adrian leaned close.

"I'll come to you tonight," he whispered.

Good thing she didn't choke on her mouthful of mutton tart.

❧❦ ❦❧

That night, Joanna perched on the edge of the narrow bed in Adrian's room, twisting the faded coverlet in her chilled fingers.

The concept was difficult to absorb, but she was now a wife. Soon she and Adrian would consummate their marriage. Her ear and the side of her neck still tingled from his warm breath when he told her he'd come to her.

Though she yearned to touch him, kiss him again, nervousness mingled with desire. Would he behave as any husband with a new bride? Or would the constrictions of their agreement stifle any hope of passion, relegating any intimacy of their joining to mere necessity?

Margery's off-key humming intruded into her thoughts. Her half-sister moved briskly about the narrow room, placing a small bouquet of dried flowers in various locations and rearranging the stems over and over. She looked lovely as ever in her best gown of imported wool.

"Margery, what have I done? Marrying a man I hardly know, committing myself under God?" Joanna asked.

"Of the choices you faced, you've surely made the best one," Margery said.

"Yes. I wanted this," Joanna reminded herself. She took a deep breath and let it out, but anxiety remained. "I still don't know why a man of noble birth would want to marry me. Surely there's some lady who'd want him. Or is he less desirable because of the stories that once circulated about his father?"

"Perhaps his lack of funds hinder him. Even nobles prefer to marry someone who can increase their wealth and stature," Margery offered.

"What if I'm not elegant or refined enough? Think of the women he must be used to."

"Whatever his reasons, he married you. Though not in the most festive of ways." Margery clamped her lips together, but Joanna knew what she meant to say.

"The wedding meal was delicious, though. I've not tasted mutton tart as good. Now you can begin your new life," Margery fidgeted with the flowers as though the safety of the world depended on their arrangement. "Joanna, we must talk. You need to know some things. Do you know what a man does when he…? You see, a man has a…. He puts his…."

Joanna felt herself flushing. Her life was her work. She'd barely considered any intimacies with a man beyond kissing, which had thus far proved most interesting. "No, I don't know. How do you? Have you already…?"

Margery kept her back turned. "Not exactly. But I wanted to find out beforehand, so I asked a married friend or two. Not an easy topic to discuss."

Did Margery feel as awkward as she did? Embarrassed and nervous, not an auspicious way to begin a marriage. Did other brides feel this way? Margery joined her on the bed and took her hands.

"How I wish your mother or mine was here to have this conversation," she said. "You see, when married people share a bed...." She continued in a rush, "A man has a male part called a penis. A cock. It gets hard, and then he can put it in—"

"How does it get hard?"

"I'm not exactly sure. Then he puts it inside you."

"How?"

"He'll know," Margery answered. "And the act can hurt the first time, and sometimes after that."

"If 'the act' hurts, how do women bear doing it more than once?"

"They want more babies, of course," Margery said. "Then once he's in, he moves around until he's done."

"Done with what?" Joanna asked, awash with naiveté. How could a woman her age not know such things? Why were women kept in the dark about such an important topic?

"Men feel pleasure, and then they're done." Margery walked back to her flowers, moving the blossoms back and forth. Bits of colorful petals dropped to the ground, dislodged by her repeated agitation.

"How long does it take?"

"I'm not sure. If he wants to kiss and touch you, maybe a long time. That I do know. Kissing can be very nice, with the right man. But then again, kissing can be very wet and sloppy. Did you know they use their tongues?"

Joanna remembered the night she and Adrian had signed the agreement, when she'd thought he was about to kiss her. How she had wanted him to. Then when he had, she'd not wanted him to stop.

"Yes, I know. We've only kissed that way once, but I liked it." She couldn't bring herself to mention the yearning she'd felt, the tingling in her most private place. "Do women feel pleasure too?"

"Some, I think."

"What am I supposed to do?"

"Act as though you enjoy it?" Margery surmised. "I wish I knew more. But soon you can tell me all about lovemaking."

"'Tis so very discomfiting to talk about. But I'll try."

"Oh, Joanna." Margery crossed to Joanna and enveloped her in a quick hug. "Congratulations," she said with a teary smile, and left Joanna alone.

Though she knew Margery had been trying to cheer her, Joanna's heart sank.

"Thereto I plight thee my troth," she'd vowed.

For the rest of her life.

But what should she expect from her partner by contract? She must've imagined that suspended moment in her studio when he'd looked at her with such intensity, the way she thought a man would look at a woman he desired. The anticipation she'd felt was real.

Now she waited for her husband. How odd that appellation seemed. Husband. She wiped her hands on her wedding gown of blue wool, much as she had the day of Adrian's sitting, hoping to remove the dampness before he arrived. She didn't want him to know how nervous she was. Not only about the impending loss of her virginity, but the beginning of their life together. She wanted their marriage to start off well. But the sand melted through the hourglass after Margery left, the candles burned ever lower.

Despite her intent to wait for Adrian, she fell asleep. A soft knock on the door woke her. As she sat up, he opened it, pausing at the threshold. Firelight from the small brazier illuminated him. He still wore the black, short tunic with full sleeves and tight woolen hose he'd worn at the wedding. The same garments he'd had on the day she met him. The jacket, with a stamped diamond pattern on black velvet, outlined his broad shoulders, while the belt delineated his waist. The hose revealed his muscular thighs and the curve of his calves.

Joanna's mouth went dry, from a mixture of nerves, desire and curiosity about her handsome husband. Reading his thoughts was impossible. Did he find her attractive in the least? He'd once said she was beautiful. Did he want, even the tiniest bit, to make love to her, or did he only want his heir? Whether he desired her or not shouldn't matter in this marriage of convenience, but it did.

Joanna wished she knew how women made men desire them. The confidence that filled her while she painted her windows and discussed commissions had fled.

Adrian walked to the bed and unbuckled his belt. He pulled off the tunic, leaving the short doublet underneath. He untied his collar and sleeves, then the ties on his doublet, exposing dark hairs and a hint of his chest. His shoulders flexed as he removed his undergarment. That left his hose and pointed shoes.

Joanna continued to meet his gaze, refusing to look away. She wanted him to know she wasn't afraid. Moistening her dry lips with her tongue, she moved her hands to her waist to untie her robe.

"Wait." Adrian's voice was low and deep. "Not yet."

Joanna's hands stopped on her belt. Already she'd done the wrong thing. She drew the robe tighter about her.

The ropes creaked as he sat sideways on the bed. She turned to face him, trying not to stare at the well-muscled expanse of his chest. Soon she'd see all of him. Touch all of him. The first foray into intimacy. Into secrets.

She took in a deep breath and let it out. Tension combined with budding desire made her heart pound as she felt the heat of him warm her.

Adrian ran his hands through her hair, gently brushing it back from her face, watching as the curls straightened then recurled. He took a single curl and wrapped the strands around his finger.

"How I've wanted to do this again. So soft." He bent toward her and inhaled. "And smells even better."

At least he liked her hair. Joanna felt that strange tingling in her most private parts as he leaned closer.

He tangled his hands in her hair and gently drew her near, so their mouths were only inches apart. His eyes, darker blue now, filled with warmth and sparks of hunger. His breath smelled of mint.

Anticipation built within her.

"I've wanted to do this again too," he whispered.

He did want her. Joanna rejoiced.

Adrian lowered his lips to hers and kissed her softly. He pulled back as if to see how she reacted to his touch. Seemingly satisfied, he shifted closer. He kissed her, his mouth firm on her own. Then he showered light kisses on her lips, her face, her neck. Everywhere his lips touched, she felt a rush of incredible warmth. Joanna captured his and kissed him, gasping as his tongue met hers. He deepened the kiss, taking possession of her with the force of his desire.

She slid her arms behind his neck and drew him against her, savoring the heat and solidness of his chest through her thin robe. Joanna wanted to spend hours enjoying the feel of his mouth on hers, the warmth and hardness of him against her.

He broke the kiss. He untied her belt and slipped the soft wool from her shoulders. Adrian groaned softly as he exposed her nakedness. He reached out to take her breasts into his hands.

"Yes," he murmured.

Slowly he explored them, gently lifting, sliding his fingers over the taut nipples. Ripples of pleasure spread through her.

"Oh, yes," she agreed.

Her husband wanted her. The heady power heightened her arousal.

He leaned forward, looking up at her as his tongue flicked out to lick her nipple. Then he closed his eyes, sucking her gently, swirling his tongue over her flesh. She swayed, twining her fingers in his hair to draw him closer. She relished the wondrous sensations flowing through her at Adrian's touch.

Margery hadn't mentioned anything about this.

His lips still doing marvelous things to her skin, Adrian picked Joanna up and set her on her back. He pulled away, leaving her wanting more. She reclined against the pillows and waited. Adrian kept his eyes on her as he removed his shoes, then dropped his hose.

For the first time Joanna looked upon an aroused man. And wasn't sure she liked what she saw.

Had Margery known how big a man's cock could be?

❧ ❧

Adrian watched Joanna as he removed his clothes, hoping to encourage her natural passion. She presented an incredibly erotic picture with her curls tumbling about her in enticing disarray, her breasts partially covered by the silken strands. He liked the way she watched him, unabashed, without the shy, embarrassed mien of a virgin. The way her slight smile seemed to welcome him.

He'd known Joanna only a short time, but he knew that no woman from his past could compare to her. For no other woman was Joanna. He wanted to bring her pleasure while satisfying his own desires. But what if—

All would be lost unless he lived in the moment.

Her mouth dropped open as his hose slid to the floor. He should've remembered sooner that lovemaking was new to her. But she'd come so willingly into his arms, her kisses had been so arousing. Still, he should move slower, for her sake. Theirs may be a marriage of convenience, but that didn't mean they couldn't enjoy each other.

He should add a stipulation: intimate conversation about making love was more than welcome.

"You're so beautiful," he said. "I'm a fortunate husband."

Her smile was his reward.

Slowly, he pushed her hair from her breasts so he could see them better. Her curls shimmered fiery red in the brazier's glow. He resumed his gentle assault, stroking her softness. Savoring the fact that she was his.

He leaned forward and sucked gently on her nipple, swirling his tongue over her flesh. She tasted sweet as honeyed wine. His erection pulsed as she swayed against him, her hands in his hair drawing him closer.

Adrian had to feel her skin against his. He eased himself onto the bed alongside her.

Exquisite.

"What should I do?" she whispered.

"What do you desire?"

"I want to touch you."

"I want that, too." He needed it.

Joanna sat up, her hair tumbling about them. Her small hands slid leisurely over his shoulders, down his arms. She caressed his chest, letting her fingers trail over the ridges of muscle. His heartbeat quickened, sending heat through his veins. He responded to her so quickly, so thoroughly.

Seeing and touching her, being touched in return heightened his arousal to the limits of his control. If her exploration went any lower, he wouldn't last. He'd never ached so strongly with the need for release.

Could Joanna tell how much he wanted her? How much she affected him? Despite their agreement, he wanted her to know how special she was to him. He'd show her. He moved over her, bracing himself on his knees as he kissed her. Not the pretty kisses they'd shared thus far, but a deep, thirsting kiss to convey his yearning. He put his arms around her and pressed against her. She kissed him back with equal fervor.

Adrian reached between them to stroke her secret softness. She squeezed her legs together, trapping his hand.

"Open for me," he whispered. "Let me pleasure you."

She released her grip, giving him access.

So wet. So ready. He had done that. She wanted him. Another surge of desire charged through him. Straight to his groin.

Joanna moaned as he established a soothing rhythm, lifting her hips against his hand. He had to be inside her.

"Adrian, more...." she gasped.

Her demand pleased him to the depths of his soul. She was as caught up in passion as he. Next time, he'd prolong their lovemaking. But his wife wanted him now, and he'd do his best to surpass any expectations.

He positioned himself. The tip of his erection pressed against her, sending fervid pulses through his very core. Carefully, defying the urgency within, he eased inside to allow her to adjust. He pulled away, then entered her again, moving a bit deeper into her moist heat. Joanna wriggled beneath him, as if to help him embed himself.

Adrian wanted to plunge into her, but pushed as gently as he could, moving past the tight barrier. Joanna gasped again, in pain, not pleasure, Adrian was sure. He hoped she'd soon join him in relishing the rightness of their joining, in the need for completion.

Her hands tightened on his arms as he waited, motionless, enjoying the incredible sensation of being enveloped by her. Soon, soon they'd reach the pinnacle and release the wonderful tension building between them.

Suddenly his head started to pound. Next came the severe ache behind his eyes. He stiffened over her. Intense dread consumed him, obliterating arousal.

No, no, not now of all times! Not now. Though he tried to will the vision away, there was nothing he could do to stop it.

"Adrian?"

Joanna's voice was low, sensuous. Her clear green gaze, so trusting, marred by slight confusion.

How many times would he have to betray that trust before she had none left to give?

His vision began to blur. He had to leave. Now. Or she'd learn his deepest secret. Any moment he could lose consciousness or enter a trance-like state where he might say anything. Do anything. For both their sakes, he couldn't risk exposing her to his Sight.

"Adrian? Is something wrong?"

He felt Joanna's concern through his pain. "I must go."

Adrian pulled away and fled to his room across the hall, immersed in his suffering. Hands shaking, he slammed the door and managed to lock it. He staggered to his bed, then collapsed onto it, not having the will to cover himself.

The power of the vision gripped him, sucking him into its otherworldly depths.

His last rational thought was of Joanna. How could he ever explain this to her?

CHAPTER 9

"This is nothing to laugh at!" Joanna cried as Margery doubled over on a stool in Joanna's workshop. Peals of glee echoed off the walls. Joanna threw a small brush at her half-sister. The brush missed its target and dropped to the floor. "Stop that. You should be more concerned for my welfare. I've been miserable ever since."

After several long moments, Margery's laughter subsided. She wiped tears from her cheeks, then caught her breath. "He left in the mi—middle?"

She collapsed again in a helpless fit of laughter, resting her head on the counter.

"Well, I think it was the middle. Perhaps closer to the end. How was I to be sure?" Joanna asked. "I didn't realize how complicated lovemaking could be. This is most embarrassing. I never should've told you."

She picked up her grozing iron and furiously snipped the edges off of a piece of glass. Out of the corner of her eye, she saw Margery bite her lip to hide another smile.

"Forgive me for laughing. I do want to help. Tell me." She leaned on her elbows. "Was it good?"

Joanna felt herself blush. "Really, Margery. All right, yes, quite good at first. The kissing was truly wondrous. He did want to kiss and touch me, as you'd said he might. Then he, he…he put…his hardened male part…which seemed large…."

She fervently wished she was less desperate for an explanation of his sudden departure. Worry consumed her like a raging bonfire. What had happened last night? Had she done something wrong? She'd waited, tense and hopeful at the same time, but he didn't return to her room. His closed door seemed an unbreachable wall. After she heard him leave at first light, Joanna hurried to the studio and waited for Margery to awaken.

"So he was inside you."

"Well, yes."

Joanna thought back for the hundredth time. She had relived their aborted lovemaking over and over, analyzing every move. She'd been so intrigued by him and what he'd do next. His hands on her, the feelings and sensations engendered by their closeness had been more intense than she'd thought possible. A strange need had built inside her.

Adrian had seemed as pleased as she, the look in his eyes more tender than she'd seen.

She couldn't figure out what had gone wrong. Had she disappointed him when she involuntarily stiffened at the sharp sting of losing her virginity? Even during the brief discomfort, she was steeped in desire. Surely he could tell that. Had there been something she was supposed to do or say?

Joanna cursed her innocence. But Adrian had known it was her first time. He had to have known there'd be some pain.

She sighed. "He was inside me for just a moment. Then he froze. He had the strangest expression on his face. Then he hurried away without a word of explanation," she said. "The kissing and touching took some time, but the other didn't take very long. How long should that part last?"

"Different amounts of time for different men. Did he moan and groan a lot? Grunt?"

"Men grunt?" That didn't sound appealing. "Not really."

Adrian's eyes had clouded over. He'd tensed above her, then whispered, "No," before clambering off the bed and running from her and the room without his robe or his clothes. She'd remained on the bed, clutching his tunic as if the garment could explain its owner's strange behavior.

The physical pain of losing her virginity had been nothing compared to the agonizing mystery of his abandonment mixed with unfulfilled desire.

"Hmmm." Margery frowned, then retrieved the brush Joanna had thrown. Idly she flicked the dry brush across the counter. "At first I thought he might have finished too early and was embarrassed. Did some fluid come from him? Or did you scream, or pull away? No, he wouldn't have left if you had," Margery answered her own question. "How did he look?"

"Sick, actually."

"Sick? I've never heard of such a thing. Unless he prefers men to women," Margery mused.

"What?"

"No, surely not Adrian," Margery continued as though Joanna hadn't spoken. "Hmmm. Maybe he had a touch of ague and didn't want to vomit all over your pure flesh."

"Margery!"

"Maybe he too was new to lovemaking and was nervous?"

"I doubt that. I've never seen Adrian nervous." Joanna forced herself to voice her greatest concern. "I must've done something to offend or disappoint him. I fear I've failed him. Perhaps I shouldn't have listened to your advice, but I tried to show him I enjoyed his touch. Is it possible to be too enthusiastic?"

For a few moments she'd feared he thought her wanton. She'd wanted to ask, but just couldn't. This was too personal for her, whether talk of what went on in their bed fell under his definition of personal or not. Maybe, over time, she'd grow more comfortable.

"I don't know much about the marriage bed, but I do know yours is a strange tale. Like as not he'll return this evening with sweet apologies and make it up to you," Margery said. "You worry too much, as usual. You barely know the man. Who knows what he has up his sleeve?"

❧ ☙

Ignoring bitter winds, Adrian paced the streets of York, pondering his problems as he often had over the past few days. Walking once helped him uncover answers, the methodical movements somehow freeing his thoughts.

Not this time.

He couldn't bear to face Joanna. How could he explain what had happened on their wedding night? Not only would the truth endanger her, she'd be appalled and likely want nothing more to do with him. What woman wanted a husband who had visions of what was to come? A man who was so different from other men, whose affliction, if discovered, would lead him to be thought a heretic or a sorcerer so the authorities might put him to death.

On the other hand, he couldn't bring himself to lie to her. For several days he'd taken the coward's way out, though he hated doing so. He slipped into his room in the wee hours of the morning and left before she woke. Each time, he had to force himself not to turn back and tell her everything. Adrian knew she'd keep to their agreement and not approach him on so sensitive an issue. But the issue had to be broached. He needed to know what she was thinking, how she felt. To find a way to apologize.

He missed talking to her. Their visits to her clients and time spent working together to satisfy the guild had filled a need for companionship he hadn't known he had. She'd unearthed it and made him want more. He thought of her constantly. Which made him wonder what was wrong with him, for he'd never spent so much time thinking about a woman. Then again, he'd never had a wife.

What if she needed him and he wasn't there? He'd be breaking their agreement. He'd fail her. There had to be a way to free himself from this awful coil. Because of his Sight, he was no closer to fathering another heir than the day they married.

Which brought him back to their bizarre wedding night. The vision that interrupted their lovemaking was of a battle between the king's men and the Duke of York. He didn't know when, but he knew where. And he knew who would die.

As always, he wrestled with the difficult choice of whether or not to disclose his knowledge. And if he chose to share what he'd seen, how to explain. Perhaps he could tell Warwick he'd found some correspondence from the king's party detailing the battle plan. But if Warwick asked to see the documents....

Lies upon lies, weaving a web stickier than a spider's.

Who should decide: Adrian, York, or the king? And at what

risk to the future? Did he see destiny? How might the future be altered if the deaths were prevented?

That might be the worst thing of all about his "gift," worrying what would happen in the changed future if he helped someone avoid death or injury. Would more people suffer later because he saved someone now? Or was he supposed to save the subject of this particular vision so the future would be changed?

He couldn't come up with a way to decide whom to warn. Nor could he keep what he knew from haunting him.

He could eke out one bit of good news. Usually his visions came several weeks apart, sometimes as long as a month. It was safe to go to Joanna now and spend a few days in her company, letting her goodness soothe him. He could be her husband. He could pretend his troubles were over.

Another problem ensnared him, one he had to resolve before the others. Adrian stood at the front door of Bedford Castle, on schedule for his weekly visit with Lady Anne. For the past few weeks he'd sent word he was too busy to meet with her. She hadn't replied.

He couldn't avoid her forever.

Disgust curdled in his stomach as it did whenever he thought of his peculiar arrangement.

Now he had another unusual agreement with another woman, his wife. To touch Lady Anne now that he was married would be a desecration of his vows, not to mention a betrayal of Joanna's trust. But if he didn't follow through, and if Warwick couldn't help him, he'd lose his house and his father's fortune, the cornerstone of his family's future. He'd fail the goal he'd pursued all of his adult life. Unless he could convince Lady Anne to let him find another way to regain his house.

He needed more time at Bedford Castle or he'd fail Warwick as well.

Stomach churning, Adrian knocked on the door. Seconds later, it opened.

"Lady Anne awaits you," her plump servant, Pamping, said with a bow.

Adrian gritted his teeth as he followed the short, bald man inside. He knew the way to each room with his eyes closed. Pamping insisted on leading him to Lady Anne each week, which made Adrian seethe. He didn't need reminding that the house was no longer his.

"Ah, my Adrian." She reclined on the bed, her velvet robe tied loosely. The harsh morning light fell through the windows onto her. "Wherever have you been? Come to me."

She opened the robe.

He closed the door as the servant bowed and left them, then crossed to the bed. "Lady Anne, I need to tell you something. I can't continue this liaison."

"Whyever not?" She toyed with her belt, her eyes narrowing.

Days ago, he'd relieved Joanna of her robe. Before disaster struck. He blinked, remembering again the look of confusion on Joanna's face.

Focus. There was no way to prepare Lady Anne for his news.

"I have married."

Lady Anne flew off the bed with the speed of a young woman.

"What?" she shrieked. She clutched her robe closed, as if to deny him the supposed pleasure of viewing her body. Adrian didn't recoil from her stale breath. "Why didn't you tell me? Is that what you've been off doing all these weeks, fornicating with your bride?"

Lady Anne looked so angry that for a moment Adrian believed she'd hit him.

"Who is she?" She waved her hand in the air as if wiping it clean of her own thoughts. "You think you can break our agreement by marrying? You can't. Not if you still want this house. Which I know you do. So come to bed. Now. Or I'll leave the house to a convent, and you'll never set foot in here again." She rubbed against him. "You want your house and I want you. Nothing has changed."

Adrian swallowed. He watched his dreams tumble away and was powerless to stop them.

"Everything has changed. We can't continue. I will remain true to my vows and to my wife." No matter the cost. *For they're all I have left to be proud of.* "Let's agree upon some other way for me to acquire the house. Perhaps there are repairs you need done?"

She laughed. "What of your wrist? It might amuse me to see the proud Sir Adrian Bedford debasing himself with manual labor."

The irony would've made him smile if he had less at stake. Repairing his own home was degrading while having sex with her to earn it wasn't?

"My wrist improves each day." He rubbed the scars, a constant reminder of what war could do to a man. "Please, Lady Anne, let us find another way."

Adrian cringed at the wheedling tone in his voice. So much for the proud Sir Adrian Bedford. But he was willing to do a little groveling for his house.

And he'd never have to touch Lady Anne again.

"No," she said, wagging her finger at him. "We made a deal. With no provisions for alteration. You'd best forget this house and go back to your bride. Is she worth all you have lost?" she hissed. "You'll be sorry you crossed me, I'll see to it. I may be old, but I can still wreak havoc."

"Name your price. I'll buy the house from you."

"Ha. Even if you could afford to pay, which I know you can't, I'd never sell *my* house to you. Not now." She drew her robe tighter and rose to her full height. She tied her sash belt with finality. "Leave. Don't come back until you're ready to return to my bed. I will not give you up."

Worse and worse, Adrian thought as he left his house for what could very well be the last time. He looked over his shoulder at the familiar façade to make sure every brick, every mullioned window was implanted in his memory. His dreams crumbled at his feet, years of effort obliterated by a single conversation. For a moment, he allowed himself the luxury of mourning his loss.

Ending his visits to Lady Anne was the right choice. He'd rebuild his dreams. There had to be another way.

Lady Anne had threatened trouble. Finding out whom he had married wouldn't be difficult. If she went to Joanna and told her they'd been lovers, and why, Joanna would be devastated. And what if Lady Anne cancelled her commission for the new windows, which he knew Joanna needed to achieve her own goals?

Adrian had to outthink and outsmart Lady Anne.

He shuddered. He felt sullied by his past, haunted by the sacrifices he'd had to make. How could he go to Joanna, so fresh, so lovely? Could he ever cleanse himself of his mistakes and his secrets to be worthy of her?

Not a very auspicious way to begin his role as husband. If he didn't make things right with her, his marriage would be over before it started.

And he'd hate himself forever.

CHAPTER 10

To complete the restoration of her reputation, Joanna spent every waking moment finishing windows her clients had commissioned, so she focused on her designs, the painting and firing of her glass. When she looked up, a week had gone by.

"A week. We've been married for seven days and he hasn't come to me since that first night," Joanna confessed to Margery, who'd stopped by Adrian's rooms to tell Joanna of a possible new client. "He's gone with me to visit clients to make sure William and John don't try to harm me or my business again. Then he leaves. I've tried to concentrate on my windows. But it's not easy. The expressions on the faces I paint all come out confused. I have to force myself to think serene thoughts to get them right."

Margery's own expression had given her away when Joanna let her in, as though she'd forgotten how sad and unwelcoming Adrian's rooms were. To her credit, Margery hadn't said a disparaging word about Joanna's new home.

No, not a home. Not yet. Maybe not ever.

Each woman sat on a plain wooden chair without even a cushion for comfort, drinking watered wine. A musty odor lingered in the air despite Joanna's best efforts to eradicate it with a thorough cleaning and dried herbs.

"Seven nights," she repeated. Lying alone in Adrian's bed. Worrying.

Under the terms of the agreement Joanna already despised,

she couldn't ask why he stayed away or where he went. Asking him what was taking so long to return to her bed, why he was no longer anxious to produce an heir, would also be too personal, because he'd said he would come to her at his convenience. She'd fooled herself into thinking she'd seen desire in his gaze. That he'd care about her.

"Adrian still hasn't spoken about his behavior on the night you wed?" Margery asked. "I've done some investigating. Men don't often leave in the middle, never to return."

Embarrassment washed over Joanna anew. "I must've done something so awful he couldn't bear to stay and can't bear to face me now. He left to spare me discomfort. What other explanation could there be?"

Margery set down her cup of wine and paced the narrow room. "You don't think he has another woman?"

They gasped in unison.

"Oh, Joanna, you know I speak before I think. He wouldn't have married you if there was someone else…"

Joanna couldn't breathe. She wanted to vomit. Surely Adrian wouldn't break his vows. Could she trust him that far? Was another woman the reason for their agreement forbidding personal conversation?

"Perhaps he has preferred another all along but couldn't marry her for some reason," she whispered, because despair clogged her throat.

His kisses and caresses had thrilled her. She hadn't known she could experience anything like the marvelous fullness of him inside her. She hadn't known she could be so drawn to a man, especially in such a short time. What should she have done to show him how she felt?

"You haven't asked what's bothering him?"

How could she tell her sister that their marriage agreement prohibited her from asking such questions? The more she thought about it, the sillier the dictate seemed. If only she'd had more time to make her decision before signing, more time to negotiate the unusual terms.

"It's almost as though he is two people. Before, he was courteous, charming, and helpful. Now, when he is here, he's distant, unapproachable, even bordering on sullen." She took a sip of wine to erase the bitter taste in her mouth. "He disappears for long stretches of time, not returning 'til almost dawn."

"Does he drink? Remember Uncle Frederick, how he used to behave strangely after drinking all that ale?" Margery returned to her chair and picked up her cup.

"I haven't seen him drink much of anything since we wed. Who knows what he does when we're apart? I feel like a fool waiting for him night after night but I can't help myself," Joanna confessed.

How could I have known I'd miss him so? The desire to touch him, to taste his kiss, to be with the Adrian she thought she'd married never left her.

Now that Margery was seated again, Joanna started pacing. "I was worried this might happen. Thoughts of him follow me throughout the day. I must focus on work to stay on schedule." She turned and started in the other direction. "Yet in other respects, my work has improved. My muse is free again, since Adrian helped mend my relationships with the clients William had John try to sway against me."

"I don't think you've heard the last of them," Margery said. "But we were speaking of Adrian. Joanna, you must find the courage to talk to him, or you'll suffer in silence until...if...he's ready to explain." Margery took in the sparsely decorated room. She shook her head. "You're obviously besotted. You'll lose yourself if you go too far. But desire for your husband is a good thing."

"Not if he doesn't desire me in return. I can't believe we're talking about these things but, Margery, there are moments when his presence is with me so strongly I stop what I am doing, close my eyes, and enjoy it. I didn't know I could feel this way about a man."

"I wish I could find a man who made me feel that way." Margery said, wistfulness coloring her tone.

"On the other hand, each minute this remains unresolved is painful, right here," Joanna said, pointing to her chest. "Each time I think on it, the pain returns anew and spreads. How can I trust him, with so many secrets between us? When he kissed me, touched me.... I don't have the words to explain how wonderful I felt."

"Do you love him?" She paused in the midst of pouring more watered wine.

"Love?" Joanna scoffed. "How can you even ask? Love, if it exists, is a spell that destroys those who succumb."

"Just because Father fell in love with my mother after yours died...."

"Love consumed him. As you said, he went too far. He rarely worked. Anything she wanted, at any time, was hers. No matter what he had to do to fulfill her requests. If Father hadn't had me to assist him, he'd have run the entire workshop into the ground to please her. We would've starved.

"All for something you can't see, can't hold, can't eat. All for love," Joanna said, hearing the rancor in her voice. But words continued to spill forth. "Do you recall how devastated Father was when your mother died? He was so consumed with grief. People use love as an excuse to avoid responsibilities, to focus their energies on hedonistic pursuits. Love makes people completely happy or completely miserable. I've never seen any other type. Have you? I can't be that vulnerable. I can't allow anyone to have that much control over me."

Not even Adrian.

She needed this reminder why a marriage of convenience was a good thing.

"Love can make people stronger, make them better because they have another person's support. Knowing a man cared enough for me to worry about me, to want to be with me, to make love to me would give my life more meaning," Margery said. "A man who would hold me in his arms all night long..."

"Love makes you vulnerable. Father doted on your mother. He couldn't stop himself. The best marriages are based on companionship, mutual support and compromise. That I have, and that's all I need."

Even as Joanna said the words, she knew she wanted more from Adrian. She did want him to care for her. She wanted to be more important to him than anything else. As he was becoming to her, in spite of his behavior on their wedding night. In spite of her will to remain immune.

What if she was already lost?

"Are you sure you aren't saying these things to protect

yourself? Because Adrian hasn't told you how he feels about you?"

Hasn't and never will. She took a large sip of wine to keep from telling Margery the truth of their marriage.

"Perhaps no one is meant to be too happy," Margery said. "Concentrate on the good, and pray that the rest will resolve itself with time," she advised. "Where is he now?"

"I wish I knew."

🙚 🙘

"Joanna."

Adrian's deep voice woke her. Feeling groggy, she sat up. She must've fallen asleep at the small table she'd squeezed into her room. The square piece of glass she'd been painting teetered on the table's edge. Joanna rescued it with a small push from behind.

Where was Adrian? She squinted, but couldn't see him in the dim candlelight. She was imagining things. He wasn't there.

Another troubled night. She sighed and stretched, straining to see if Adrian was in the room. No, just wishful thinking.

But he stepped into the candle glow, his shirt untucked and flowing over his hose. Her heart raced. The first time in seven nights he'd come to her. He paused, as if uncertain how to proceed. Flickering light danced over his face, highlighting his strong cheekbones.

His presence reassured her. She didn't need an explanation of his strange behavior, she needed him. If he made love to her, it would prove he still valued their marriage. Now, he'd surely take her now.

She raised her face, hoping for his kiss. She didn't try to hide the passion in her eyes. He might harbor secrets, but she didn't. They were married. She was ready to fulfill her part of their agreement. It was long past time.

He raised his hand and lifted her chin, sending his warmth through her.

Yes, yes, kiss me.

"You have charcoal all over you." He selected a rag from the pile on the table and gently wiped her face.

Joanna's heart sank. She wouldn't let her disappointment show. She had agreed to this, hadn't she?

"Up late again?" Adrian asked, moving a step closer.

She relished having him so near. The heat of his body encompassed her, sending shivers down her spine. He awoke a sensual nature she hadn't known she had.

She smiled. Despite their separate rooms, despite the odd hours he kept, he'd noticed her late night sessions.

"And what keeps you awake?" She leaned toward him, making it easier for him to reach her. If this was all the contact she was going to get, she'd make the most of it. Ah, he smelled so clean, so enticing. So Adrian. If only she could tell him how much she wanted him or ask if he felt the same. No. She wouldn't break their agreement. Even though the reason was honorable, she didn't want to risk losing a fragment of his trust. She'd promised to uphold the rules, no matter how difficult that was to do.

※ ※

Adrian admired the lovely face of his bride as he wiped charcoal smudges from her smooth skin. Her parted lips were so tempting, the curling hair he longed to touch so soft against his hands. The need in her eyes fed his own. That gave him hope. He feared their aborted lovemaking had crushed her interest.

Just being near her, in her delicate nightgown was enough to make him hard.

There was so much he wished he could tell Joanna, but he didn't dare. Only time could earn trust.

One more thing he didn't have.

How could he tell her he had visions like his grandmother, who was burned at the stake? That he was afraid to come to her because to have a vision in her presence, as he almost had on their wedding night, would be worst of all? He couldn't bear to see the desire and trust in her eyes turn to horror as a vision assaulted him.

Even if he dared trust her, he couldn't place the burden of knowledge upon her. For she'd have to struggle with her conscience as his father once did. As Andrew did now. If he was taken and she knew his secret, she might be tortured until she told. Or she too might be arrested and punished with him.

How could he watch her suffer because of him? The sights, sounds and smells of his grandmother at the stake flashed before his eyes. She'd burned. He'd been spared. Grandmother had kept his secret and he must honor her memory.

Far better for them both that Joanna know nothing. Then she couldn't testify against him if forced, or, God forbid, do so voluntarily. What could be worse than if she turned him in as his father had his grandmother?

Far better to trust no one. *For when a relationship falls apart, your friend becomes your enemy.*

Joanna had returned to her painting, fine black lines on green glass forming an arm and part of a shoulder. Glass-painting remained a safe, neutral topic that would give him the chance to spend time with her and talk. He found himself wanting to know more about the beauty she created. About such an important part of her life.

He looked over her shoulder. He couldn't help himself. He needed to be close to her.

"It's part of St. Mary Magdalene," she said. Her brush moved from the paint pot to the glass in a slow, soothing rhythm.

"You're very good."

"My father taught me everything I know," she replied.

"Certain skills can be learned. But talent is a gift."

Joanna looked up at that, a flash of green.

His heart pounded. He couldn't talk about glass forever. As surely as their strange wedding night hovered in his mind, it must in Joanna's. Yet she didn't reveal petulance, anger or fear as many other women might've done.

Coward. How could he, a grown man, six feet tall and strong enough to battle several men at once, continue to avoid his new wife? Never had he feared anything as much as he feared hurting her. He'd have to find strength enough for both of them to face their future.

Adrian couldn't speak of their wedding night. But he wanted her forgiveness and would win it with his kisses, his body, his passion. He felt strangely like an untried youth. He hadn't wooed a woman before. Women had come and gone in his life, willingly offering their bodies with the mutual goal of finding release. He hadn't wanted anything more.

With a slight smile, he took her paintbrush from her hand. He set it on the table, careful not to get paint on anything.

He slowly wrapped one of her curls around his finger again and again, letting the strand draw him to her like a lure. His face was inches from hers when her lips parted. His smile widened. He hadn't scared her away.

Releasing the curl, he slid his hands against her scalp, again reveling in the softness of her hair. He tipped her head back and kissed her. Gently at first, then with determination. He was already fully aroused, as if his body remembered where they'd left off so many days ago.

He couldn't wait to consummate this marriage.

Joanna wasn't kissing him back with the same fervor she had on their wedding night, but he hoped he could reawaken her passion. The memory of her kisses had haunted him all week, beckoning like a siren's song.

"Come," He held out his hand.

Together they walked to his room. Once there, he kissed her and kissed her as best he knew how, but she didn't respond with kisses of her own. Where were the enticing sighs he remembered? Her hands rested on his shoulders, but didn't explore or caress. She stood like a woman doing her duty, as proscribed by contract. Had he imagined her enthusiastic response? Despite their restrictive agreement, he wanted her to want him.

Gently he undid her ties and undressed her. He ran his hands over her breasts, her arms, again admiring her beauty. Desire pulsed as she stood before him, remote as a marble statue, cool and composed, looking off into the distance.

Should he think of eloquent words to praise her beauty? Such talk didn't come naturally to him, but might help relax her. Maybe she had need of a cup of wine? He was willing to try almost anything to make Joanna return his desire. Anything but telling her the truth of why he'd left her on their wedding night.

Adrian turned to remove his clothing, draping it over a small trunk. He took his time, hoping to give her time to adjust. When he turned back to Joanna, she lay flat on her back on the bed, her arms and legs rigidly outstretched. She looked for all the world like a martyr awaiting torture.

What had he done to her?

CHAPTER 11

As Adrian undressed, Joanna climbed onto the bed. Carefully she stretched out her arms and legs. If her eagerness had turned him away before, surely her emotionless acceptance of his body would please him.

This had to be the way.

Not kissing him back as she wanted to do seemed wrong. Not running her hands over his shoulders, exploring his body seemed unnatural. She'd squeezed her fingers tight to keep from running them through his hair. Kissing him on their wedding night had pleasured her. This self-restraint didn't. But providing an heir was her duty. Pleasure and enjoyment were not part of their bargain.

The night air raised gooseflesh, but she didn't dare cover herself. She felt uncomfortably exposed and awkward. Fighting the urge to close her eyes, she concentrated on the feel of the worn linen beneath her. She wasn't afraid of what lay ahead.

When he turned, an expression of horror crossed his face.

"My God, Joanna, no! Not like this."

Embarrassment smacked her. Wrong again. Tears filled her eyes. She couldn't remain another minute and subject herself to this humiliating misery. Barely containing a sob, she scrambled off the bed, grabbed her gown and ran out of his room into hers. She slammed the door, pushed the bolt into place, then slid to the floor, oblivious to the harsh wood scraping her bare skin. Her week of waiting and hoping had been for naught. She'd failed him, again.

What if he wanted to end their marriage?

"Joanna, let me in," Adrian said, his voice low and measured.

The door shook as he knocked. She was so mortified she couldn't speak. How was she supposed to know what to do?

"Joanna?"

She stayed motionless, her gown crushed in her hand, until the cold floor permeated her bones. Slowly she crawled to her bed and climbed in. She drew the covers over her head.

Adrian called to her a few more times. Then there was silence.

How could she face him again?

🍀 🍀

Adrian paced outside Joanna's door. He felt disgusted with himself for not handling the situation better. He'd thought he could make her want him with kisses and caresses alone, had thought his touch would convey his desire, but he'd failed miserably. His heart filled with dread as he realized what he'd have to do.

He would have to talk to her, really talk.

He was going to have to reveal something of himself to make things right between them. He wanted that more than anything, even more than he desired her and the blazing release he knew they could share.

What if he couldn't bring himself to do it? What could he possibly say? If he didn't find the courage to resolve this tonight, she might be averse to making love for the rest of her days. Instead of a willing lover, he'd have an uninterested, obligation-filling partner.

He put his hand on the door, as if the portal could somehow connect him to her and her thoughts. Far better to have this discussion with some clothing on. Adrian hurried back to his room and pulled on his robe, then returned to her door and took a deep breath for fortification. And another.

"Joanna, I need to talk to you," he said. "Please let me in."

He put his ear to the door but heard nothing.

"Joanna, please. I would very much like to see you."

The bar clanged against the wood and the door slowly

opened. A tear-streaked Joanna stood before him. She'd put her gown back on, but it slipped off her shoulders. He appreciated the smooth expanse of skin she displayed.

Panic hit Adrian as he looked at her pale, beautiful face. He didn't have the words. He needed more time. His left hand clenched as he thought about what to say. Soon his wrist would be fine, proof that wounds could heal, even grave ones. But the only way to heal the breach he'd created was through honesty. As much as he dared give.

"We must talk. About our wedding night. And tonight," he began.

Her gaze dropped to her hands. She scratched at a smudge of paint on her thumb. Her hair fell forward, blocking her face.

"I'm sorry if I displeased you," she whispered.

Shock and dismay coursed through him. It hadn't occurred to him Joanna would think their mishaps her fault. And he'd let her suffer for over a week. Adrian felt worse than he had since he left her alone. His attempts at creating an impersonal marriage were hurting them both.

Gently he pushed her hair back and wrapped his fingers in her curls. The anguish in her eyes stabbed him like a dagger.

"Ah, Joanna. I'm the one who is sorry. It was me, all me," he began. "You see, from time to time, I have…severe, debilitating headaches. They come on suddenly and can last for days. When I get such a headache, I have to be alone," Adrian explained. He stroked her hair. "It was pure mischance that one came on during what should've been a special time for you. For both of us. But I felt so ill, there was nothing I could do but flee. My head pounded so, I couldn't even speak." That was true.

"Oh," she said, her voice small. "I'd have tried to help had I known. I thought you thought I was too eager."

"Never that." Understanding dawned, but made him feel worse yet. "So that's why tonight you—"

"Then I thought because of our contract that bed sport should be, well, less emotional," she said. "I didn't know what else to do. I didn't know how we should be."

Adrian hung his head. How his demands had wounded his bride. Could he make this up to her?

"Bed sport can be however we want it to be," he said. "We should enjoy lovemaking… together. It would please me very much if you were eager."

He paused, leaning closer to her, inhaling her rose scent. He wanted her still.

"Oh. That's good. But I wish I knew what to do."

He whispered into her ear, "Do whatever you feel like doing. Then both of us shall find pleasure."

He moved even closer. She hadn't pushed him away. Yet.

"I can never change your memory of our wedding night, but perhaps we can create new memories," he whispered. "Will you let me try?"

Joanna's eyes filled with tears. The pain in Adrian's gut stabbed him again. He'd made her cry. How many more times would she suffer because of his affliction?

One shining droplet rolled down her cheek. He wiped it away with a flick of his thumb.

She didn't answer.

A new fear gripped him. What if she'd given up on him?

As another tear followed the first, she whispered, "Yes."

❧ ❦

Joanna couldn't stop her tears of relief, though they were embarrassing. Adrian didn't blame her for their wedding night or their aborted attempt this night. He'd apologized, even revealed something about himself that was outside the purview of their agreement. Though Joanna sensed he'd left a huge piece out, enough of the puzzle had fallen into place to reassure her for the moment.

Adrian was here.

He wanted to be with her again. He wanted her. Nothing else mattered.

Despite his encouragement, a small part of her remained nervous. The rest surged with anticipation as his hands warmed the sides of her head. She liked the feel of his fingers threaded through her hair, as though he couldn't bear to let her go. As though she meant something to him. Something special.

"Yes," she whispered again.

He dropped his head, briefly closing his eyes. Had he feared she'd refuse him? Then he met her gaze, his brilliant blue eyes holding her a willing prisoner. A smile raised his lips as he slid his hands behind her head and gently drew her closer. Her whole body tingled.

Joanna clasped her hands behind his neck. For an endless moment, they gazed at each other.

"Joanna," he breathed, "I'll not disappoint you this time. That I promise."

Ever so slowly, he bent his head toward hers until their mouths almost touched. At last he kissed her, his mouth warm and reassuring. Joanna collapsed against his chest and Adrian drew her to him. He deepened the kiss as his tongue found hers.

Desire swirled through her. She needed to feel him, feel his skin, against her.

"Do what you feel like doing," he'd advised. And so she would. Without breaking the kiss, she felt for his belt and untied it. He groaned as she slipped her hands inside his robe, her cool fingers meeting his warm skin.

The robe had to come off. Now. No barriers between them.

She hadn't expected her body to ache for his touch, but she welcomed the yearning building within her.

"Off," she whispered, surprised by her own boldness. But Adrian complied with a sensual smile, moving away to slide out of his clothing. The candlelight delineated the contours of his chest.

He was beautiful. No other word described him. Wearing only his hose, he stood before her. She could see the bulge between his legs, and reveled in the fact that he desired her.

Adrian lifted her and carried her to the bed. The intensity of his passion fueled hers.

He set her on her feet and kissed her again. His hands slid up and down her spine, leaving tremors of excitement in their wake. As his tongue delved into her mouth, he pulled her against him so she felt every inch of his hard body. Joanna kissed him back, conveying her desire by matching his fervor.

Adrian broke the kiss. His gaze seemed hot enough to sear her. Before she could fully admire his muscular arms and well-defined chest, he reached behind her to undo the loose laces on her gown. Slowly he worked them free, rubbing himself against her. She couldn't wait to be rid of the fabric separating her skin from his. After sliding the gown from her shoulders, she raised her chemise. Together they pulled the cloth over her head. His hands grazed up her sides, imparting delicious thrills.

The tiny brazier in the corner proffered just enough light for them to see each other.

"Joanna. You are exquisite."

That this powerful, magnificent man found her appealing filled her with sensual power. He pulled her against him, sending his warmth flowing into her. Ah, yes. She could stay this way forever, held securely in Adrian's arms, their bodies as one.

He kissed her as he lowered her to the bed. With a fluid motion, he joined her. The narrowness of the bed required Adrian to lie partially atop her, but his weight was comforting and she enjoyed their closeness. He kissed her until she thought she'd melt into the mattress, hot as molten glass.

Her hands roamed his back and arms. He turned so they were on their sides facing each other, leaving more freedom to touch. His hands cupped her breasts, then he bent his head and kissed her there, taking a nipple into his mouth and sucking gently. His tongue spiraled over her sensitive flesh.

Joanna tightened her grip on his shoulders.

His hand slid past her stomach to rest between her legs, his fingers seeking the moist folds. Joanna arched off the bed as he found her core. She gasped at the sensations that gripped her, at the pressure building inside.

"Adrian, I…." She could say no more, for he found a rhythm so enticing she didn't want him to stop. Inner tension mounted as she approached some unknown goal.

Then he stopped his magical pressure. She felt bereft.

Adrian moved over her, holding most of his weight on his hands. He was breathing hard. "Open for me, Joanna."

She looked down the length of his body poised over hers, marveling at his physical beauty.

"Do what you feel like doing," he whispered.

She had to touch him as he'd touched her, had to give him the same pleasure. As her hand closed over his erection, he caught his breath. He watched her hand slide over him.

"Tell me what pleases you," Joanna whispered.

"You seem to already know," he answered. "But I need to be inside you. Now."

He took her hand and kissed her palm, then positioned himself above her.

"Now," he repeated, pressing his length into her.

Joanna's body erupted with pleasure as he filled her. He moved, slowly out and slowly in. The pressure within her increased, bliss heightening and expanding until she thought she might explode with the joy of it.

More, she needed more.

"Adrian...."

"Be one with me, Joanna." He moaned softly as he plunged into her again.

Her world burst into a million sparkles, brighter than the sun on jeweled glass.

❧ ❧

Adrian started. They'd fallen asleep on Joanna's bed. He was practically on top of her, but she didn't seem to mind. The coals in the brazier had dimmed, but he could still make out her face. Her hand rested possessively on his back.

Amazing. Never before had he experienced such urgency with a woman, nor enjoyed such a powerful release. Joanna's honest passion had sparked both intense desire and a need to please her.

He wanted to do it again.

In repose, her beauty touched him. He noted her flawless skin, her delicate nose, her lips slightly parted, her tousled red-gold curls fanning across the pillow. He couldn't resist twisting one around his finger.

Adrian watched her sleep. How lucky he was to have found her. He hadn't realized how much he needed someone to care for. He had to admit that he wanted to be cared for in return.

Until now he hadn't known a woman with whom he'd want more than a causal connection. Which was a good thing, given his unusual situation.

Making love with Joanna was more than the physical joining,

more than the exchange of great pleasure. And what he'd felt for her wasn't just because she was his wife. He'd experienced a sharing, a giving, one to the other, far beyond anything he had expected or known was possible.

That could be the most dangerous thing of all.

CHAPTER 12

The three ales William downed hadn't taken the edge off his woes. He and John shared a table at The Mermaid, leftovers of their mutton stew congealing in a chipped bowl between them. Smoke trailed about, carrying the smell of burned meat. Raucous laughter filled the room. William slammed his cup down and glared at the happy people. Did no one else have concerns as grave as his?

Time was running out. Unless he could make Joanna fail in the next five months, the glass-painting workshop would be hers forever.

"There must be something I can do," William muttered.

John laughed. "Still worrying over Joanna?" He set his cup on the table. "That man won't let you anywhere near her. Doesn't matter anymore what we want."

"Time for something drastic," William said.

"Like what?" John asked.

"I could kill her. Better yet, I could cut off her hands."

John's mouth dropped open. He leaned closer, not that the swilling crowd could hear anything he said. "You jest. But you don't amuse."

William swished a mouthful of ale to clear the sudden disgust he tasted. John was right. Even he couldn't go that far. Besides, he needed her talents. "But what else can I do?"

"You've often said your father should've left his supplies to you instead of Joanna," John said. "Why haven't you contested the will?"

"What are you talking about?"

"My father contested his father's will. Didn't think he got a fair share. So he tried to prove the will was a forgery. He went to someone called an escheator," John related. "And to the ecclesiastical court."

He pronounced "ecclesiastical" with great care, as if the word was too big for his paltry brain to contemplate.

William signaled a passing waitress to bring another round. "Why didn't you tell me this before? I've never heard of such a thing. But you seem to know a lot about it."

"Lived through it. Was all my father could talk about."

"Can contesting be done quickly?" William's fingers tapped the table in his eagerness to get started on this venture.

"Don't know. My father's took more than two years. Besides, there's another part. Having the will proved up."

"And that means?"

"You have to convince the court the will they have is the actual will of the person who died. Takes up to a year, I think," John finished.

William fumed, hitting his fist on the table. "Joanna. That little sneak, keeping all this from me. She's got the damned will. I never saw it. I have to get it from her!" he hissed. "Maybe I missed something useful when the will was read to us. Maybe I'll claim forgery. Or I could take the real will and make another one, with new witnesses. Then it'd be her word against mine."

He chortled with glee as ideas filled his brain. He rubbed his hands together. This would work. It had to.

But he might need help. He looked at John, assessing the hulk of a man who hid a certain level of intelligence behind his coarse features. "Do you still want Joanna?"

"Aye." John folded his huge arms across his equally huge chest. "I can make her want me if I have the chance."

A scuffle broke out in the corner, raising the noise level. William clenched his teeth.

"Are you with me?" he asked.

John thought a moment, then nodded.

William let out a breath he hadn't known he held.

The buxom waitress wove through the crowd to deliver their drinks. She bent low as she set down the foaming cups, displaying her ample wares with a wink. William smiled and patted her ass. She responded with a welcoming smile.

His mood had much improved.

⁂

Two days later, William crouched behind a low stone wall across the street from the workshop—he wouldn't think of it as Joanna's. His knees ached and his nose and toes were freezing.

Upon his arrival hours ago, he'd checked the door, hoping to take a look at the will while Margery was upstairs in her room. He should've known she'd keep the door locked at night. So he waited all day for her to leave. When Margery came out, she turned the key in the lock. His heart sank. Now he'd have to wait for her to return or for Joanna to show up for work.

There, at last. Joanna. With jealousy burning his icy veins, he watched her open the door. Would his patience be rewarded? Had she left the door unlocked? He hurried closer and peered in. There she stood! If only she'd go upstairs....

A niggling bit of conscience reminded him that sneaking was wrong. No. *The workshop and its contents should have been mine from the start.*

Still he waited. He stomped in place, hopping to revive his numb feet. At last Joanna went up the stairs.

He had to hurry. Who knew how long she'd stay up there?

Glancing about to make sure no one was watching, he checked the door. It opened. He hurried inside. Luckily he knew exactly where Joanna kept her important documents, and wasted no time opening the drawer. William pushed aside a few pieces of parchment until he located his father's will.

Victory.

Footsteps sounded above him. He froze, poised to run. After a few tense seconds, he realized he was safe. For the moment.

The will. His hands shook with excitement as he scanned the document.

He swore. "Latin," he hissed. "I can barely read as it is. What am I supposed to do with this?"

Only one thing to do. He concealed the will inside his cloak, then slipped out the door.

Three long days later, William held the translation in his hands. He'd had to borrow the money from John to pay the translator. The last thing he needed was more debt, with his creditors due on his doorstep any day. He began to sweat, as he did every time he thought of losing another finger. He had to get his hands on some money.

At least he'd attained this goal. Alone in his small room, he read aloud, carefully sounding out the words.

"'In the name of God, amen. I, whole in mind and of sound memory…make my testament in this form…bequeath my soul to God.' What? Look how much Father left to the Church for masses to be said in his name. No wonder my portion was so small. 'Pay the following debts….,' let me see. He couldn't avoid paying debts, I suppose. Aha!" He hurried closer to the cloudy window to capture the best light. "'I give and bequeath my glass-painting workshop and all pertaining supplies and materials appurtenant therein to my daughter Joanna, unless within a calendar year from my death she has earned less income than I earned the calendar year before. Should that be the case, all above-mentioned transfers to my son, William. The residue of goods I give and bequeath to my son, William.' Damn." He sighed. "This cursed thing seems clear enough."

So much effort for nothing, and more time and money wasted. But he had to be sure of what the will said before he could create a believable new will.

"Time for the forgery, then."

Then he'd have Joanna just where he wanted her. At his mercy.

❦ ❦

"Joanna, Joanna!" William yelled through her studio door. "Let me in. I have news!"

Joanna set her grozing iron aside and opened the door. William swept in and headed straight for her, not even sparing a glance for her works in progress. Once again he proved how little glass-painting meant to him.

"Where is he?"

"Adrian isn't here." Perhaps she should've lied, or told William to return when he was.

Her brother plopped onto the stool before her table, haphazardly shoving glass pieces aside.

She flinched. "William, take care!"

"I don't know how to tell you this, but I must," William said. "Father's will is a forgery!"

Joanna wanted to laugh at this new tactic. "You heard the will. You saw it witnessed."

"Yes. I saw Father sign *a* will, but not *the* will he meant to sign," William began. "You know how ill he was. He didn't read the document over before he signed, did he?"

How could two children from the same parents turn out so different? They had the same curly red hair, the same pale skin. He had more freckles and a longer nose. But his pleasant features concealed a deceitfulness and mendacity she couldn't comprehend.

"I don't know. I do know what you're trying to do." She reached over to pick up the pieces of her window before he knocked them to the floor.

She had to protect everything she had, everything she was from him. "You're trying, once again, to get the shop." Then it hit her. "What did you do, create a fake will that says Father left the contents to you?"

Though his affable expression didn't change to reveal his guilt, Joanna knew she'd guessed right. "How low will you sink?"

He answered, "I happen to have in my possession a will that says Father left everything to me. But it's not a fake. It's the true will. Somehow you made sure Father signed your version. I've met with the escheator and am going to contest this in ecclesiastical court."

"I can't believe you're going to attempt this. His will, the real one, hasn't even been proved up yet," Joanna said. "How did you come by this 'new will?'"

With a flourish, William dropped the document in the space he'd cleared. "Among the 'residue of the estate' Father left to me. I knew deep down he'd never leave the workshop to you," he said as he picked the parchment up and untied the pink ribbon around it. "You trapped him by begging so often that he felt sorry for you. He could never bear to hurt his precious Joanna's feelings," William sneered.

He held it out to her. "Read. As you can see, this will is dated two weeks after the one you have. That means he must've changed his mind, and mine is the valid will. Don't you see? Everything belongs to me."

Joanna studied the parchment for a few minutes. "It's in Latin, so I can't make out all the words. I have to admire your cleverness, William. But you'll fail." She tossed the document back onto the table. "Father filed a copy of his will and a letter of intent with the glazier's guild, because leaving the contents of a studio to one's daughter is unusual when there's a son to inherit. Father wanted to be sure they knew exactly what he wanted. They'll all serve as witnesses, if need be."

William's face fell. "This isn't like you, Joanna. You're being selfish, trying to keep me from pursuing the truth. You see the new will is dated the day before he died. Obviously he didn't have the time to take this one to the guild. You see father's seal affixed."

William couldn't resist a smile at that. How clever he was to have thought of adding that most important element of proof. He'd carefully melted one off an old letter he'd found and affixed the wax to his new will.

So very clever.

🥀 🥀

Joanna was stunned. William seemed to have thought of everything. She fingered the seal. Clearly their father's. William's surprising thoroughness combined with his ability to twist everything to make her appear in the wrong made her nervous. He meant to pursue this fake will. Was there some grain of reality to his tale?

"Do you know how long this could take? Where will you get the coin to pursue this in court?" She tried to keep panic from her voice. "You'd best leave before Adrian returns. I'd hate to see his reaction to your latest attempt to wrest the shop from me."

William snatched up the will. "This is not the end. Time will tell."

"Just remember I have never lied to you," she called out as he left.

Joanna slumped against the door as she locked it behind her brother. She lacked the coin, time and energy for a court battle. Though William's will had to be a forgery, if he could convince a court to take the case she might have to devote so much effort to preserve her rights she might fail under the time limit of the real will. William could prevail even if he'd committed forgery.

She'd ask Adrian for advice. Perhaps he could recommend a solicitor. For now, work first, worry later, as her father always said.

Before she could pick up her grozing iron, another knock sounded at the door.

"Joanna, it's Margery."

Joanna opened the door once again.

"You just missed William," she said as Margery walked in, her wool cloak covered with glistening snowflakes. "He tried to get me to believe Father made out another will leaving the contents of the studio to him."

"Is it true?"

"I suppose there's a slim chance. More likely William had someone write words he dictated. I called his bluff and told him there was a copy of Father's will at the guild, but he's determined to bring his claim."

Joanna could tell Margery wasn't giving her full attention to this latest problem. She had her back turned and hadn't met Joanna's gaze once.

"Margery, if something is wrong, your problem had better be more important than the fake will."

"Oh, yes, this is worse. Worse and worse. But I'm not sure how to tell you." Margery walked to the window, then turned. She busied herself with removing her cloak, shaking it and hanging it on a peg. She warmed her hands by the fire, still keeping her back to Joanna.

"Margery, you're making me nervous. Tell me."

"I brought the final changes to Lady Anne's for her approval this morning. I was waiting in the small room near the back door when I heard her arguing. With a man. I couldn't hear what was said. I thought perhaps she was disciplining a servant. Then Adrian came storming past and went out the back door," Margery said. "What could he have been doing there?"

Joanna frowned. "The first time I saw him was at Lady Anne's. She actually kissed his cheek and held his hand. He told me she was going to let him buy Bedford Castle back. But why did he have to go there, then or today?"

Something felt strange, out of place. Her mind painted vivid yet disgusting pictures of Lady Anne and Adrian together. Could he possibly be involved with her? Was Lady Anne the source of his secrets?

Her stomach threatened to rebel. The need to know burned. She'd find out what was going on, agreement be damned. For if he was sleeping with Lady Anne, she couldn't stay married to him.

Joanna drew in a sharp breath as jealousy stabbed her heart, sharp as a shard of glass. Could that be the reason for the "conversations of a personal nature" clause, so he'd be free to keep a mistress? Joanna grabbed an apple and took a bite to quash the bitter taste in her mouth. The fruit didn't help. She was still nauseated. First John, then William, now Adrian.

Would every man she knew betray her?

❧ ☙

She and Adrian had finished eating their evening meal before Joanna felt ready to broach the topic of Lady Anne. He'd seemed angry since she told him about John's latest ploy. Her hands shook every time she picked up a spoon or bowl. Adrian didn't seem to notice, immersed in his own thoughts as he ate.

Her nails bit into her palm, she clenched her spoon so tightly. "Margery was at Lady Anne's today," Joanna began.

Did Adrian's shoulders stiffen? Did his eating knife pause briefly before he cut his meat?

Please, Adrian, please tell me you were there. Don't lie to me.

What if the truth was worse than a lie? She couldn't finish her food. The smell of roast capon made her stomach turn.

"Oh?" He placed his knife in his bowl.

"She dropped off the final changes for the new window designs."

"Joanna—"

She held her breath.

"Are there any more peas?"

Joanna collapsed against the hard back of her chair. She was going to have to drag the tale out of him. He must harbor some secret involving Lady Anne or he'd have told her on his own. She couldn't glean anything from his bland expression.

"Margery said she saw you there." Good, she thought. Much better than accusing him as she wanted to.

"Oh. I didn't see her," Adrian said.

Joanna went cold inside. He'd admitted to being at Lady Anne's. Though theirs was a marriage of convenience, his revelation hurt. She'd been a fool to be drawn in by his handsome face, his kindnesses. His amazing caresses and kisses.

Perhaps she should give him the benefit of the doubt and assume he had a good explanation.

"Joanna, I don't know how to tell you this," he said.

Apparently not.

The dull tone of his voice, the somber look on his face, sparked tears. She wouldn't cry, wouldn't let him see how this conversation disturbed her. She swallowed back her tears despite the burning in her soul.

Her husband had a mistress.

Disgusting. No wonder he'd had to marry. Lady Anne was too old to be his precious heir or provide children. The food she'd eaten threatened to leave her stomach. She swallowed, wincing at the burn in her throat.

Marriage of convenience, marriage of convenience, marriage of convenience. If she focused on those words, maybe she could protect herself from the pain.

Adrian pushed his bowl away. "Before I met you, I…. There's no way to sweeten this tale. You deserve to know, though I fear you'll despise me for it." He ran his fingers through his thick hair, leaving the dark waves messier than they had been. "Until we agreed to marry, I…visited Lady Anne every week."

Joanna's throat constricted. She had to swallow several more times before she could speak. "Would I be naïve to assume you helped her with chores? Read to her or some such thing?" Her voice sounded like she'd squeezed out the words.

"Joanna, I too am disgusted. I could see no other way. That was what she insisted I do to earn back my house."

"You had sex with her, to...." Joanna fled to the slop bucket and bent over, sending her curls flying. She pushed them out of the way and vomited.

Joanna felt Adrian behind her. For the first time since she'd met him, his presence was no comfort.

"Please," she whispered, "don't touch me. I can't bear it." She couldn't look at him. Any pity in his gaze would be her undoing.

"I haven't touched her since you and I decided to wed. I swear to you," he said. "I never wanted to be with her at all. I told you Lady Anne had agreed to let me buy back the house. We struck a deal so I could earn the manor because I didn't have the coin to purchase it."

"What?"

"She said my visits would earn back my father's fortune and she'd leave the rest of his gold and the house to me when she dies."

Her jaw dropped.

"A morbid plan, I agree. Realistic, nonetheless. She is five-and-fifty, and her son inherited her late husband's riches. Her husband was my father's largest creditor, but being wealthy in his own right he never spent my father's coin.

"I did what I had to do to get my family's birthright back. I never thought I'd care what anyone thought of my actions."

Adrian stepped so close she could feel his body heat. Unconsciously she flinched and moved away. She couldn't be near him.

"Now I do care. Don't condemn me, Joanna." Adrian's voice caught.

Adrian's tale seemed so far-fetched it might be true. But her nausea remained. Could she accept his actions and continue living with him, sharing his bed? What recourse did she have? Could she ever look at him and not imagine him with Lady Anne?

She retched again.

✂ ✂

The sight of Joanna hunched over the bucket, clutching the counter beside it as if it provided her last link to sanity, and the sounds of her retching made Adrian sick, too. He felt worse than after one of his visions. He felt more sullied now then he had each time he left Lady Anne.

Yet his past, who he'd been with before meeting Joanna, shouldn't matter to either of them. Especially when his relationship with Lady Anne had been a means to an end, not an affair of the heart or even of passion. Why did it matter? Because it mattered to Joanna. Because he hadn't brought the issue up before. He'd insisted on their agreement so he wouldn't need to tell her anything he didn't want to or couldn't.

He wished he felt worthy of his wife.

Adrian yearned to comfort her, but she'd asked him not to touch her. He clenched his fists behind his back, watching as she wiped her face.

He'd told the truth, but he couldn't tell her that he had left out a major part of the story. Something even more important than his happiness or hers.

Yes, he'd had sex with Lady Anne to earn back his house. But another, more far-reaching goal had made him agree to the liaison.

His overlord, the Earl of Warwick, had asked Adrian to spy on Lady Anne's son. Adrian agreed for three reasons: the income Warwick offered, the rightness of the cause and because Warwick agreed to use his influence to help restore the Bedford name to its former standing. After years of struggling on his own, Adrian had been willing to accept some aid.

Lady Anne's son, Lord Berkeley, remained a close advisor of the king's. Warwick and several other Yorkist supporters believed Lord Berkeley kept extensive notes, perhaps even a journal, of his meetings with Henry and his council. Those notes could prove invaluable in assessing the king's strategy. Adrian's job was to find them and share his discoveries with Warwick.

With his goal of wanting his family home back, he had reason to approach Lady Anne and spend time with her. With his intimate knowledge of the manor's layout, who better to search?

Whenever Lady Anne dozed, he ventured through his house seeking Berkeley's papers. Avoiding her servants was difficult at first, but over time he learned their routines. He'd looked through every drawer and rifled through every stack of documents without finding anything of use. Since he'd stopped his weekly visits to Lady Anne, so must his spying come to an end.

He'd never regain his home, nor complete his service to his overlord. But his regret at that didn't compare to his misery over hurting Joanna.

Joanna believed the worst, but he couldn't allay her fears by telling her about being a spy. The outcome of the civil war between King Henry's Lancastrians and the Yorkists could depend on him. He couldn't compromise the fate of his country or those who'd placed their trust in him. Even for Joanna.

Her curls were a mess, her face ashen. Adrian wanted nothing more than to take her into his arms, but he knew that wouldn't ease her suffering. Only time could do that. Time he didn't have.

"I'm sorry I've upset you," he said. "But all that is in the past."

Joanna stumbled toward the door. "I must go to my shop."

"I'll go with you," he said.

"No."

"Let me—"

"Go away. Just go away," she whispered.

Then she crumpled to the floor, unconscious.

CHAPTER 13

"The bleeding has finally stopped," the physician stated. The balding man in dark robes shook his head. "You should've called for the midwife instead of me. Send for her now. If not for the emergency, I wouldn't have tended to her. I'm sorry. She lost the child."

He gathered the pile of rags stained with Joanna's blood and dropped them in a basket.

Adrian choked. "Child? Oh, God. No. I didn't even know she was pregnant." He stared at his wife, motionless on the bed. She looked dead. He took her chilled hand in his. "This is all my fault."

"Did you hit her?"

"Of course not!"

"Many men beat their wives." The physician picked up his satchel. "If you didn't, then you aren't the cause. Did she fall?"

"Not that I saw or know of," Adrian replied.

"Did she take something to rid herself of the baby?"

"What?"

"Oft times women who don't want the child for one reason or another drink concoctions of savin or tansy with willow leaves to induce miscarriage," the physician explained. "At any rate, women often lose their babes early on. Godspeed. I'll show myself out."

The physician left Adrian alone in his misery.

He wished he could suffer in Joanna's stead. His fault, no

matter what the physician said. Shock from his abhorrent tale had caused Joanna to lose their baby.

Joanna had seemed quieter than usual last night, but he hadn't suspected she was upset or had known he was at Lady Anne's. Then everything turned upside down. Adrian thought the discussion about Lady Anne was as bad as things could get. Joanna's anguish became his as he unveiled the truth. Never before had he cared so much about how someone else felt.

When she'd collapsed, he'd reacted instantly, catching her just before her head hit the floor. His heart still hammered from the jolt of seeing drops of bright, red blood and realizing they came from Joanna. The moments of indecision when he couldn't decide if he should stay with her or run to fetch the physician haunted him. He hadn't thought to send for the midwife. Panic during the physician's examination continued to race through his veins.

He cursed himself. His marriage to Joanna had been a mistake. The emotional suffering he'd caused his new wife was bad enough. Leaving her on their wedding night, ignoring her for days at a time because of his visions. Now she'd miscarried. All because of him.

He had killed their child. His heir. How could Joanna ever forgive him? How could he forgive himself? At that moment, watching his beautiful, still wife, all he wanted was for Joanna to get well. If there was a way to make up with her, he'd find it.

Adrian arranged another blanket over her. Taking care not to disturb her, he eased onto the bed and stretched out beside her. Except for helping Joanna with her clients and the guild, he had failed her. The only thing he could offer now was his warmth and comfort.

Time crept by as he worried about Joanna and the mess he'd made. Would he ever sleep again?

Joanna woke in a haze. Her heart pounded and nausea from a horrible nightmare threatened to overwhelm her. In her dream, Adrian had told her Lady Anne had been his mistress. Then she'd taken ill and lost their baby. The dream had been so real she remembered the terrible cramping and the raspy sound of the physician's voice.

Thank God it was only a dream.

She tried to get out of bed but couldn't. Why did she ache all over? Why was Margery dozing on a chair in the corner?

"Margery?" Her voice cracked. Her tongue was so dry she could barely lick her lips.

Margery started and stood. "Joanna, how do you feel?"

"Awful. Like a kiln fell on me. What happened?"

Something must really be wrong to make Margery oblivious to her own appearance. Her hair was tousled, her gown was wrinkled and even bore a brownish stain near her waist.

"Joanna, let me get Adrian."

She turned to go, but Joanna reached out to clasp Margery's skirts. Her hand brushed the fabric but lacked the strength to hold on.

"No. I don't want to see him," she said. "You tell me."

Tears filled Margery's eyes as she held Joanna's hand. "You had a miscarriage."

Joanna retched, but there was nothing left. She collapsed on the bed, shocked and aching. A miscarriage. If part of her dream was real, did that mean the rest was true? Had Adrian told her he'd slept with Lady Anne?

She couldn't bring herself to tell Margery, not yet. "How could that be? I didn't even know I was pregnant."

"I talked with the midwife who came after the physician left. Adrian fetched them, and sent for me. She said some women have no symptoms of pregnancy at first, and that early miscarriages are common. You must rest for a few days, then you should be fine."

Joanna turned her head away from the concern in Margery's gaze. How could she ever be fine? Her marriage was a sham. Adrian had promised to be there for her, but he had betrayed her, then disappeared. Despite their argument, he should be at her bedside, sharing the loss of their child. His precious heir.

What irony. She'd been on her way to helping Adrian achieve his dream and they hadn't even known. Now that dream was shattered along with her hopes of a real marriage.

"Please, let me get Adrian," Margery said.

"No." Joanna sank deeper into the pillows. "Perhaps someday I'll feel able to tell you what he was really doing at Lady Anne's. Ours is a marriage of convenience. He cares nothing for me."

Her eyes burned with tears and she closed them.

"Joanna, that's not true. He stayed beside you all night, holding your hand. I just convinced him to leave to change his clothes and get something to eat. I thought he might make himself ill."

A hot tear trickled down Joanna's cheek and into her ear. It itched, but she couldn't summon energy to wipe it away. She desperately wanted to believe Adrian cared for her, but she knew better.

"He feels guilty. Nothing more," she said.

"By the stars, Joanna, what happened?"

"Please, I'd like to be alone now," Joanna whispered.

Margery looked at her for a long moment, then left.

As soon as the door closed, pent-up tears burst forth. She needed Adrian, but couldn't face him yet.

More hot tears dripped down her cheeks. Her life was a disaster. She'd lost her baby. Her brother threatened her tenuous security with a forged will. She could no longer trust her husband. As if that wasn't enough, enforced bed rest would delay completing her windows, which would lead to more trouble with the guild and her clients.

Not that she felt strong enough to get up anyway. Why fight it? She was a failure.

There was no reason to ever get out of bed again.

※ ※

Two days after the miscarriage, Adrian paced outside Joanna's door. She still hadn't asked to see him. He could've forced his way in, but kept hoping she'd change her mind. He needed to talk with her, to tell her how sorry he was. To see for himself how she fared. The only chance he had to be with her was after she fell asleep, when Margery took pity on him and allowed him to sit by his wife's side.

For once he wished he could control his visions, so he could see if she'd be well. If she would ever forgive him. If they'd ever enjoy making love again.

Margery came out of the room and closed the door. "She sleeps."

"Did she eat?"

Margery shook her head. "Maybe tomorrow. Adrian, you look awful. Have you eaten? Have you slept?"

"That doesn't matter. Did she ask for me?"

"I am sorry, but no."

"Did you tell her I waited here?"

"Yes. Several times," she said.

That hurt.

"Please tell me what happened." Margery put her hand on his arm. "I can't bear watching you both suffer so. I can't try to help if I don't know what went wrong."

"Go get some rest," he said. "I'll stay with her until you return. She can't turn me away if she doesn't know I'm there."

"The midwife said she can get out of bed tomorrow if she feels up to it. I hope she will, but I doubt it. Godspeed, Adrian. Until morning."

She clasped his hand between hers, then left.

Adrian went into the room and resumed his position on the bed. Joanna's corpse-like stillness scared him. Carefully, he reached for her hand. It felt icy and small in his. He hoped in her sleep she sensed his presence and concern. He needed to touch her, do something to make her well.

He needed her forgiveness even more.

❧ ❧

"Here. I brought your favorite," Margery said.

She handed Joanna a cup of hippocras, but Joanna pushed the drink away. Nothing appealed to her except sleep. And staying in bed, though the midwife had permitted her to resume her activities two days ago.

Margery took a drink. "This is quite refreshing." She set the cup aside.

Joanna dreaded the conversation she knew would follow the confession she was about to make. But unless she dragged

Margery from the tiny bedroom, Margery would have her say. The price she'd have to pay for the comfort of confiding in her half-sister and receiving her advice.

"Adrian had been having a liaison with Lady Anne."

Margery's jaw dropped.

"Though he swears it stopped after we agreed to marry." The effort of admitting the truth drained her. The hurt lingered.

"Did you expect Adrian would come to your bed a virgin?" Margery asked softly. "An incredibly handsome, virile man such as he?" Margery didn't wait for a response, but continued, "Do you think he was taking advantage of Lady Anne?"

"No, based on what he told me, if anything it was the other way around. Lady Anne insisted upon it if he wanted her to leave him Bedford Manor when she dies." She shared everything else Adrian had said.

"If you believe she wanted him, then they weren't any different than thousands of other people who become lovers out of wedlock," Margery said. "In fact, they weren't lovers in the truest sense of the word," she mused. She picked up Joanna's comb. "Now that he's abandoned his bargain with Lady Anne, how will he get his home back?"

"I don't know. I don't care." Joanna put her arm over her face to block the bright morning sun.

"You do care. Your anger is speaking," Margery said. "Don't you see? Adrian must care for you far more than you're willing to acknowledge." She took a section of Joanna's hair from the pillow and began to untangle it. "He sacrificed his dream, one you said he's pursued his entire life, to marry you. He didn't violate your vows. Surely that has to ease your misery. Would you have given up your dream, making your father's workshop thrive, to marry him?"

Margery and her romantic ideals.

"Why are you taking his side?" Joanna closed her eyes again as Margery carefully tended to her curls. The slow brushing soothed her, easing the tension of their conversation.

"Everyone has faults, Joanna. Despite his mistakes, Adrian is a good man. He proves that every day."

But Margery didn't know of their impersonal bargain.

"Could you forgive him if you were me?" Joanna asked.

"No." Margery stood and looked down at her. "I already forgave him because I am not you. Joanna, I love you. But your rigid views of right and wrong won't warm you on a cold night. Nor do they bode well for the rest of your marriage," she cautioned. "Don't make a mistake by blaming Adrian. He obviously felt he had no other choice than to...visit Lady Anne. He didn't know he'd marry in the near future. It's not as though he's still sleeping with her or desires any other woman. Despite the cost to his future, he broke off their arrangement after he met you."

Tears welled in Joanna's eyes and dripped down her cheeks. She'd been so busy feeling sorry for herself she hadn't even tried to look at the situation from Adrian's point of view. What if Margery was right?

More than grief, more than mistrust, one emotion seared hottest. Jealousy. How could she admit she was jealous, and jealous of a crone Adrian had sworn meant nothing to him, when feelings fell far outside their agreement?

"He thinks you blame him for the miscarriage, too."

"I did, at first," Joanna admitted. "But no one else agreed with me. The midwife sees no reason why I can't have another child." Joanna sighed. "Well, except for the fact that I may never sleep with my husband again.

She pushed herself into a sitting position. Margery hurried over to plump the pillows behind her.

"A joke! That's a step in the right direction," Margery encouraged. "Joanna, your situation is grim. But you'll heal. To my view, the only question you have to ask yourself is this: do you believe Adrian told the truth about not touching Lady Anne once you agreed to marry him?" She paused to let her words sink in. "If so, then you must forgive him."

CHAPTER 14

Adrian's heart thumped in his chest. His knees didn't want to support his weight. He hadn't been this nervous since his first battle.

After six endless days of waiting, Joanna had finally asked to see him.

He walked into the room. For the first time since the miscarriage, Joanna was dressed and sitting on the bed. She was still pale, and he knew she must've lost weight from not eating much. But what hit him hardest was that the light seemed to have drained from her eyes. Like one of her windows looked on a rainy day…lifeless. Another person, a cold and spiritless one, inhabited Joanna's weakened body. He ached for what she'd lost and couldn't fathom how to help her get it back.

For a few moments, they simply looked at each other, Joanna stiff and silent on the bed and he awkward and uncertain just inside the door. He itched to hold her, but feared she'd turn him away.

"How do you feel?" he began.

"Better," she said, without moving.

"Is there anything I can get, anything I can do for you?"

"No."

Adrian tamped down his urge to go to her, to shake the life back into her. He sensed it was up to him to bring her back, that if he couldn't do or say the right things she'd be lost to him forever. If he could revive her, maybe then he could begin to redeem himself in her eyes. Begin to salvage their marriage, which he wanted more than he'd thought possible.

"Joanna, I am so, so sorry." He couldn't think of anything to say that wouldn't sound maudlin.

"Margery tells me you stayed by my side every night. She says you haven't been able to eat either." Her voice lacked its customary lilt.

Adrian moved a few steps closer to the bed. If he hurried or spoke too loudly, she might shatter like her finest glass. He felt her suffering deep in his chest. He hadn't known he could experience such agony without having a physical injury.

"I've been doing a lot of thinking," she began. "I don't care about the agreement."

Had his heart stopped? He felt as frozen as she looked. Was she going to leave him? Or worse, divorce him?

In that moment he realized he wanted her as much as he wanted an heir.

With great effort, she shifted on the bed, the slight rustle of her skirts the only sound. She sighed as if the movement had sapped her strength.

"I meant to say, I hope this won't be considered a 'conversation of a personal nature' that would violate our agreement."

Damn that agreement. At the time he'd thought the careful wording would satisfy his needs. How could he have known what would happen? That he'd come to care for his wife?

What he wanted to say was, "Let's tear the damn thing up." But the conditions that led him to write the terms hadn't changed. So he said, "Unfortunately, I agree we need to make an exception." He forced himself to continue, "Just this once. The rules still stand."

Her eyes changed from a chilly green as they filled with a strange sadness. "I don't blame you for what happened, Adrian. I wanted to, I even tried to, but I can't."

Silently he thanked God for giving him another chance. "You must know I never meant to hurt you."

"I'm sorry I lost your heir." She collapsed onto the bed and burst into tears.

"Oh, Joanna."

He couldn't have felt any guiltier. She'd apologized to him, when clearly it should be the other way round. He was in perfect alignment with their agreement, but still felt he should have told her sooner about his past with Lady Anne.

He flew to the bed and gently took her into his arms. She threw her arms around his neck and wept. Despite their shared misery, holding her again felt good. Her body shook as she sobbed against him. He clutched her tighter.

"I'm the one who is sorry. For hurting you. All I want is for you to be well again," he said. "What can I do to help?"

"Just hold me," she answered.

"For as long as you want."

Eventually she pulled back a bit to look at him. Her teary face deepened his sadness.

"You don't look well," she said.

"I am, now that you agreed to see me. I wish I could undo the past and make things right between us. I wish you'd told me about the baby...."

"While you continue to keep secrets from me?" The bitterness in her face hit him like a slap. "I didn't mean that," she continued. "I had no idea I was with child. No symptoms or signs until that night," Joanna said. "The miscarriage is no one's fault. As to my reaction to your past...affairs, Margery helped me accept that most men are experienced when they go to their marriage beds. More importantly, she reminded me that you gave up part of your dream to marry me and remain faithful. I'm honored but also surprised. Have you thought of another way to get your house back?"

"I'll think on that when you're well. For now, I'll concentrate on getting some color back in your cheeks and getting you back to work, which is where I know you want to be."

"Yes. But later, I hope we can, well, I hope." Joanna stopped and took a deep breath. She blushed. "I hope you'll want to return to my bed."

He touched her cheek. "When you're ready, let me know."

Thank God. She had forgiven him.

This time.

Joanna set down her brush, stretched and rubbed her back. She'd lost track of time and probably pushed herself too hard on her first day back at work. Though she still had much to finish, she'd made good progress on the border of St. Edward's robe. The bright colors cheered her.

It was time to go to Adrian, but she couldn't bring herself to leave her table. Or make sense of her feelings. She had and did mourn the loss of their child. She'd accepted Margery's advice about Adrian's past and now yearned for things to be as they were before. Yet she was afraid to trust him completely. She had a strange feeling that he still kept something from her. A secret that must be worse than his having had a liaison with Lady Anne. Why couldn't he tell her?

How could she trust him, knowing he couldn't trust her?

She still wanted him. No denying that. Maybe sharing the pleasures their bodies offered would be enough. But she wanted more. She craved his trust. His love.

If only she could turn to her father for advice. She smiled, knowing he would've said, "Treat him as you would want to be treated."

Meaning that to earn Adrian's trust, she'd have to trust him. No matter how hard doing so would be or how difficult the obstacles she faced, that's what she'd do.

❦ ❦

"Let us in or we'll break down the door," a deep voice cried.

William scurried under the bed, joining mounds of dust and a pair of squealing rats.

Baldwin, the hatchet man, had come for the money he owed. William didn't have the full amount. His fingers twitched.

Mayhap if he stayed silent they'd leave.

"He's not there," said Baldwin. "Try again tomorrow."

If they found him, he was doomed. Pure fear smacked his guts.

"He's in there, I say," said another man, Wat. "Start on the door."

The hatchet whacked against the door. Bam. A splintering

sound followed by a heart-wrenching pause. Bam. Bam. He trembled as each strike shook the floor.

The door slammed against the wall. Feet pounded before him.

William reached out to pull down the edge of his coverlet, but knew it wasn't enough. A cold sweat burst from his skin.

"Told you, he's not to home."

Hope flitted in his chest, then died.

Because he was going to sneeze. No, no! "Aaachoo!"

"Aha."

Two heads appeared beneath the bed. Four hands grabbed his legs and dragged him out. His head hit the wood frame. He remained on the floor, dazed by pain.

"Where's my money?" Baldwin demanded. The thick scar snaking down his face was white against his mottled skin. He pulled the hatchet from his belt and knelt by William's head.

"I...I—"

The short, wiry Wat took William's mutilated hand and spread his fingers wide. Slowly Baldwin positioned the hatchet. The blade hovered inches above his last finger.

"Do you have the coin or not?" Baldwin hissed.

William almost gagged on the smell of his sweat. "Please, please, a few more days. I'll have it then, I swear."

"That be what they all say." Wat laughed.

Baldwin raised the hatchet. He started to swing.

"Wait!" William cried.

The hatchet thunked into the floor just beyond his finger.

He panted with relief. "Perhaps there's some service I could perform instead of paying you in gold," he offered. Could anything be worse than losing another finger?

Baldwin and Wat exchanged a meaningful glance.

"Hmmm. That might work. You bought yerself some time 'til we see if our commander will accept services instead of gold," Baldwin said. "We'll be in touch. Soon."

They stomped out, leaving William collapsed on the floor in relief.

He had "some time" until "soon." How long was that? Not enough to use his forged will to obtain the workshop. He'd hoped Joanna would save him the trouble of pursuing the matter in court. But she'd stood firm behind the first will. Will contests, he'd learned, could take years. Especially if there really was a copy of the first will at the guild.

With those thugs after him, he'd be lucky to have a month. Enough to try to scare up money some other way. He could only guess at the unsavory tasks Baldwin's and Wat's superior could make him do. He'd never met the man, but he had to be even more determined and fearsome than his underlings.

William shivered.

Who did he know with enough coin to cover his debts? Only Joanna, if she handed over all of her profits, which she'd never do. Mayhap her lordly husband could rescue him, but why would he? Surely Sir Adrian would believe whatever Joanna told him, which wouldn't be good.

Unless he could uncover some secret of Sir Adrian's. Everybody had something to hide. What if he kept a mistress? Had a bastard? If William couldn't unearth a secret, he'd make something up and threaten to expose it as truth. Everyone knew what gossip could do. Look at how the rumors John spread almost ruined Joanna.

William slowly pushed himself into a sitting position, at the mercy of his throbbing head. The rats skittered around him then ran back under the bed. William sighed as he saw what his life had become. But he had far more important concerns than rodents at the moment. His very flesh was at stake.

Never had he been more desperate. And desperate people took desperate measures.

☙ ❧

Joanna didn't quite have all of her energy back, but she pushed herself to meet her deadlines.

Thomas Osbert needed far less direction than John and was far less surly, so she and her clients liked him better. One less thing to worry about. Adrian's occasional comments about Thomas's good looks and pleasant demeanor amused her. Not that he was actually jealous. But he did look in on her at least twice a day, ostensibly to see if William or John caused any trouble.

Though his brief visits were distracting, Joanna enjoyed spending a few minutes with him. And looking at him. His deep blue eyes, well-defined features and long, thick hair combined with his unique presence continued to fascinate her. As did her desire for him. She hadn't known want could be so strong or so constant.

"Two and a half months left," he said, looking over her account book.

"Yes," she replied, not looking up from her design table. "So short a time. I'll be close, but can't be sure I'll meet the goal."

"You can't possibly work any harder, or you'll make yourself sick," Adrian said.

"Thomas works faster than John, and Margery has been surprisingly helpful. Barring any major difficulties I hope to earn enough by the end of February."

Neither referred to the miscarriage. Not that she could ever forget, and she could tell by the slight frown it still bothered him. But they had to move on.

"Until this evening," Adrian said. He bent to kiss her. She expected a nice, short farewell, but he put his hands on her cheeks and kissed her thoroughly. Her whole body tingled, leaving her wanting more.

How would she concentrate on her work now? *Do you see what caring about someone can do?* Her heart kept forgetting their practical arrangement and wanted to believe this was a true marriage. What was wrong with her? And why had Adrian kissed her so passionately?

Then she noticed that Margery and Thomas had entered. She smiled. Adrian's possessive behavior pleased her, even if it was just for show.

As he left, Margery plopped rather ungracefully onto a stool. "Lady Anne is going to make me a lunatic," she groaned. "She demanded changes to her changes. But that's not as bad as cancelling her commission, which I feared she might do. Maybe she hasn't heard about your wedding. Or, if she did, maybe she doesn't care."

Joanna had considered ceasing contact with Lady Anne, but losing a good client wouldn't help her coffers. She'd made a promise to deliver, and though Adrian might not regain his home, she could still save the windows. For the home they'd share some day.

"Again? This has been going on too long. We need her to decide and pay."

"I know why you send me to meet with her, but she sorely tries my patience."

Margery had been watching Thomas the entire time. Was she planning to practice her wiles on him?

"I must run an errand. I shall return shortly," Thomas said.

Margery definitely looked after him with longing.

"I thought you spent so much time working because I'd been ill. Now I wonder if you have a different motivation," Joanna said. She walked over to inspect the large window Thomas had been working on.

"He is attractive."

"And kind and available, but he has far less money than you've claimed to want. What happened to your dream of marrying a noble?"

"Dreams can change. As much as I'd like fine things, there's no guarantee they'd make me happy. I've only known Thomas a short while, but he makes me believe marrying someone you truly care for would be more than enough."

"I agree." Joanna wasn't ready to tell Margery how her feelings for Adrian grew with each passing day. He acted like he cared for her, so why keep to their agreement?

"You had to marry. But I don't," Margery said. "At least you found someone magnificent in face and what can be seen of his body."

"What you cannot see is pleasing as well." Joanna couldn't conceal a smile or stop the warmth spreading through her. "When you're ready, let me know, and we can discuss what really happens when you have a man in your bed."

If only their agreement didn't stipulate that only Adrian could choose when he visited hers.

CHAPTER 15

ndrew entered the back of the church, on his way to morning prayers. This was his favorite time of day, peaceful and full of potential for virtuous behavior. In the past few weeks since he'd joined the Franciscan friars and donned their grey robes, he'd prayed and worked hard for God's aid in controlling his tendency toward licentiousness. He'd not yet accustomed himself to their vow of poverty, but made great strides toward finding the right path. Soon he'd know what to do about Adrian.

Soon he'd make the decision that had tortured him for most of his life. Accept his brother, or follow in his father's footsteps and the Bible's commands by handing over a heretic.

As he paced slowly down the nave of the friary's church, he still couldn't believe how Adrian had forced him to go on that horrible pilgrimage. By now his twin should have earned enough to support them, but no. Adrian had failed. Andrew needed money to ensure the church would grant indulgences for his sins.

For years he'd spent hours on his knees in repentance, yet he feared his sins were so great they couldn't be absolved by prayer alone. So he'd waited so long and so patiently, needing Adrian to come through for him. He had to accept Adrian would never regain their family fortune.

The time had come to take matters into his own hands.

His brother's secret powers had frightened and haunted Andrew since he'd seen his twin in the throes of a vision. Once had been more than enough. As if Adrian's writhing and moaning as though possessed wasn't abnormal, the scene was all the stranger because watching Adrian was like watching himself.

Adrian had been ill afterward, obviously from fighting off the Devil's attempts to claim him. Only his strength and will had saved him. Andrew had to admit a lesser man would've succumbed to evil long before. But he couldn't take any more chances.

Andrew's pilgrimage should have served two purposes: absolution and a means to clearly see what to do about Adrian. But it had been hard work, too hard. Traipsing for hours through the cold had made him ill.

He moved toward his favorite pew, ready to kneel and lose himself in prayer. He froze at the sight of a beautiful woman entering the church. What was Temptation doing here? Why was God doing this to him, when he was trying so hard to be good?

The beginnings of desire seeped into his flesh. He couldn't avert Lust. The more he tried to avoid Her, the more he prayed for her to go away, the more She followed and goaded him. Tempted him to stray. His second greatest sin.

This woman was a test. He'd prevail despite his body's urges.

Even as he prayed for the will to resist, he felt drawn to her like a scrap of metal was to a magnet. His erection couldn't be helped. He was weak and Lust was strong. Thank goodness for the concealing robes he wore.

His natural charm should encourage her to converse with him. His handsome features would do the rest. Andrew started toward her, but stopped when Friar Newton came into the church. He ducked into the shadows under one of the arches lining the nave.

"Mistress Joanna, I'm Friar Newton," the friar said. "We are so grateful that the tailor's guild wishes to provide us with a stained glass window."

Andrew watched him waddle down the aisle, his sandals silent against the stone floor. "We'd like your window to replace this plain one on the back wall."

"A good location for light," Mistress Joanna said as she followed him. "I brought several small preliminary sketches for you to choose from. The tailor's guild has approved them."

Andrew stuck his head out as far as he dared. Her body perfectly curved. Her skin so pale, so pure. An angel, with a voice to match. His body throbbed. The sunlight outlined her delicate profile as she presented Friar Newton with her small drawings. Andrew watched as the portly friar paged through them.

"Each is lovely, but I believe this will suit our needs." He selected one and placed it on top of the others.

She nodded, her slim neck bending enticingly. "An excellent choice. I'll take initial measurements, then return after I have finalized the design."

Andrew had to see the beauty again. He had to touch her. *When you will be back?*

"When do you think that will be?"

Surely God spoke through the friar.

"In three days," she replied.

Andrew watched as Joanna stretched to measure the window, her full breasts pressing against her gown.

When she finished, Joanna and Friar Newton walked out of the church. Andrew pressed flat against the cold wall. He caught a whiff of rose as they passed by his arch.

"I believe felicitations are in order. I heard that you recently wed," Friar Newton said.

Of course a beauty like her would be married. But, curse his desires, that'd never stopped him before. Married women perversely brought more pleasure because the sin was greater. Why, oh why was he so weak?

"Yes," she said, "to Sir Adrian Bedford."

Andrew jumped and hit his head on the stone. He couldn't even gasp in pain, for complete shock took his breath away.

Adrian had married.

Because he knew his twin so well, he knew why. Adrian believed Andrew's religious devotion invalidated his own twin as a suitable heir. Adrian would find excessive prayer dangerous, being a servant of the Devil as he was. Thinking his twin was off searching his soul, Adrian rushed to find himself a bride. And managed to find a true beauty. A bride who could bear him a child, despite the chance of it being afflicted with Adrian's curse. How had he done all of that in such a short time?

How could Andrew let Adrian bring more of Satan's spawn into the world? Perhaps he'd been planning to betray Andrew all along.

Adrian would pay. On the morrow, Andrew would tell the authorities about Adrian's Sight. In vivid detail. Overhearing Joanna in his church must be the sign he'd been seeking. God had spoken.

He closed his eyes, imagining the scene. Adrian, humbled on his knees before him. Perhaps he'd be bound, or in chains. Mistress Joanna, standing at Andrew's side, appalled by her husband's sorcery, realizing he was the better twin as Adrian spouted more lies. The authorities, dragging Adrian away to burn.

His outlook brightened, as though the sun had come out from behind a cloud. Andrew knew what he had to do. Something far better than accusing his brother.

God had sent Andrew the perfect revenge.

❧❦ ❦❧

Three days later, Andrew waited in the front pew of his small church, his hands clasped before him. He was grateful for the respite after his busy morning. Up before dawn, he'd hidden outside the rooms he and his brother once shared, waiting until both Joanna and Adrian departed. The sight of them smiling and exchanging a brief farewell kiss had stung. Using his key, he'd gone inside and taken what he needed. All was ready.

At last he heard footsteps. She'd returned.

There, at the back of the chapel, stood Mistress Joanna. She was alone. Good, now Friar Newton wouldn't spoil his plans. God had heard his prayers.

Today she wore a blue gown that offset the little he could see of her red-gold hair to perfection. How he longed to run his hands over her softness, to hear her cry out beneath him.

All in good time.

"Joanna," Andrew said, deepening his voice slightly.

She turned. "Adrian, what are you doing here? Did you follow me?"

Why didn't she look happier?

"I wanted to talk to you. I missed you." He endeavored to sound sincere.

She frowned. "Since this morning? Has something happened? This isn't like you."

❧ ☙

Tension coiled inside her, despite the calm of the church. Why was Adrian here, saying he missed her? This was the most personal comment she was likely to get, yet it seemed off.

He wore a hat she hadn't seen before. Though most men wore hats every day, Adrian disdained them whenever possible.

She didn't resist when he brought her closer and kissed her. But she felt nothing. Not when he touched her, nor when his mouth closed over hers. Every other time they'd kissed, she'd wanted more. He didn't taste the same, but she knew he'd cleaned his teeth mere hours ago. She pulled away abruptly, knowing her consternation showed on her face. Where was the desire, the melting sensation she'd come to expect?

Something wasn't right.

He held her face in his hands and gently caressed her cheeks, the way she loved. But she felt empty. She took a deep breath, hoping the clean, fresh scent that was distinctly Adrian would ease her anxiety. He smelled too sweet, with a cloying tang that made her nose itch.

She had to figure out what was wrong. He bent toward her again, but she gripped his hands to stop him. She didn't want him to kiss her. Not until she understood the changes in him. Her breath caught as she felt smooth skin on both of his wrists. She pulled his left hand closer and stared at it.

"What happened to your scar?" she whispered.

Adrian grabbed his wrist self-consciously, then jerked his sleeve down.

"It has healed," he said.

"Scars like yours don't heal so quickly, if ever." Joanna took a step back. Her heart pounded. This man wasn't her husband, yet looked so very like him.

She saw the handsome, chiseled features she expected to see, the same dark eyebrows. There was something eerie about his eyes, slightly shadowed by the hat.

Joanna snatched the hat off his head and recoiled. The man before her had shorter hair than Adrian. And the gleam his eyes scared her.

"Who are you?" she cried.

The hat dropped to the floor.

"What the hell is going on?"

Joanna gasped, frozen with shock. The Adrian she knew stood in the arched entryway, his blue eyes blazing, his hair as it should be. But the other man looked so like him....

Adrian strode toward the stranger and grabbed fistfuls of his clothing. He said in a flat tone, "Joanna, meet my brother, Andrew. Andrew, I see you've already met my wife."

Joanna stared at the two men before her, so alike except for their hair. One looked furious, the other smug. Her mouth dropped open in surprise as her stomach roiled. Adrian had a twin, yet he hadn't told her. Why?

Was his twin the missing piece of his puzzle, the reason for prohibiting personal conversations? Could she trust him at all?

Then it hit her. She'd kissed Adrian's brother. She wiped her mouth on the back of her hand, but his cloying scent remained.

"What are you doing here? And with Joanna?" Adrian demanded.

She'd never seen him so angry, so formidable. His clenched muscles could barely contain his energy, which she feared might burst forth with the force of a fired cannonball.

Andrew choked. "Let me go."

Adrian complied with obvious reluctance. He positioned himself in front of her as though shielding her from his twin. Though the brothers were of a height, Adrian's aura of restrained power overshadowed Andrew.

"Joanna, I need to speak with my brother. Alone." He turned to look at her. "I know you are beyond curious, but I ask you to do this for me." His words were slow and measured.

Shock froze her in place. Could she forgive him for keeping this secret?

He took a deep breath. Then exhaled through his mouth, as if the stream of air helped him remain calm. He took her hands, then stroked her cheek. His eyes gave no clue as to his thoughts. "Please. I promise to discuss this. Later."

She wanted to stay, but couldn't refuse his sincere plea especially when coupled with a promise of a personal conversation. Fighting the temptation to linger outside the door and listen, she left the chapel. Later, despite their agreement, she'd learn about Adrian's twin. Somehow she'd endure the wait.

❧ ❧

The rage that besieged Adrian upon seeing Joanna in Andrew's arms hadn't faded. Scorching possessiveness consumed him, as surprising as it was fierce. She was his. Neither careful breaths nor the soothing quiet of the church could ease his fury.

"What in God's name were you thinking?" he demanded.

Andrew held out his hands, palms up, looking for all the world like an innocent friar instead of the conniving zealot Adrian now knew him to be.

"We often pretended to be each other as children." Andrew backed away, holding his hands out as if to ward off an attack. Adrian half-expected him to make the sign of the cross.

"Nice try. But you can do better."

Adrian matched Andrew's retreat with a steady advance, aware that his twin could sense his fury.

"She seemed upset," Andrew said. "I thought if I could offer comfort...."

"By wearing my clothes and pretending to be me? Have you been following her, too? Again," he growled. He backed Andrew against the wall. The stone gritted against Andrew's back. "I want the truth."

"She is beautiful," Andrew whispered.

Adrian shook his head in disgust. He couldn't talk about Joanna any longer or he'd strangle Andrew. He stepped back, needing to breathe something other than his twin's oversweet scent.

"What are you doing here? What happened to your pilgrimage?"

Andrew slithered away from the wall and out of Adrian's

reach. He sat on a pew. "I did visit a shrine or two," he said. "But I didn't realize how draining such a journey could be. Rome is so far away. I've been staying with these good brothers."

The panic Adrian felt before Andrew left returned in a flood. "Why?"

"My brother," Andrew said, "I came here to seek guidance through prayer. You fight wars for England. I fight a war with myself. I don't know which side of me will win."

"What the hell does that mean?"

"I ask myself, can I allow you to live, tainted as you are, or should I commend your soul to God? I do love you. You're my twin. The only family I have."

Adrian clenched his teeth. Another lie. No male in his family, including him, knew how to love. He wanted to beat some sense into Andrew. Though releasing his anger would probably make him feel better, violence wouldn't change anything.

A pair of brothers walked into the chapel. Adrian and his brother nodded, waiting for them to pass.

Andrew might turn him in to the authorities. No news could fill him with greater fear. Of utmost concern was how easily something could happen to Joanna. Something harmful, yet unforeseen and sudden, the minute his back was turned. His possessiveness increased. Joanna had married him for protection. How could he shield her from every danger? Could he anticipate Andrew's next move?

And what of William and John, who'd been quiet for too long?

When the brothers had moved on, Adrian cursed himself for not accepting sooner what Andrew had become. He had a sudden urge to take Joanna and go somewhere, anywhere, away from his brother and hers. But he'd never been one to run from his troubles.

He couldn't conceal his hostility as he walked to his brother, who slid along the polished wood pew until the carved end of the bench trapped him.

"Stop acting the hero." Andrew laughed, a dry, hollow sound. "So much for earning back the family honor. You've gone and married a commoner, a woman who engages in trade at that. What would our precious father have had to say about that?"

For the first time, his brother's harsh words didn't affect him. "I'm still working to have our family titles restored. You know very well that no nobleman would give me his daughter until I do."

"Then why marry now? If you're so sure of your impending success, why not wait?" Andrew persisted.

Adrian wasn't about to share his reasons for a hasty marriage. And he certainly wouldn't tell him how he'd felt drawn to Joanna from the moment he saw her.

Behind Andrew, sunlight streamed through a small, round stained glass window set high in the wall. He thought of Joanna, of all that she represented: goodness and light. He had to go to her and explain that which could not be explained. The stunned look on her face, the near daze in which she left the church made him wonder what his reception would be.

This was precisely why he'd insisted upon such a strict agreement. He hadn't wanted to reveal anything about Andrew. If he'd given her one drop of information about having a twin, unasked questions about Andrew's whereabouts, his occupation and their relationship would constantly swirl around them. Far better that she know nothing.

Too late.

He held out his hand. "Give me your key."

Thank God Andrew hadn't shown up at their rooms while Joanna was there, and he, Adrian, was absent.

"What if I wish to leave here?" Andrew asked, palms up as if he were an innocent petitioner. "You'd keep me from our lodging?"

"I pay the rent. And I don't want you sneaking around and bothering my wife. Or taking more of my belongings," Adrian said. "Give me the key."

Andrew pulled the key from a pocket in his robe and held it out.

As Adrian's fingers closed over the cold metal, Andrew asked, "What happens now?"

CHAPTER 16

"Joanna!"

No answer.

Adrian hastily unlocked the door to her workshop and looked inside. She wasn't there. She hadn't been in their rooms, either.

"Joanna!" he shouted again.

He couldn't keep panic from his voice or his heart. Had she left him? Had his secrets finally pushed her away?

The back door was ajar. He ran up the stairs, his blood pounding. No one in the small living area. The bedroom?

At last.

"I found you," he whispered, relief rushing through him.

She sat crumpled on the bed, like an abandoned doll with her head down and her hair covering her face, her hands limp and resting in her lap. He wanted to take her in his arms and soothe her.

Adrian dropped to his knees, placing his hands on the bed in front of her. He struggled for words. The easiest solution would be to blame everything on their agreement. Yet she deserved more. Worse, he wanted to give her more.

Their gazes met and held. Hers was replete with an odd mix of anguish and wariness. Like a battered puppy, wounded to the core, afraid more abuse was to come. He couldn't bear it. Again she suffered because of him.

The longer he waited, the harder speaking became. Sentences formed in his head, but he couldn't make them come out of his mouth.

"I have a twin." Not a promising beginning.

"So I saw."

He could barely hear her.

"I'm more than sorry that he bothered you. That he dared to touch you."

Joanna shuddered. He took her hands. They were cold and pliant. She didn't pull away. He folded her fingers over his.

"What troubled me most is that he is so like you, yet at the same time somehow not," Joanna said. "At first I thought he was you. But the minute he touched me, I knew something was wrong. So strange, like living a bad dream. I couldn't figure out what was different at first."

She shivered again. He took off his cloak and draped it over her shoulders.

"Why didn't you tell me about him?" she asked. "Never mind. I know why. The agreement. 'Tis no marriage when the wife can't even ask her husband something simple as, 'Do you have any brothers or sisters?'"

She bit her lip as if to keep from crying or saying something she might later regret.

Joanna looked so hurt he felt her distress. He'd never heard her voice sound so empty, not even after the miscarriage.

Theirs was a marriage based on a contract. Perhaps the terms were more specific than most marriages made solely for political or financial reasons. But they'd both signed it.

Willingly. She'd needed a husband, but hadn't been forced to wed him. He had no obligation to tell her anything unrelated to her glass-painting or begetting an heir.

Then why did he care how she felt and what she thought of him? Why did he need to earn her trust?

There was only one solution. He had to show her he trusted her. The only way to do that was to reveal more of himself. But sharing his secrets, confiding in someone, was unfamiliar and frightening. That side of him had rusted like abandoned armor. He wished he could be restored as easily, with nothing but elbow grease and oil.

He took a deep breath, then released air slowly. "Do you remember when I told you how my father told the authorities about my grandmother?"

"Yes."

"There is more." He joined her on the bed.

They sat side by side, backs against the wall, facing straight ahead. He didn't want to see sympathy or pity, if she had any, for it might break him. If she didn't understand, if his explanation wasn't enough, he didn't want to see that either.

"My mother died shortly after my grandmother. Some said the cause was grief, though the physicians said she had a weak heart. My father blamed himself."

"As you blamed yourself for the miscarriage," she said softly.

A lump formed in Adrian's throat. He hadn't acknowledged the similarities until this moment, when his youth and recent past merged with agonizing misery. He could still see the flames, hear the wood crack and smell his grandmother burning. He ached with the loss of his and Joanna's child and the anguish of her recovery. Would the pain ever cease to haunt him?

"I suppose so," he said.

"Go on," Joanna whispered, as though the sound of her voice would scare him away.

Adrian couldn't resist the lure of her hair. He reached for a perfect spiral and wrapped it around his finger. He needed to be connected to her, even in this small way.

"I've never shared this with anyone, but I want you to know. Father began to gamble. He kept gambling until he lost everything except his title. But he wasted nary a thought as to how his foolish actions would affect his family, his children," Adrian paused, determined not to let distressing memories overwhelm him. "Andrew and I begged him to stop before all of our money and possessions were lost to his gaming. He didn't listen. After several years, we were impoverished. One day we returned from school to find Father dead on the floor, lying amidst several empty wine bottles."

That image stayed with him. A once powerful and respected man, destroyed by the consequences of his own actions. Alone with his insurmountable sorrows.

What if he ended up the same way?

He shifted to escape the lumpy ropes poking him from beneath the thin straw mattress. How did Joanna sleep here? He'd find a way to get her a fine, freshly stuffed bed.

"Perhaps he regretted his choices," she suggested.

"I think he regretted only what his choices cost him," he said. "Just before he died, King Henry put him under a bill of attainder."

"For what?" Joanna looked at him, clearly engrossed.

"The king had Parliament issue a bill saying my father was guilty of treason. Last July, the Duke of York, his sons and several others were attainted, too."

"Whether or not their cause is valid, York and the rest took up arms against their anointed king," Joanna said. "What crime did your father commit?"

"Father was so absorbed in his own concerns he refused to fight when the king needed him. He lacked the resources to send men in his stead or pay a fine. The attainder gave the king the right to confiscate all of his possessions and execute him. Without a trial. My father had no opportunity to defend himself.

"Most of his estates and possessions were gone by then. The king gave what was left, including Bedford Castle, to Lady Anne's husband, father's largest creditor. Father died the day before his execution date."

Telling the tale reopened wounds that wouldn't heal. His heart ached. He sighed, as if doing so could whisk away the cobwebs of the past.

"After Father was attainted, we had nothing. No choice but to work to keep a roof over our heads. At fourteen, Andrew and I were penniless and alone in the world. We no longer had estates to manage or rents to collect, no servants or tenants to supervise as other nobles did. In fact, legally we weren't noble any longer. The king had taken Father's title, too. I owe everything I have now to Warwick's support, not to any inheritance."

Joanna squeezed his hand. Her sympathy didn't hurt as he'd thought it would, but eased the tightness in his chest.

"I am the eldest, though only by five minutes. It fell to me to restore what my father had destroyed. I earned my spurs and was knighted, but fighting wasn't enough. So I did what I had to do." Adrian instantly regretted those words. The last thing he wanted to do was bring up his arrangement with Lady Anne.

"I've worked for years to get the attainder reversed, which would restore Father's title, but the king has refused. To honor my mother and grandmother, I want my family name to be as respected as it once was."

"What a story." Joanna sighed, but said no more.

He couldn't tell if she was merely intrigued or if she now forgave him for not telling her about Andrew. Still, he hadn't revealed the whole truth and told her of his visions. Or spoke of his work as a spy for Warwick. He rode a powerful wave of guilt. He hadn't known he'd want to tell her things about himself against his better judgment.

Joanna had no right to know about his past. 'Twas not his fault if his silence displeased her. The agreement would stand.

She knew too much already.

"Adrian, what now?"

He shook his head. First Andrew, then Joanna. Everyone looked to him, assuming he had answers to all the problems looming before him.

"I wish I knew."

❧❧ ❧❧

The next night, Joanna was alone in bed. Adrian hadn't come to her, leaving her restless and chilled beneath her coverlet.

She could add a few pieces of precious coal to the brazier, but every groat counted.

What was that? A slight scraping noise sent her heart racing. Could someone have broken in? She snatched up the candlestick, crept out of bed and peered through the slightly opened door.

To glimpse Adrian on his way out of their quarters.

Her heart sped still faster. She set down the candle, then threw on her boots and cloak to hurry after him. But he'd disappeared into the night.

Where could he possibly be going at this hour? And why?

As she trudged back inside, Joanna recalled the night they signed their contract, when she'd vowed to uncover his secrets. She hadn't guessed how painful knowledge of them would be: his strange dealings with Lady Anne, a fanatical twin and a mysterious past which left scars so deep they might never heal.

But he'd protected her, helped her retain her father's

workshop. He introduced her to the wondrous pleasures of making love.

Tears filled her eyes. Just when she'd thought they were growing closer, she discovered he had more to hide.

What secret assignation had lured him from their home?

She didn't know how much more she could take.

❦ ❦

Ensconced in a dim corner of the Boar's Head alehouse, Adrian clenched his tankard of ale.

On occasion he wished he could drown his troubles in drink, but found that excessive imbibing made him maudlin. Not only did good ale require coin he couldn't spare, he feared an excess might loosen his tongue. He sighed, missing the costly foods, furnishings and clothing he'd taken for granted as a boy.

Andrew had been right about one thing. A poor man's life didn't suit them.

He ignored the clamor in the narrow, low-ceilinged room and the aroma of cooked mutton in the air. Foam frothed over the side of his tankard and onto his fingers, but he didn't wipe it away.

This night he awaited his lord, Richard Neville, Earl of Warwick, whom he trusted with his life. Not even Warwick knew about his visions. But he alone understood that Adrian walked a fine line between treason and service to his country.

How he wished he had someone to talk to about his deepest concerns. His recent conversation with Joanna showed him the benefits of companionship, something he'd never appreciated before.

Adrian had spent the journey to London analyzing his options. He hadn't slept, struggling with the daring choice he'd made for this secret meeting.

Would he live to regret it?

I'm not making the same mistake my father made. Though he was about to do something his father had done, something he'd sworn never to do. He was going to gamble. Not with money or possessions, which was bad enough, but with people's lives.

The risks were great. The reward could be greater. If this

worked, most of his problems would be solved. He couldn't think about what would happen if he failed. For then he might not have the courage to proceed.

"You were right, this place was hard to find," Warwick said as he slid onto the stool next to Adrian's. He tugged his plain, coarse wool hood further over his face, shedding melting snow onto the table. He bent closer. "But obviously popular. No one will notice us here. What have you learned?"

Adrian forced himself to swallow some ale. The path he'd chosen could alter the course of history. Yet he believed he was doing the right thing. He leaned forward, not wanting to shout over the patrons' conversations. "Unsettling news. The Lancastrians plan to attack York while he is at Sandal Castle."

Warwick looked at him, his lean face rife with disbelief. "What? 'Tis near Christmas. Both sides agreed to hold the fighting until after Epiphany."

The serving wench slammed a mug of ale in front of Warwick and continued on her way.

"I've also learned York is low on supplies." Adrian had learned these things by seeing York and his men in his most recent vision. "The Lancastrians know they can't breach the defenses of York's castle. So they plan to lie in wait and attack when his men leave to forage for food."

Warwick shook his head. "I can't believe that. How do you know it isn't a trick?"

Adrian shrugged. "I don't. But you asked me to spy and that's what I've done." At least that part was true. "Perhaps we should send reinforcements. If we're not already too late."

Richard, Duke of York, was the key to England's future. His supporters believed he was the rightful king, having descended from an older son of John of Gaunt than King Henry himself. Thus Henry VI and the Lancasters were usurpers.

York would be a far better king than the weak Henry, oft ruled by his unpopular French queen, Margaret of Anjou. But he also knew York would never be king.

Because he'd seen York's death.

If Adrian didn't try to prevent York's demise, all of their efforts would be for naught. But his conscience still questioned the ethics of using his visions to change the future. Perhaps York needed to die so his cause would fail. Or so someone else, perhaps his son, Edward, Earl of March, would pick up the gauntlet. Edward had but eighteen years, while the duke was a powerful, experienced lord, better suited to rule.

"York wants me to remain in London," Warwick said. He took off his gloves and placed them on the table, then took a swig of ale. "I trust you, Adrian, you know that, but your information must be wrong. York is a shrewd commander. He'd not leave the security of Sandal Castle."

"I could ride ahead and warn them," Adrian offered.

"No, I'd rather you return home. I need someone in York I can trust. Keep seeking information. Don't doubt yourself, Adrian. If anyone can do this, you can."

Had Warwick read his thoughts, sensed his doubt? Nay, his commander couldn't know the depth of his lack of confidence. Warwick would expect him to succeed as he had in the past. But never before had so much been at stake.

"I must go. Send word as soon you know more. More facts, not rumor." Warwick took another drink, then tossed some coins onto the table. He picked up his gloves and left.

Adrian sagged with a mixture of relief and frustration as Warwick went out into the snow. He'd tried to do what he thought was right. But York would soon die as God or Destiny had decreed.

He was thankful Warwick had seemed preoccupied and hadn't pressed for details about how he acquired his "information." He'd done as promised, continuing to spy on Lady Anne's son despite ending his liaison with her. Using his key, he'd risked visiting Bedford Castle in the middle of the night, hating feeling the thief in what should be his own house. And he despised himself for sneaking out and keeping more secrets from his wife. So he'd decided to stop going.

Since he hadn't found anything to alert him to the king's plans, he'd used knowledge gleaned from his visions. Only rarely had he done that before, and only when he believed there was no other way to reveal essential information.

If Adrian was caught spying before the Yorkists succeeded, or if Andrew turned him in, his gamble would fail. He'd be executed for treason.

Just like his father would've been.

Disgust and guilt wracked him. He could lose all. His best efforts could end up tainting his family name beyond redemption. And his home would be lost forever. Far worse than anything that could befall him, his mistakes would leave Joanna alone and unprotected.

He froze, shocked by his own thoughts. When had he come to care for his wife more than his lifelong ambition? Somehow her well-being had become more important than his own. Somehow his once self-serving instinct surrendered to her needs. What had happened to his marriage of convenience?

Did he love Joanna?

No. Because he couldn't love. Everyone he thought he'd loved had turned on him, from his father to Andrew. Or they'd died, like his mother and grandmother.

Love didn't bring comfort and security as most people seemed to think, only fear of loss, disaster and death. He cared for Joanna more than anyone else because she was his wife, his legal responsibility. He desired her because she was beautiful and giving. God, Church and contract bound him to her. That had to be all.

But he realized that for weeks almost everything he'd done had been for Joanna. Concern for her had made him cease both his visits to Lady Anne and his secret nocturnal visits to Bedford Castle. He'd been so obsessed with trying to help Joanna and protect her from William, John, Andrew and even himself, he hadn't focused on what might happen if he failed.

Because he'd come to care for Joanna, and for her had forfeited the opportunity to spy on Lady Anne's son, the future of England was at stake.

What had he done?

CHAPTER 17

Adrian awoke, his head throbbing. A week had passed since the confrontation in the chapel. He hadn't seen his brother since.

Adrian feared each day with Joanna would be his last, worried that any minute the sheriff and his men would haul him to prison for witchcraft. He'd spent hours racking his brain for something he could do, some action he could take. Waiting both to see what Andrew might do and for news from Warwick grated on him.

He and Joanna had been living under a wary truce. Their nights were filled with passion, their days cordial and cooperative. He no longer returned to his own chamber after their lovemaking because he enjoyed sleeping with his wife. And slept better with her beside him.

But not this night.

Joanna was wrapped securely in his arms, her hair spilling over his chest. He couldn't appreciate the wonders of her because a vision approached. Fast.

He needed to flee, to avoid disturbing Joanna or exposing her to what was to come, but knew he wouldn't make it across the room. His head pressed into the pillow as the swirling mist overtook him.

He stood in the midst of a vast field. In the distance, a castle loomed high on a hill. York's castle, Sandal. Woods ran to both sides. Up ahead, a bridge spanned a rushing river.

A small, mounted force rode into view. York's men, he could tell by their blue and white livery. Suddenly soldiers spilled out of the woods, swords drawn. More soldiers ran into view, bearing the badge of bear and ragged staff. Warwick's men.

Warwick's men were attacking York's. But they were allies. How could this be?

Rushing blood, screaming, drowning...field and river crowded with corpses.

The faces of the dead floated before his eyes.

Adrian burst up in bed, gasping for breath, unintentionally bringing Joanna with him.

What should he do about all he'd seen?

"Adrian, what is it?"

Her heart thudded against his chest. Sweat chilled on his skin. As the remnants of the vision faded, unavoidable queasiness seeped in. He struggled to speak, but couldn't. He'd never talked to anyone so soon after an episode.

With great effort, he found his voice. "Just a nightmare."

Another living nightmare about Richard, Duke of York's death. He now knew why York and his men would leave the safety of Sandal Castle. They thought they rode out to meet allies. But awaiting them were traitors garbed in friends' clothing, who'd then be joined by thousands of enemies. He had to warn Warwick about possible traitors in his ranks. But wait. What if Warwick himself was behind this? Should he warn York instead?

Glowing coals in the brazier lit the room enough for him to see Joanna's distress. But he couldn't bring himself to meet her gaze when he was being dishonest. He turned away, drawing the bedcovers close to his chest. He hadn't anticipated the pain of keeping the truth from her. She snuggled against him and wrapped her arm across his waist.

Her trust and support made him even sicker.

Why had he married? He'd set himself up for a lifetime of torture from the constant strain of keeping secrets. He'd hurt Joanna and most likely would again, even as he tried not to.

She deserved a husband who could make her happy. He'd believed helping with her glass-painting would be enough. He didn't even know if he could keep her safe as promised.

"Adrian." Her gentle voice stopped his wild thoughts. "This isn't working, is it?"

His gaze snapped to hers, showing him tears threatening to spill from her glorious green eyes. She couldn't have caused him more anguish had she stabbed him with his own sword.

What could he do, what could he say, to comfort her? Adrian slid an arm around her, trying to ignore the menacing sickness clinging after his vision. She felt icy cold, making him shiver in response. He moved closer, trying to restore her warmth with his.

She blinked. A fat tear plopped onto his chest. The proof of her sadness sizzled like acid. He held her against him, hoping to offer some reassurance.

"Joanna. It isn't you," he said. "No matter what happens between us, you must believe me in this. You are everything good, everything wonderful. Our troubles stem from me, from things I can't reveal without endangering us."

Concern slowly replaced the misery in her gaze. "What things? How can I help?"

She was so forgiving. He wasn't worthy of her.

He closed his eyes as despair washed over him. She wanted to take his problems as her own. She believed in him. As much as he relished her trust, it encumbered him.

"If I could…."

What was he doing? He couldn't burden her with the truth. His very existence hinged on secrecy. Guilt—he hated the way it gnawed at him. The alternative, to let her go, to live without her, would be worse. Was it selfish to reduce his pain by staying married to her? Would she be happier if he released her from their agreement?

If he left her for her own good, would she be able to bear the stigma of divorce? And what of the dangers she'd face alone?

He opened his eyes. The look in hers seared his gut. She did need a formidable husband. He'd have to be satisfied with offering what protection he could, if not himself. Despite the misery their marriage brought her, there was another reason he could never let her go. He didn't want to.

He and Joanna had made amazing love numerous times since the miscarriage. She could be pregnant again. Despite his need for an heir, the risks still besieged him.

Should Andrew accuse him to the authorities, if he were

found guilty, his taint might or might not spread to his family. He hadn't uncovered enough similar cases to find a clear pattern.

And his child. How he prayed he or she would be normal. The affliction seemed arbitrary: his grandmother had the Sight but his mother and twin didn't. If his child did have the Sight, perhaps he'd be able to help conceal and deal with the problem better from the start. There was a slim chance the world would grow more tolerant and leave the child in peace.

Even so, Adrian accepted that he could be subjecting his child to a lifetime of loneliness and fear. A life like his. But now, he had Joanna. He'd worked so hard and so long to preserve his family, his heritage. How could he let his purpose fade away? Let all of his efforts go to waste? Then his life would have no meaning.

Nothing. He had to keep reminding himself of that.

More tears spilled down her cheeks. "Adrian, I...I wish I could say...I want to tell you...." Joanna squeezed out a breath, then burst into loud, gasping sobs. She pushed away from him and scrambled out of the bed, then sped toward the door.

Without thinking, Adrian ran after her. He fought off dizziness, knowing that if he let Joanna leave the room he'd never get her back. He pulled her into his arms, raining small kisses all over her wet face as her hair tumbled over them.

"Joanna, I will make it right. I promise."

His words sounded weak even to his own ears. He held her close, wrapping his arms about her as though his strength alone could resolve their problems. Her sobs subsided as she stood motionless in his embrace.

Are you proud of yourself now? You've broken this wonderful woman.

"I'm truly sorry the agreement comes between us. I hope you believe I have your best interests at heart, and do this to protect you," he said. "Please say you understand."

He'd beg if doing so would make her stay.

She turned her red, swollen face to his. Her eyes were bright, brilliant green. She was as fresh and unsullied as he was soiled by his quagmire of a life. She looked all the more lovely to him at this moment. Adrian wanted to kiss away her pain. To give the comfort with his body that he couldn't offer in words. He inhaled, appreciating her rose scent. He bent to kiss her, but her words stopped him.

"I've tried to understand, Adrian. But how can I, when you won't tell me anything?" Her voice caught in a sob. "All I hear is 'trust me' or 'it's for the best,' yet you obviously don't trust me enough to share your concerns and problems. Yes, our marriage is a based on a contract, which we both agreed to, but things change, and I hoped...." She sniffled. "I hoped...."

He couldn't bear it. How painful caring for someone in agony could be, as with his grandmother and mother. But this time, the fault was his.

"I hoped too, Joanna. You must believe that. You must," he said, smoothing back her hair. "It can't be. Not now, perhaps not ever. That doesn't mean I don't care about you. That I don't want you. Because I do." He wrapped his arms around her, feeling the warmth of her skin through her nightgown. "We have more than many couples do. We have this."

His mouth captured hers in the tenderest of kisses, slow and soothing. As arousal swept through him, he pulled away. With his finger, he outlined the soft curves of her lips. He wanted her so, no matter their problems. But if she didn't want him in return.... "Please let this be enough."

He slid his arms around her, kissing her gently. Then he slid his tongue into her mouth, coaxing, caressing, until she responded. At last.

When she wrapped her arms around him, relief mingled with gratitude. She'd accepted him once again. He clasped her tighter, welcoming the press of her breasts against his chest.

"Ah, Joanna," he breathed as need surged through his veins.

He couldn't get used to this need for her. Each time the intensity surprised him, coming out of nowhere. Like his visions, almost as overwhelming. Surely he should've had his fill of her by now. Yet whenever he saw her, he wanted her. Judging by her response to his kisses, she wanted him, too. Her desire was arousing in itself.

She kissed him back even as her tears fell, her tongue joining his. He tasted salt. She clutched him as though she couldn't bear to let him go.

"My Joanna," he said softly. "Do not cry. It breaks my heart to see you so unhappy."

Gently, he wiped her tears away.

"I'm not unhappy," she said, her fingers brushing his hair from his face. Her eyes were so green and clear. Yet so full of anguish. "Just so sad you must keep secrets from me. Sad you can't trust me. Don't you know I'd never do anything to hurt you?"

"Yes. I do. Not of your own free will, at any rate. That's part of the problem. If I relied on your trust, I could be putting you in danger." He knew all too well how persuasive his enemies could be in getting answers. "I can't allow that, even if it makes you sad."

"Even if it comes between us?" Her voice was so low he could barely hear her. Her hands rested on his shoulders, as if ready to push him away. "Even if I have to break the agreement?"

His heart wrenched. She'd become essential to him, like the very air he breathed. He didn't know what he'd do if she left. He'd lived most of his life for his family. Now he knew he lived for Joanna too. He stroked her hair, praying his words would reassure her.

"Even then. Your safety is more important to me than anything. Joanna, when we signed, I didn't know how hard keeping the agreement would be. I didn't know how I would come to care for you." His own tears stung his eyes, the sensation unfamiliar and disconcerting. "Let us share what we can," he said, his voice breaking.

He bent to kiss her again but she pushed at his chest. His skin burned under her fingers as she held herself from him.

Tears dripped down her cheeks. She seemed to be fighting a silent battle with herself. Adrian prayed his side would win, even as he wondered if Joanna might be better off without him. But he needed her now, needed her understanding, more than anything he'd ever needed before.

As if she couldn't help herself, her hands began to make small circular motions on his chest, tormenting him with desire. He forced himself to stay still, awaiting her decision.

She said, "Kiss me, then. Make love to me. Make me forget everything else."

He whispered into her ear, "That I can do."

❧ ☙

Several days later, Joanna and Adrian stood in front of Micklegate Bar, one of York's fortified gates. Dismal skies and wailing winds echoed their emotions as they stared upward, horrified by what they saw.

The severed head of Richard, Duke of York, stared blankly down from its perch on the stone wall. His head and two others had been impaled as a barbaric reminder of what befell traitors to the crown.

"Who else is there?" Joanna asked.

"The Earls of Salisbury and Rutland, York's younger son." The wind snatched his cloak. He raised one side and wrapped it around Joanna, drawing her against him.

"Did you know them, too?"

"Yes."

His scratchy voice revealed how affected he was by the animosity prompting York's enemies to impale his head and what the act portended.

Indecision after his second vision had wracked him. How to explain what he'd seen? He'd sent Warwick a carefully couched warning, as he had no physical evidence. He didn't know if the message reached him, if he'd received but ignored it or tried to heed it but failed.

Adrian should've done more. But what?

For the first time, he wondered if the stronger choice was accepting what his vision foretold, not worrying about how to change the outcome. He'd been given the opportunity to address painful reality before it happened. Was his Sight a gift then, not a curse?

The Yorkist cause would continue on with York's eldest son, Edward, the new Duke of York. He had to believe that was meant to be.

A tattered paper crown sat on York's head in ironic reflection of his belief that he was the rightful king. A lifeless leader looked over his namesake town.

Joanna shuddered at the gruesome sight. "For once I'm glad you couldn't inherit your father's high-ranking title. You're free of these political quarrels between the Lancasters and the Yorkists. How many must die before they come to terms?" She shook her head. "Yet I'm surprised Warwick didn't call upon you to join the fighting."

He hated that he couldn't tell her how involved he was. The more he came to care for Joanna, the worse his hidden truths became. He hadn't yet lied outright, but significant omissions stung just the same. If she'd asked why he didn't fight, he didn't know what he'd have answered.

Concealing the truth from his wife was tearing him apart.

They walked back to their rooms through bustling streets. People bargained for goods, horses and laden carts lumbered along. Cold air whisked away the usual smells produced by ale-makers, fishmongers and animals.

For years his focus had been on redeeming his family name. He still wanted that, for the memory of his mother and grandmother, for his children and Joanna. But when he married her, he'd had no way of knowing he'd want his life to be better, not for himself, but for her. How he'd need her. He, who had never needed anyone.

Had the time come to let go of the anger fueling his life? Should the part of him that couldn't resist Joanna claim victory over his heart? Could he truly care for her as she deserved?

He admired her skin, so pale beneath the gray skies, her natural elegance as she walked beside him. She met his gaze with a sad smile and took his hand.

His heart thawed. He could actually feel it.

She meant more to him than he wanted to admit. Accepting that Joanna was essential was easy because she belonged with him, difficult because he couldn't stop trying to resist her pull.

The rest of his secrets stood between them, an impenetrable barrier. And they always would. Somehow she'd accepted him, even as she peeled away a few distasteful layers of his past.

He should appreciate that his visions and his spying would preserve some distance between them. But more and more he wanted to belong to her completely. He wanted to love her.

If only he could.

CHAPTER 18

Joanna listened to Adrian's even breathing. Despite the weight of his burdens, he'd finally fallen asleep.

Her feelings for her husband were so complicated. He amazed her, for despite the problems he had, he'd been strong enough and willing to take on hers too. She was thrilled he'd begun to open up to her. On the other hand, she couldn't forget the strange meeting with his twin, and still couldn't understand why Adrian hadn't told her about him. What if Andrew's appearance hadn't forced his hand?

His passion overwhelmed her. He made love to her so tenderly, almost reverently, as though he wanted to remember every moment. She felt cherished, her body still resonating from his touch. She had gotten far more than she bargained for in that regard.

But he held something back, clearly the biggest secret of all. His hints of danger scared her more than the truth ever could. The unknown lurked in every shadow. But she wouldn't add to his problems by letting him know how his secrecy and her own fears bothered her.

Slowly she turned, enjoying the sensation as the warmth of him against her shifted from her back to her front. Gently she combed back his hair, revealing his handsome face. In the gentle radiance of dawn, she admired the sculpted muscles of his chest. If only she could help him as he had helped her. Was it enough for him that she listened? Would he relish knowing she trusted him, no matter what?

Joanna relaxed into the lulling rhythm of his breathing. A horse clip-clopped outside, momentarily disrupting the quiet. Adrian moved closer and wrapped his arm around her. She smiled.

She hadn't expected to or wanted to care deeply for him. Nor had she anticipated the disturbing vulnerability that came with caring.

In the face of all that had happened, somewhere along the way their marriage had become more than a mere agreement for her. Her heart swelled with an emotion far beyond tenderness. Her heart swelled with...love.

Love.

Joanna gasped as she accepted the truth, reveling in the joy flooding her. Despite her resistance, for the first time in her life, she was in love. She loved Adrian. For one blissful moment, that awareness was enough.

Until reality returned. She knew all too well how love worked strange magic, destroying those who succumbed to its capricious lure. Take her father's almost desperate attachment to Margery's mother...there was no controlling love once it struck. Would loving Adrian ruin her, too?

She'd crushed the blanket in her fist. She smoothed the fabric, wishing she could even out her concerns as easily.

He'd never know how she felt, for she could never tell him. She couldn't share her feelings, for they were far outside the boundaries of their agreed upon marriage. She sighed, and nestled against Adrian, her pleasure in the moment shattered. What good was love if you couldn't share it?

Now she too had a secret.

⁂ ⁂

William reeled down the winding lane, a half-dressed whore at his side, a surfeit of drink making her oblivious to the cold night air. She tried to pull him against her for a wine-laced kiss, but instead stumbled and laughed.

What time was it? Very, very late. The best time to be drunk and far from central York. They bumped into a house and burst into laughter. The bottle she held smashed against the wall.

Red wine dripped onto his shoes, shining like blood in the moonlight. The scent filled his nostrils as the pieces of broken glass sparkled, an unwelcome reminder of Joanna and his sad financial state. Too much bad wine could bring on very serious thoughts. He didn't want to think, didn't want to remember. Best to keep moving on.

After the night he'd had, he needed more wine than he could afford. Now the last of it was slithering down the frozen stones of the street.

"Again?" the whore asked, pushing him against the wall, into the shadows. Glass crunched under his shoes as she grabbed his crotch.

"Don't have any more money," he said.

"Well, then, that be that."

William didn't even care.

A church bell rang out the hour. One, two. He yawned. Better wend his way back to the city and get some sleep.

Wait, what was that? He grabbed the whore's arm and pulled her in front of him.

"Stand there a minute," he whispered.

"Why?"

"Shhhh!" Had he seen what he thought he'd seen? He stared into the mottled areas of light and dark.

A man moved swiftly down the street. A man he recognized. Yes. Adrian, in this unsavory neighborhood. He wore the grey robes of a friar, the hood pulled over his face. If he hadn't tilted his head, if the moon hadn't shined just so, William wouldn't have recognized him.

Luck was with him for once. His chance to discover Adrian's weakness had landed at his feet. But he couldn't be recognized, or word would shoot straight to Joanna.

"See that man?" he whispered in the whore's ear. He pointed past her shoulder, and she craned her neck to see. "Follow him, then send word. I would know where he goes, what he does."

"For that, I'll want double me usual. But ye got no coin to pay."

"Go. You get the information, I'll get the money," he promised. "Now hurry, he's getting away."

The whore rushed into the night.

CHAPTER 19

Caught!

Adrian froze in the entrance to the great hall of Bedford Castle, the iron door handle cold beneath his hand. But not as cold as the expressions of Lady Anne's two servants who he turned to face.

"What do you here, Sir Adrian?" Pamping asked. His bald head gleamed as he raised his candle. "'Tis not your usual visiting hour, Sir."

The servant couldn't know he was leaving after a final search of Berkeley's study. Nor could he learn that Adrian finally had the proof of the king's plans he desperately needed secreted in his cloak.

"I must speak with Lady Anne about a matter of great urgency," he said in his most arrogant tone.

Pamping looked skeptical, but nodded. "Very well, I shall ask if she will receive you."

A draft made the candle flicker as he turned to go. When the other servant followed, Pamping said, "Stay with him. Don't let him out of your sight."

Adrian stared at his guard until the man looked away. He wracked his brain for something so urgent it couldn't wait until morning. The high ceilings of his home loomed above him, vast and unwelcoming. A dog barked. The guard's rapid breathing annoyed him.

No good topic came to mind.

A woman screamed.

"Mary preserve us," shouted another.

Adrian tensed and instinctively started down the hall toward the noise. Pamping intercepted him. Three more servants in assorted sleep attire ran to them.

"Lady Anne is dead," he reported in a flat tone. "And we know who killed her. You."

Adrian jerked back in surprise, bumping into the man behind him. Lady Anne, dead?

Pamping continued, "You weren't coming in, you were going out. Hold him!"

Two men grabbed his arms and pulled them behind his back. The third held a dagger to his neck.

Adrian tipped his head back to avoid being sliced. If he wanted to, he could've escaped. He'd taken four trained soldiers before. An equal number of servants wouldn't pose much of an obstacle. But breaking free and running would only make him look guilty.

He found his voice. "Let's be reasonable. If I had killed her, would I have waited here while you went to get her? You couldn't have stopped me if I wanted to leave."

Pamping glanced at the other servants, as if to read their expressions.

"Perhaps," he said doubtfully. "But she was well when she went to her bed. Now you're here and she is dead. I shall send for a sheriff. He'll know what to do with the likes of you."

Stay calm. There has to be a way out of this.

At the moment he couldn't see one. He hadn't killed Lady Anne, hadn't been near her sleeping chamber. What could he say to make them believe him?

He'd say a prayer for her soul after he got out of this situation. But now he had to worry about himself. If they hauled him to prison, Joanna would be alone. And when she heard he was in jail for killing Lady Anne, he might lose her. He couldn't bear that.

Who knew what William or John would do to her if they found out? Or Andrew, for that matter? The thought of anything happening to his wife made his stomach tighten.

He had to go to her, to explain. But he couldn't tell her the truth, and anything less would no doubt make her feel betrayed.

How ironic that in working to aid his country he might bring further dishonor to his name by being tried for murder. He could never get the bill of attainder against his father reversed if he himself was labeled a felon. Worse, what would they think when they found the letters hidden in his cloak? He had to get word to Warwick, to tell him what he'd found, to seek help. But how?

"Pamping, you must come at once," someone called.

"Don't release Sir Adrian until I return," the servant said as he scurried back down the hall.

A presumed criminal in his own home. The silence bore down on him. He could feel the servants' tension as they held him, feel the man whose knife was against his throat tremble slightly. The hall was poorly lit at this hour, but he knew every shield, every sword on the wall, every banner that hung from the rafters.

What had transpired? Maybe she'd fallen and was merely unconscious.

A moment later, Pamping returned, a contemptuous expression on his sallow face. The candle made his bald head gleam.

"Well, well, Sir Adrian Bedford. Make that Sir Adrian Bedford, murderer," he said.

"I didn't kill her."

Pamping laughed. "There's no point in lying. We have proof."

❧❦ ❧❦

Pounding on his door awoke William from a fitful sleep. He clutched the covers to his chest. Had Hatchet Baldwin returned already? Only two days had passed since they'd given him a repugnant task to complete in exchange for his debt's cancellation. He hadn't even had the chance to tell them he'd done it.

He couldn't move. He'd die of fright, just as he was, naked in his bed. He should've known they'd chop him up despite their unholy bargain.

"William, let me in!"

He fell back against his meager pillow in relief, then dragged on a tunic and hose before he opened the door.

"John, what's wrong with you? It's the middle of the night!"

After lighting a tallow candle stub, he turned to see John leaning against the closed door, crossing his bulky arms over his bulkier chest.

"It's almost dawn. I have news that won't keep," John said.

"Well, what then?"

"About that Sir Adrian. He's in deep."

William wanted to jump for joy. All good things come to those who wait. What had Adrian been up to when William ikop0lsaw him near the stews? The whore hadn't yet delivered her report.

"What happened?"

"They say he killed Lady Anne, the one who lives in his house."

William struggled to conceal his excitement. "How do you know that?"

"Friend of mine is a servant there. Said Sir Adrian got caught on his way out the door. Lady Anne was found dead in her bed. Stabbed right through the heart with a fancy dagger. He's been hauled off to prison."

"Maybe he had a reason for being at her house. Besides murder."

John shrugged his shoulders. "Not likely."

"How do you know?"

"They say the dagger bears the initials 'A.B.,'" John said.

Most excellent. A marvelous detail. How could he best use this turn of events to his advantage? William tapped a finger against his upper lip. Something wasn't right.

"What time did he kill her?"

"What does that matter?"

"The time, what time was it?" William demanded.

"Don't know exactly. But my friend said he was in jail by four."

How could this be? William had been drunk, but not too drunk to count. He'd clearly heard the clock strike two, and had seen Sir Adrian a few minutes later. Sir Adrian could never have returned to York proper, gone to Lady Anne's house and get carted off to jail in only two hours. How could Adrian be in two places at the same time?

Something wasn't right.

Another knock sounded at his door.

William tensed. His missing finger ached, as it always did when he got upset. Thank God John was here. Even Hatchet Baldwin wouldn't try anything with this lout in the room.

He opened the door. A woman in a tattered cloak hurried in. The whore.

She glanced at John, scanned his large frame, then nodded approvingly. She turned to William and held out her hand. "Pay up."

"John, loan me some coin."

"More?"

"I need to pay her."

John smirked. "You run off without paying?"

The whore laughed.

William didn't appreciate being the butt of their humor. "I paid for that. This is for information."

John dug into the worn purse at his waist. He handed William a few coins. Painstakingly, William counted out what he needed, then dropped the coins into her outstretched hand.

"I should ask triple for what I know." She closed her fingers over the coins.

"There. Now spill," William ordered.

❦ ❧

Where could Adrian have gone...this time? Joanna picked at her breakfast of bread and cheese. Shortly after falling asleep with him beside her, she'd awoken in an empty bed with fear lacing her thoughts. The rest of the night had been long and lonely. Now she was tired, annoyed, and her head ached.

What could he be doing? The last time she'd caught him disappearing, he'd been home by dawn. Why hadn't he sent word?

"Joanna!"

William. How did he know where they lived? She didn't reply. She feared being alone with him.

"I've news, important news about your husband!" William shouted through the door.

Was this a trick? Joanna stood, her hand hovering above the handle.

"He's in prison!" William cried.

That did it. Joanna opened the door, letting in both William and a burst of freezing air. She shivered, more from concern for Adrian than the cold.

"What happened?" Joanna asked. "How do you know?"

William's nose was red and his hair mussed. "I had to tell you as soon as I heard. John told me. A friend of his is one of Lady Anne's servants. Then I talked to John's friend, who confirmed everything."

Dread mixed with fear in Joanna's heart. "What about Lady Anne?"

"Adrian is in prison for murdering her," William said.

Joanna felt herself dropping to the floor. William caught her and half-dragged her to a stool.

"A mistake." She held her whirling head in her hands. "It has to be."

"There's proof. Are you ready for the rest?"

She'd never be ready for such a tale, but she had to know. She steeled herself to remain calm no matter what William said. "Tell me."

"Lady Anne's servants caught Adrian as he was leaving Bedford Castle. In the middle of the night, I might add. One wonders why he was there in the first place."

Joanna wanted to collapse again, but forced herself to remain upright. Adrian had gone to see Lady Anne last night, leaving her alone. Had he been lying to her all this time, still carrying on his liaison?

She was sure she'd vomit.

"Maybe he had a good reason," she said, though she didn't believe her own words. But she wouldn't let William see her confusion and pain.

"There's more." He fairly sang his excitement.

"More?" she repeated.

"Lady Anne was stabbed in the heart. With a dagger."

No. It couldn't be true. Believing that kept her from panicking.

Clearly her brother enjoyed every moment of this. Despite her shock and disappointment, she'd remain stoic.

"The dagger had the initials 'A.B.,'" William crowed. "Adrian Bedford."

Joanna closed her eyes. Could Adrian have done this? She loved him, and though the evidence was clearly against him, she'd do her best to view the situation in his favor. Until she looked into his eyes and saw the truth.

"Did he admit it?" she asked.

"Of course not. But they raised the hue and cry, and the sheriff arrested him."

She smiled. Perhaps Adrian was innocent. A.B. also stood for Andrew Bedford and dozens of other names. What if Adrian's twin was the murderer?

William shook her, and she cringed away from his grasping fingers.

"Are you well?" he asked.

She nodded.

"How does it feel to be wed to a murderer?"

"Stop it. I see how glad you are to bear these tidings. You make me sick," she said. "How can you be so cruel? You feed on other people's misery. Go destroy someone else's life and leave me alone."

She opened the door, but he pushed it closed and leaned against it. A frisson of fear ran through her.

"I am sorry to cause you upset, Sister, but what I say is true. You can verify all as I have done." William acted appropriately apologetic, but Joanna knew he was faking. He was truly glad Adrian was in prison.

"I'm also sorry that your marriage is over," he said. "Now you're back where you started. And time is running out."

William's gloating made Joanna even more determined to find out the real truth, not the version William put forth.

"You can't know for sure what happened, nor can John. I won't believe you. I'm going to find Adrian and talk to him."

"Suit yourself," William said with a shrug. "But whether he killed her or not, he can't help you while he's in prison. He can't protect you.

"I'm certain you'll be hearing from the guild again in a few days. They'll find that you have relapsed. They'll think you've started drinking again, because of your grief over what your husband did. Then you will lose, Joanna. You will lose all."

He smiled, and in that moment she hated him.

CHAPTER 20

Joanna jumped and squealed at the rats darting past her feet as she followed the Keeper of the prison down yet another corridor. She fought back tears as she hurried to keep up with the gangly man. This morning she'd been so shocked, so upset by the accusations against Adrian and the possibility that he might've done murder she hadn't spared a thought as to what prison would be like. How he might be suffering.

The stench alone was enough to make a person faint. She couldn't identify the foul odors assaulting her nose. Between the smells and the closeness of the air, she couldn't draw a full breath.

"Ye got some shillings?" the Keeper asked. He scratched his head, making Joanna shudder at the thought of the lice that must be roaming among the mangy strands.

"No," Joanna said.

"Some groats, then? Who be paying for his food? His sheets and blankets? Food or candles?" The Keeper paused under a spitting torch on the stone wall. His eyes were red-rimmed and bloodshot. He grinned, then leered at her. "'Course, if there be no coin, there be another way he can earn his keep. I'll take ye as payment."

He grabbed her arm.

"No!" she cried. She yanked her arm from his grasp, but knew if he wanted to maintain his hold he could. "Just take me to him. I'll get you some money."

"I get paid first." He grabbed her again and kissed her, his lips slimy and his breath fouler than the air. One hand dug into her arm, the other clutched her backside. Then he let her go.

"That'll buy ye ten minutes."

Joanna bit back a scream and the urge to spit in his face. But the Keeper held all the power and had what she wanted. Access to Adrian.

The Keeper clomped down the corridor, whistling. As soon as his back was turned, Joanna used her sleeve to wipe the taste of him from her mouth. Disgusting.

He turned down another hall lined with prisoners' cells. Some men moaned, others cried out, their agony pitiable whether they were true criminals or not. Hands reached out of the bars, grasping for her. She stayed in the middle of the corridor to avoid their straining fingers.

At last the Keeper stopped.

"In there." He opened the door with a large, black key. "Five minutes."

"You said ten!"

"Ten, then. But it'll cost ye."

She shuddered at the thought of him touching her again, but what choice did she have?

"Take this. For free," he said with a chuckle as he handed her his candle. He locked the door behind her with a clang.

The corridor wasn't very bright, but the cell was dark as pitch. The faint illumination floating down from a small window high in the wall ended well above her head. Something scampered over her feet, making her stumble.

The slow, uneven drip of water was barely audible over the other prisoners' clamor. Metal clanked nearby.

Where was Adrian? Her eyes adjusted. Beneath her feet, darkened straw—damp or dirty or both—covered the floor. The air smelled old and complex, as though remnants of all the prisoners caged through the ages still lingered. Slowly, she moved forward, the candle slim defense against what might lie ahead.

Adrian sat motionless before her, his chin on his chest, his eyes closed. She held the candle closer, then gasped.

Chains. They'd fettered him to the wall he sat against, manacles encasing his wrists, chains pulling his arms taut over his head.

"Oh, Adrian," she whispered.

Was he asleep or unconscious? More clanking accompanied his shift of position, but he didn't open his eyes. The rise and fall of his chest was visible through his shredded tunic. An encrusted bruise marred his forehead. Something, dried blood she guessed, matted his hair. The right side of his face was swollen.

Tears filled her eyes and dripped unnoticed down her cheeks. What had they done to him?

"Adrian, wake up." She reached out, then stopped, afraid to touch him and cause him more pain.

He moved again on the filthy straw and moaned softly. His ankles were chained too, his feet were bare. She could see no food or water.

The frequent skittering all around and occasional high-pitched squeaks were enough to drive her mad. Every inch of her skin crawled as if the vermin were on her instead of the floor. Perhaps it was better that Adrian was unaware of his surroundings. But she had to talk to him, and the Keeper had only sold her ten minutes.

"Adrian," she said.

His eyes opened. A long "aaaah" escaped him as he lifted his head. His arm muscles bulged as he adjusted his body.

"Joanna," he rasped. "What are you doing here?"

His words came out slightly garbled, as if he'd been drinking.

"Did you do it?" she blurted.

She wished she could seize back the question. She'd meant to ask how he fared, what she could do to ease his conditions. But she had to know the truth.

He shook his head slightly, then winced. "No, but I don't blame you for doubting me."

"Look at me. Tell me, and I will believe you."

His gaze met hers. His blue eyes were clear as glass jewels in the candle's glow.

"I did not kill her." His voice was low and hoarse.

She let out a breath she hadn't even known she was holding. Adrian was innocent.

"Why were you there?"

His eyes closed again. "I cannot tell you."

The answer pierced Joanna to the core. He expected her to

trust him and believe in his innocence, but wouldn't ease her concerns by explaining why he'd been at Lady Anne's house, and in the middle of the night. Chained to the wall, beaten, charged with murder, he still couldn't bring himself to trust her.

How could she love him?

Joanna wanted to scream. The drip, drip of the water, rustling vermin and Adrian's silence corroded her already taut nerves. She tried to keep the hurt from her voice. "I came here to see if I could help you. Obviously you don't need me."

"I would tell you if I could. But knowledge means danger. I've already put you at risk by ending up in here, unable to protect you. That's all I can say." His voice faded, as though he lacked the strength to continue.

Joanna had no response. So many times he'd asked her to trust him without reciprocating. All he did was warn her of danger. This marriage was far more difficult than she'd anticipated.

"Is it enough?" he asked.

Not this time.

But her proud, strong husband had been reduced to captivity. He could barely stand, chained as he was. She couldn't deny him. She wished the only reason she'd help him was because she was his wife, but her concern exceeded duty, despite his actions and his secrets.

Was she a fool?

"As soon as I can, I'll bring money to buy your way out of these chains, at least. Can I do anything else? Hurry, we only have a few minutes left."

"Thank you." He sighed, then coughed. "First, I want you to have this."

Adrian lifted his hip. Beneath it rested the gold signet ring he always wore. She took it.

"I never gave you a wedding ring," he said. "This ring is my only possession that means anything. Will you wear it?"

"Why did they let you keep it?"

"They didn't know I had it. I hid the ring in my mouth at first and would've swallowed had they thought to look there. They took everything else, but I refused to let them have this." His tongue moistened his lips. "I'll rest easier knowing it's safe with you."

"I'll wear the ring until I can return it. When you are free." She pushed the jewel into the deepest recesses of her cloak pocket. She'd never forgive herself if the Keeper somehow found out what she concealed.

Adrian nodded, but she wasn't sure if he believed that day would ever come.

"Now I need one thing more. A kiss."

She couldn't contain her surprise. "That's what you need? Now?"

"Now. Only you can give me something pleasant to think on while I'm here."

"Aren't you in pain?"

"I've had worse. Kiss me."

Her kiss. At least he wanted something of her, something intimate. She pushed some straw out of the way with her foot to make a place for the candle, then set it down. The narrow circle of light hid some of the horrors of his cell while highlighting his face, so handsome despite the bruises. She needed to feel his arms around her to give her strength. She could hold him instead, and offer him her strength. Bending down, she slid her hands behind his neck.

"Yes, Joanna. This is what I need. You smell so fresh, your fingers feel so cool," he whispered. "I prayed you wouldn't come here, wouldn't have to see this. At the same time I wanted you to come. I needed to see you."

She'd do anything to ease his pain. She kissed him.

The familiar feel of his mouth against hers obliviated their miserable surroundings and his dire situation. All that mattered was that they were together. He wanted her and she still had time to show him how she felt. The kiss evolved, slow and bittersweet. As she pulled back slightly, meeting his troubled gaze, she prayed this kiss wouldn't be their last.

"I'll think on that," he said with the barest hint of a smile.

"As will I." She stood, reluctant to leave.

How she wanted to tell Adrian she loved him. But she wasn't sure if the words would give him comfort, make him more worried about her or aggravate him because love wasn't part of their arrangement.

He was so strong, not complaining about his pain or his

imprisonment. The only thing he seemed worried about was her welfare. That concern combined with their kiss hung in the balance with his secrets.

"I want you to go on a journey for me," he said.

"A journey?" Adrian needed her. She liked that.

"Until you leave, please stay with Margery," he continued. "You'll be safer there should William try some new tricks."

"Yes." Joanna bit her lip. She wasn't going to add to his troubles by telling him her brother had already been to see her and had threatened her.

"Here's what you must do."

❧ ❧

Adrian had to close his eyes as the Keeper led a tearful Joanna away, as he returned to the caustic reality of imprisonment. He tried to stretch, feeling the pull of his stiff muscles.

"Help me!"

"Save me!"

The prisoners' endless cries haunted him, blinding him to his own troubles. Crystal clear memories of the day his grandmother burned replaced his squalid cell, and the prisoners' cries became hers. She'd sounded just the same, as desperate and hopeless. With as little chance of being saved.

All was lost. He'd encouraged Joanna to believe they could surmount this, but he felt as helpless as when his father told him about the bill of attainder. He could never forget that moment, for in his dreams his father read the terms to him over and over again.

As clearly as he saw his grandmother aflame, he saw his defeated father in his wrinkled, unwashed clothes, a bottle of wine in one hand and the dreaded parchment in the other.

"Sir Adam Bedford be attainted of these Treasons, and forfeit all his Goods and Lands which he had on said day or after, and his blood corrupted and disabled forever, and he be called within your Realm false Traitor forevermore," he read, his voice breaking.

His blood corrupted and disabled forever. The words rang in

Adrian's brain, louder than ever. He too could be named a Traitor and lose all hope of regaining his family name. All hope of caring for Joanna. The irony pained him as much as the manacles scraping his skin. He'd worked for years to repair damage done by his father only to end up in trouble as deep. His father's actions, equal in Adrian's eyes to murdering his grandmother, also led to his mother's death.

Adrian hadn't murdered anyone, but without a miracle the result would be the same. His gamble had failed just as his father's had, and he was just as penniless.

But he still had Joanna. She was his strength, his only reason to cling to a glimmer of hope. She made his secrets less dark, his future less grim. Without her support, perhaps he too would have succumbed to the wiles of drink and gambling. Even with her help, even with having his life with her to look forward to, too many things could still go wrong. His fate could already be sealed.

He had failed his country, failed his wife whom he'd sworn to protect.

They'd beaten him to make him confess. But he hadn't yielded, hadn't cried out. As unconsciousness claimed him, his last coherent thought had been of Joanna. Not of Warwick or the concealed letters, sure to be found in the pocket of his cloak. Disconcerting that Joanna was foremost in his mind, especially when his problems were so grave.

His head pounded, his shoulders burned. At least his hands were numb and thus spared pain. The darkness, the noises, the aches and uncertainty could drive a man to lunacy.

When he had awoken earlier—or was it yesterday? He had no way of knowing. Ah, already his thoughts rambled. When he'd awoken, he'd thought his mind conjured Joanna. But somehow she'd learned of his plight and braved the prison's filth and fetid air to find him.

Asking her for help was one of the hardest things he had ever done. He'd battled his pride until the last possible instant. He used to think asking for help made a man weaker. But Joanna had taught him that sometimes even the strongest people needed support. The key was accepting and acknowledging the need.

Now that he had, he felt both better and worse. It was hard to rely on another person to do what he couldn't. Yet knowing he had someone made him feel less alone. And not just anyone, but his Joanna.

If only he'd used some of their precious time to tell her what she meant to him. Not that he could easily put his feelings into words. He didn't want to live without her, but so much more filled his heart. He wasn't accustomed to this caring, wanting and desiring combined with the constant need to be with her.

Never had he needed anything more in his life than her kiss, the absolution and tenderness she offered. Even in this most depressing of settings, he craved the sensations that touching her brought him. Her disappointment at his refusal to tell her why he went to Lady Anne's had hurt more than his injuries did. But he could see she believed in his innocence. Her trust would see him through this.

If he got out alive.

If he survived, he'd find a way to tell her everything, from his spying to his visions. Then, perhaps they could have a true marriage, with no secrets and no agreement.

Thoughts of the day he could burn the damn document might just keep him from going mad.

CHAPTER 21

"Where is he?" Richard Neville, Earl of Warwick, demanded.

Joanna stood in the great hall of his London residence. Warwick had waved away various advisors and servants so they could speak in relative privacy. Several people came and went, others waited at the sides of the hall for a moment of their lord's time, casting curious looks in their direction. Many wore their lord's red livery, with its badge of white bear and ragged staff. They seemed a swarm of bees, buzzing and hovering, pending release from their hive.

Joanna was exhausted from the journey and from worrying about her husband. But at least she'd found Warwick, a task in itself, for she'd never been outside of York. London's vastness, crowds and sights were enough to make her dizzy.

Her travel-stained wool gown contrasted with Warwick's rich tunic, which fell in soft pleats past his ankles. His fur-trimmed sleeves, neckline and hem further accented the differences between their stations. He was younger than she'd expected, perhaps in his early thirties. This was the first time she'd ever spoken with so eminent a lord and only her experience in dealing with her higher-ranked clients saved her from incoherence.

"He is in prison, my lord." She wanted to remain strong in front of Adrian's overlord, but memories of Adrian in that horrible cell defeated her. "In chains," she whispered.

"What?"

Ashamed, she bent her head. "I couldn't gather enough funds

to feed him and buy his way out of the chains. He told me it was more important that I reach you."

"He would. Always duty before his own comfort," Warwick said. "I regret that our first meeting occurred under these dire circumstances. I'll see to it the spurious charges are dropped and that Adrian is released."

Relief filled Joanna as she curtsied. Her shaking fingers steadied as they gripped her skirts. Thank God Adrian had powerful friends. Otherwise he'd rot in prison until his trial and likely be condemned for a crime he hadn't committed.

"Thank you for your assistance, my lord."

"Don't thank me yet. Securing his freedom may take a while," he warned.

Warwick indicated a small table with two chairs near the hearth, and she sank into one gratefully. A servant brought a pitcher and two cups, bowed, and left as silently as he had come. Warwick poured wine, but she was too worried, her throat too tight to drink.

"May I offer you food? Supper isn't for hours, but there's always something cooking in the kitchens."

"No, thank you." She couldn't think about food, nor recall the last time she'd eaten. "I have a letter Adrian bade me give you."

She pulled the missive out of her pocket and handed it to him.

More than anything, she'd wanted to open that letter and devour the contents. Especially since Adrian couldn't seal it. When the Keeper came to tell her their ten minutes were up, she'd requested parchment, pen and ink. There hadn't been time to send for Adrian's seal. She'd paid dearly for the supplies and the extra minutes she'd needed to take down Adrian's words with kisses and groping that disgusted her. But the few moments of misery were worth it.

The piece of folded parchment sang its siren song throughout her travels, but she refused to succumb. Adrian had trusted her to carry his missive. She wouldn't violate that trust no matter how she yearned to read the letter. Though she knew he had no one else to ask, she felt honored that he sought her help with such an important task. And though it challenged the limits of her confidence, she would succeed. For him.

Jeweled rings flashed as Warwick opened and read the letter.

"Damn," he bit out.

His glance flicked to her, as if trying to read from her expression how much she knew. He crumpled the parchment in his fist, then threw it into the fire.

Longingly Joanna watched the edges curl and start to burn. The flames consumed her only tangible link to Adrian. And her opportunity to learn more about him.

"This could prove more difficult than I thought." Warwick ran his hands through his hair. "Do you know the contents of that letter?"

"No, my lord." She picked up the cup of wine, just to have something to do with her hands.

"A trustworthy wife is an admirable thing in these times of treachery. Adrian is fortunate to have you."

Joanna felt herself color at such praise from one of the most powerful lords in the realm.

A man in York's livery walked toward them, a rolled document in his hand. "My lord, you needs—" he began.

"Not now," Warwick said. "See to it I am not disturbed again." He turned back to Joanna. "You're fortunate you were able to find me. I've only just returned from St. Albans."

"Yes, from another battle, so your steward said."

"Another defeat, and not long after our party suffered the debacle at Wakefield. Now that the great council has acclaimed York's son Edward as the new king though Henry yet lives, there is sure to be more fighting." He sighed. "I digress. You most certainly didn't come all this way to learn the fate of the Yorkists."

She didn't know how to respond. How strange to hear such casual discussion of battles where soldiers and knights died and events changed the course of a country. How could a man inure himself to the loss of his men? How could a commander succeed if he mourned every death?

"Edward IV. To think we began this quest to rid our country of the dangerous men surrounding Henry but now put forth our own king." He took a breath, as if to continue, but stopped. "Accept my apologies. You see what occupies my mind."

"There's nothing to forgive, my lord." That Warwick would

take time to think about releasing Adrian when England was in turmoil amazed her. She smiled, for his willingness to help also showed how highly he regarded her husband.

Warwick took a deep drink of wine, then set the cup down. She sensed he was making some sort of decision. He nodded once. "Your husband is a spy. For me, and the Yorkist party."

She sucked in a breath. Adrian, a spy. At last, his secret revealed. Now she understood some of his reasons for reticence. But why from her? Did she fear those closest to him would always betray him because his father had?

"You see why I must help Adrian. He was acting on my command when he was caught," Warwick continued.

"What did he seek?" she asked, glad her voice didn't tremble.

"We hoped Lady Anne's son would lead us to key information about the king's plans. Adrian wrote that he'd finally found what we were looking for."

Joanna froze. He had gone to Lady Anne's the night of her murder to gather information…not to continue his affair? Or had he slept with Lady Anne as a means to get inside the house to search, and not to earn back his home as he'd said? Had he lied, or not told the whole truth?

The coil made her head spin.

She couldn't stand this uncertainty. When he got out of prison, she'd shred their agreement before his very eyes. He'd either stay with her without the restrictions they'd once agreed to or she'd go on alone. As much as she loved him and as miserable as she'd be without him, she couldn't bear to spend her days not knowing when his next surprise would be exposed. She wouldn't live with him unless she had his complete trust. That's what she willingly yielded to him. She deserved the same in return.

The affair with Lady Anne, having a twin, being a spy. No wonder he wouldn't marry without signing a contract such as theirs. He'd been reluctant to agree to marriage at all, accepting only because he needed an heir. How he must struggle, balancing his privacy with his plans for the future.

She had a strange suspicion that as remarkable as these revelations had been, the biggest truth was yet to come. What could possibly be so important, so horrible?

"There was more in Adrian's letter. He said he had several of Lord Berkeley's documents on his person when thrown into prison. In addition to murder, Adrian is charged with larceny. We know he's innocent of the murder, but I'll have to consult with my lawyer to learn what can be done about the other charge.

"As to the documents, they're lost to us. Adrian's knowledge of the contents could still prove useful. However, thanks to recent developments, we may not even need that."

"So Adrian's efforts were for naught."

"As a means to provide information, yes. But as proof of his loyalty to England's next king, they could prove priceless."

So much had happened in such a short time. Joanna felt her life spinning out of control but didn't know how to stop it. She knew she had to recover from her shock and respond.

"My lord, I thank you for telling me so much and for your time. I must return to York."

"You are most welcome. But you needs stay. Adrian asked that I keep you here, for your own safety," Warwick said.

The earl astonished her. He acted as if he had all the time in the world, despite the myriad details he must have to tend to, both on behalf of the new king, Edward, and his own vast holdings.

"My thanks again for your most gracious offer. But I must go to him and bring the things he'll need until he is released."

"One of my men will see to that posthaste," he said with a flick of his hand, as though with such little effort he could see it done. "The dangers of travel are heightened now. Even with your Mistress Margery and Master Osbert as companions, peril lurks everywhere. Though London has accepted Edward as king, unrest persists elsewhere."

"I'm aware of the difficult times our country faces and the hazards of the roads, my lord. But I must return to my husband."

Disagreeing with said husband's overlord wasn't appropriate, but manners weren't her primary concern. Being with Adrian when she could was.

"Stubborn as well." He smiled. "You love him, don't you? I thought yours a marriage of convenience."

Joanna was unaccustomed to confiding in anyone but

Margery, but the earl seemed to expect the truth. He deserved as much for his assistance.

"Our marriage began that way, my lord, but changed for me despite his secrets. I do love him, and hope someday he'll feel the same for me."

The first time she had expressed her love for Adrian out loud. Saying the words made her feelings more real, more permanent. Made her miss him more.

"He's been my man for years, so I know how hard it is to earn his trust," Warwick said.

"My thanks on his behalf for seeing to his needs. But I must also return to my work. I am a glass-painter, with projects that must be completed."

She wouldn't consider how much time this journey had cost her, Thomas and Margery.

"Adrian has spoken of your brother's deceit. I'll send some men with you, to protect you in Adrian's stead."

"If you could spare them, my lord, I'd be most grateful."

"Consider it done. I needs also write a letter for you to take to Adrian. Godspeed."

Joanna curtseyed, and breathed deeply. The earl walked toward a small group of his retainers, moving on to his next task. The circle of brightly dressed men parted to accommodate him.

Joanna wanted to sing with joy. Her audience was over, and she'd accomplished all she came to do. She hurried out into the antechamber where Margery and Thomas awaited. Margery had been thrilled to make the journey, eager to peek into the life of a noble and his great household, if only for a short while. Thomas, on the other hand, almost had to be pried away from his work.

They spoke at almost the same time.

"What was he like?"

"What did he say?"

She laughed at their questions, laughed because Warwick had lifted some of her burdens and because she felt real hope for the first time in days.

"He was most kind, and offered to pay Adrian's way out of prison."

"How much is that?" Thomas asked.

"Quite a sum, to be sure, with a murder charge. Warwick knows how such things are done. If Adrian didn't have him for a friend, I don't know what we'd do. He'll also send an escort to take us home. How can we repay his kindness?"

Margery threw her arms around Joanna. "Maybe all will be well now. Soon the workshop will be yours alone. Then you can concentrate on that heir."

Except Adrian hadn't told her he was a spy and England now had two kings. She knew he wouldn't be able to rest until the situation was resolved.

And deep down Joanna just knew he concealed one last, horrible secret.

❧ ❧

"I did it. I did it!" William reported to Hatchet Baldwin with bravado he acted but did not feel.

With trembling fingers, he untied his blindfold. An underling like him would never be allowed to know the location of the Lord of the Underground's lair. William glanced around the small room, disappointed that it looked like a regular study. Piles of parchment, ink and pens lay scattered across a desk. Hatchet Baldwin reclined on a scratched chair, his booted feet propped on an empty corner of the desk. Only the large hatchet next to his feet attested to the mercenary nature of the room's occupant.

There was no chair for him. Intimidating, as Hatchet Baldwin probably meant it to be.

"I did as you asked," William said.

He felt no remorse. So happy was he about saving his fingers and erasing his debt, there was no room for guilt.

Lady Anne would've died soon anyway.

"Aye, so my sources say," Hatchet Baldwin replied. "You've done me a service. I owed Lady Anne a large sum. Now no one will ever know. 'Cept for you and me," he said with a leer.

For a moment William feared the man would cut off another finger to ensure he kept silent. Or some more important body part.

Hatchet Baldwin's feet came off the desk and he leaned on his elbows. "I also heard yer brother-by-law's been pinned for the deed."

"I hope he rots in prison," William said.

But the hairs on the back of his neck stood on end. After he'd done as ordered, he'd visited several stews so there'd be witnesses to his whereabouts the night of the murder.

And he had seen Adrian. He still couldn't figure out how Adrian had been near the stews at two and at Bedford Castle at almost the same time. He feared the strange inconsistency might somehow be his undoing. Then he'd be even worse off than when he started.

Perhaps he could still work events to his advantage. What the whore had told him would certainly make Joanna leave Adrian. All he had to do was prove it to her. That is, if Adrian ever got out of prison.

And if he himself didn't get thrown in before he ran out of time.

"Clever to use a dagger with his initials."

William couldn't take the credit for that. Lady Anne, the wiry bitch, had knocked his own knife out of his hand. Luckily for him, a dagger had been on a small table by the bed. That was an awkward moment he'd rather not recall, both of them struggling to get a grip on the dagger. The old bitch was stronger than she looked and had almost beaten him to it.

Plunging the dagger into her chest hadn't been all that pleasant either.

"Now get out of here. If you need another loan, you know how to reach me. And believe me, I'll always know where to find you."

William's knees shook as he tied the blindfold again. Someone grabbed his arm and led him out.

I know where to find you. The words rang in his head.

Now that his usefulness was past, would Baldwin kill him because of what he knew? Require performance of some other, gruesome task in exchange for his silence?

Would he have to live the rest of his life on edge?

CHAPTER 22

The new king had come to York. Excitement made Joanna's fingers slip as she dressed in Margery's best gown. Borrowed finery wouldn't be as elegant as the clothing of the nobles and knights, but to her the deep blue gown with its long, full sleeves and velvet belt was lovely.

Just an hour ago, Warwick's messenger had arrived, bearing a note requesting that she meet with him at the Guildhall. Her heart hadn't stopped pounding since she'd sent the messenger with her response.

"Margery, read it again," she said, engaged in the laborious task of stuffing her voluminous hair into the confines of a headdress.

"I wish I could go with you. To be able to see the king up close," she said wistfully. "And all of his wealthy nobles. Some who must need wives."

"I don't know for certain that I'll see him. Now read."

Margery read, "'I greet you well, etc. I am with the king in York, having defeated the Lancastrians yesterday at Towton in the bloodiest battle ever have I seen. Henry has fled. Please you to know had not England's needs been so pressing, Adrian would have been freed by now. That task will be the focus of our stay.'" She clutched the letter to her chest. "To think Adrian is important enough that the Earl of Warwick thinks of him the day after a battle. And he wants to meet with you in person."

Joanna's enthusiasm was dampened by Warwick's brief mention of battle. So many more Englishmen lay dead. She whispered a brief prayer for their souls, but realized what the victory meant. "We're fortunate Warwick and Edward won this time. If they'd lost to the Lancastrians again, Adrian might never have been released."

"That is so," Margery agreed. "This war between Englishmen has gone on for years. Can it finally be over? Enough talk of that on a day like today. Joanna, you look beautiful."

"Only because you loaned me your gown. For once I wish I shared your interest in fashion," Joanna said.

"At least my gown will see the king."

"I promise to tell you all."

Margery's skirts swishing about her, Joanna hurried down Stonegate. Perhaps Adrian would already be out of prison and waiting for her. That thought made her walk even faster, though cheering people filled the streets and got in her way. Everyone, it seemed, wanted to participate in the celebration.

A crowd had gathered in front of the Guildhall, slowing Joanna down further still as she wound her way through those hoping to glimpse their new king. She spared no time admiring the large stone building with its wooden pillars but showed Warwick's seal to the guard at the door to gain entry.

"Lady Joanna. You arrived with great haste," Warwick said as he greeted her. He wore another ensemble displaying his great wealth and position, velvet robes trimmed with fur. A smile graced his face, but she thought she could see the strain of battles won and lost in his eyes.

People in Warwick's livery and others she didn't recognize rushed about on their way to do who knew what.

"Am I early?"

"No. But the king plans to say a few words, and I must stand nearby. You shall stand with me," he said.

"My lord, that is too great an honor."

"Your husband was falsely imprisoned while in my service. And I've been too busy to help. I asked you here today to tell you I'll see Adrian released as I promised. No honor I can offer is too great, nor can it compensate for your distress."

"I appreciate your kind words, my lord, and thank you again for your assistance. I realize many have suffered far more than we. My husband still lives, which is more than many soldiers' wives can say. At least I know he'll soon be home again."

As they talked, the Guildhall grew more crowded and the noise of buzzing voices increased. Warwick acknowledged with nods of his head some of the men in pleated robes of elaborately patterned fabrics who strolled by. Large jeweled brooches on the sides of their hats caught the light as if winking at her. She felt curious glances as she had at Warwick's estate. Joanna wished Margery could see the display.

Trumpets blared, their shrill notes blasting through conversations. Everyone bowed as the king approached. Joanna sank into a deep curtsy.

Edward IV was tall, perhaps slightly taller than Adrian. She barely glimpsed his face as he strode by. All she could see were his broad shoulders encased in rich patterned brocade and his reddish-brown hair underneath his black hat. He stopped in the doorway and raised his hands to quiet the crowd gathered in the street.

His voice rose over the cheers. "My thanks, good people of York. You are the first to share the celebration of my victory. The rightful blood is on the throne again. Soon we shall celebrate the official coronation.

"You will see I have already taken action. The heads of my father, brother and the earl of Salisbury have been removed from Micklegate Bar so all three great men can receive a proper burial. In their stead, you will find there the heads of certain Lancastrians, the former Earls of Devon and Wiltshire.

"Know that I will reward all those loyal to me, and punish all traitors. I bid you Godspeed."

He waved and returned to the hall, followed by his companions and the crowd's cheers.

Joanna prayed Edward would stay king, that she and Adrian could live in peace. As soon as she knew everything she needed to know about him.

☙☙ ☙☙

Back in her studio and wearing her own gown, Joanna forced herself to concentrate on her work in progress, but the red and green glass pieces blurred. In recent weeks she'd shed far too many tears over Adrian's plight. Crying made her feel a little better, but she wished she could do something for him. Only action would ease her concerns. She'd done her part and Warwick would do his when he was able. Why was it taking so long to secure Adrian's release?

Back to work, she urged herself. Adrian wouldn't want her worrying about him when she had work to do. When time was running out. Only a few weeks remained until her father's deadline, when her total earnings would be tallied by the guild. She knew she was close to the required amount, but couldn't afford to take any chances. Every pence counted.

But the brush dangled from her fingertips, creative thoughts pushed from her head by harsh reality. How had her life come to this? There was a short period when she'd felt in control of her destiny. Unlike most women, she'd mastered a craft, which should have led to independence. William and John almost brought an end to her dream. And also unlike most women, who were told whom to marry, she'd chosen her husband. Yet with his secrets and her troubles, working toward a stable, much less a bright, future was difficult.

Though admitting her love brought her much joy, in her weak moments the pain of love unrequited made her wish she'd never fallen for him in the first place. He desired her, which was more than she'd expected when they first married. Why wasn't that enough? Why did she want more?

Every day she paid precious coin to spend a few moments with Adrian. Though he was now free of the chains and had been moved to a new cell, a bit larger and cleaner than the first, he was still a prisoner. He seemed determined to triumph over his surroundings, as evidenced by his positive attitude. Leaving him each day filled her with longing for what could be. If.

She closed her eyes, remembering in vivid detail the last time they'd shared a bed. In addition to the passion and incredible satisfaction, she relished the moments spent resting in his arms. At no other time did she feel as close to him, as needed by him. The way he held her felt possessive, as though he had to keep her close. Her favourite thing was just being with him, feeling his chest rise and fall against her back as he breathed.

Warwick had promised any day now her husband would be free. With that comforting thought, she began to paint.

The door flew open, banging against the wall. She jumped off her stool.

In the doorway stood Adrian. A dirtier, thinner Adrian than the one who'd left over a month ago.

The most excellent sight she'd ever seen.

Heedless of the filth covering his tattered clothes, she threw herself into his arms. He rocked back, but gripped her so tightly she could barely draw in air.

"Joanna," he breathed.

She thought she heard his voice crack. Was he that glad to see her, or immensely relieved to be out of prison?

"It's over," he said into her ear. "I am free. Warwick had me released, and all charges have been dropped."

"That is the best news. Are you hungry? Tired? We must get you out of those awful clothes," she babbled.

His return renewed her, made her feel she could conquer any demons. That was part of love, she realized. Being with him actually made her stronger. She hadn't believed love could do that.

He laughed, a rich sound she'd rarely heard. "Are you so eager to have me?"

"I'm glad to see you haven't lost your sense of humor," she said. "I thought you might wish a bath. But there's no tub large enough here."

"I thought of stopping by the baths on the way home," he said. "But I...," he paused and looked away. "I'll make do here."

She wondered what he'd been about to say. Wishful thinking made her hope he had rushed straight here to see her.

"You look thin." She hadn't noticed the change in him during her visits, concentrating only on the few moments they had together. "Wasn't the coin I sent enough to feed you?"

"Aye, I had far better fare than the moldy bread the poorest receive. But not as much food as I was accustomed to," he said.

"I'm glad Warwick remembered your plight with all that's been happening. On the other hand," she said, "if you hadn't been in prison, you'd have been with him. And might have died with so many others."

"I might have, but I'd rather have been with him serving my king and country than rotting uselessly in a cell. Warwick said the battle last week at Towton was the bloodiest thus far, that thousands died. Henry VI and Queen Margaret fled to Scotland with some of their key supporters. Edward will remain king. The worst is over for now."

"For England and for you," she prayed.

As she followed him up the stairs to her rooms, she couldn't help averting her face. He smelled like the inside of a garderobe that hadn't been cleaned.

Margery gasped. "You're back! Wonderful. But you don't look so good." She started toward her room, then stopped. "I think I'll go somewhere and do some things. Fare thee well."

"Thank you, Margery," Joanna said, giving her half-sister a brief hug before she left.

Adrian sank into a chair, as if the journey from the prison had tired him.

"Here," Joanna said. She reached inside her neckline and pulled out his signet ring, which hung from on a ribbon around her neck. "I never took this off."

"Keep it."

"Having the ring while you were away helped, but it's part of you. Someday you can give this to our first child." She untied the ribbon, tugged off the ring and slipped it onto his finger. "There, that's better."

He flexed his hand and examined the ring. "You're right. I feel more like myself already."

"Now for that bath. I'll get the water. But it isn't hot," she warned.

He shed what was left of his clothing while she filled two large wooden buckets. She grabbed a sponge and the cake of soap. She stopped abruptly at the sight of him.

"Oh, Adrian."

In the bright light of day she could see the damage confinement had wrought. He was too thin. Still, to her he looked as handsome as ever.

"Naught that a few good meals and some training won't cure," he said. "First I must clean my teeth. The foul taste of that place is still with me."

As he did, she gathered the components of his bath and brought them to him. "I'll get more water," she said as she handed him the sponge.

He took it, wrapping his hand over hers. Gently he pulled her closer. "Stay. Help me put the past month behind me."

Together they dipped the sponge in the bucket. Their gazes locked as the water soaked and softened it. They soaped the sponge, releasing the scent of rose into the air. At first, he gently directed their movements, but they moved as one to bring the sponge up to wash his chest. Slowly their hands slid over his skin as if guided by an unseen force. Suds dripped onto the floor.

He released the sponge, and she rinsed it in the other bucket. She repeated the motions until his chest, back, arms and face were clean. She soaped his hair, working her fingers over his scalp. His head fell back and he sighed.

"Come to the basin so I can rinse," she said.

Adrian bent over the basin. She poured clean water over his head. He wrung out the excess and flung back his head, spattering her with a few drops.

Joanna had never thought cleansing could be so sensual. But as intimate as they'd been, washing below his waist made her uncomfortable. She soaped the sponge and gave it to him.

"You do the rest," she said, feeling a flush creep over her cheeks.

He returned to the chair and reached for the sponge, an unreadable smile on his now-clean face.

Joanna had planned to occupy herself elsewhere as he finished his bath. But she couldn't help but watch as he began to soap himself. The sponge moved down his legs to his feet, then up over his thighs. She felt herself becoming aroused as the sponge made its way to his groin. In helpless anticipation she waited for him to reach his private parts. The thought of him touching himself there fascinated her.

He saw her watching him. He smiled his incredible smile, rinsed and continued his progress ever so slowly. At last he slid the sponge over himself. She stood, transfixed and tingling, as he hardened before her eyes. She had a sudden yearning to wipe away the water dripping down him before it disappeared into the coarse hairs between his legs. He watched her as he squeezed the sponge over his erection. A soft moan escaped him as the sponge glided up his slick length, then back down.

"Touch me, Joanna."

She moved closer, enthralled. The sponge dropped with a soft splash into the bucket. Her hand slid over his erection. He groaned as she stroked him. His seductive sounds made her shiver.

He gripped the sides of the chair. "More. Ah, yes. Yes, like that."

He was wet and tantalizingly slippery. She felt him grow harder as she ran her fingers over him. Amazing, that her touch could make that happen. The combination of his hardness and silky wetness made her want him inside her.

She released him to tug at her gown. She tossed it away, standing before him in only her chemise.

"How I've longed to be with you. You're even lovelier than in my dreams." He stood, glistening and ready. "I'll never again smell roses without thinking of this day."

His wet hands slipped under her chemise and over her skin from her back to her shoulders as he reacquainted himself with her body. He drew the dampened linen over her head. Should she be embarrassed to be so exposed to him in the light of day? Intense need and the appreciation in his eyes pushed any concerns away.

He cupped her breasts, the heels of his hands gently kneading. Then he circled his thumbs over her nipples as she clutched his shoulders. Desire spiraled through her. But his hands weren't enough.

"More. I want more."

"Then you shall have it."

He sat on the chair and guided her onto his lap. His erection pressed against her soft folds. Instinctively she pressed closer, tilting her hips. She undulated against him, watching where their bodies touched.

He lowered his head and took a nipple into his warm mouth. As he licked and sucked, need surged within. She slid her fingers into his damp hair. His hand slipped between them, finding her center. Hot, she was so hot. She gasped as he heightened her arousal with leisurely strokes.

"Faster," she urged as need spiraled.

His fingers complied, filling her with smoldering pleasure.

He lifted his head. The look in his eyes excited her almost as much as his touch. She infused her love and passion into her kiss.

"By the stars, Joanna, what you do to me," he murmured against her mouth.

His erection pulsed against her. She wanted him inside her.

☙☙ ❧❧

Adrian knew what she wanted, and lifted her hips slightly. He wanted it too. More than wanted. He had to have her. He'd spent hours dreaming of this, how her hair would drift over his shoulders and tease his skin, just as it was doing now. How her soft moans would captivate him.

"Sit on me." He guided her with hands on hips.

The pleasure he felt as she mounted him took his breath away. She fit him so tightly, he never wanted to leave. She collapsed against him for a moment, her breasts against his chest. Then she began to move. His hands held her hips. So slowly she rose up, then pressed down until he filled her completely. She increased the speed, just slightly. until his every inch screamed for release. He strained to prolong his ecstasy to be one with her. Sharing that special moment suddenly became an urgent goal.

"Come with me," he whispered.

He forced himself to control the desperate need to thrust into her. Yet he found that letting her move as she pleased intensified his pleasure. He thought he'd explode from the sensations crowding him.

"Yes, oh yes," she breathed.

Their mutual need burst into astonishing completion.

"By the stars," he said. He could say no more.

CHAPTER 23

"What are you doing here? And this early in the morning?"

The faintest pink of breaking dawn outlined William standing on her studio doorstep.

"Joanna, there's something I must show you," he said eagerly. "Something to prove who your husband truly is. You must trust me. You've put your faith in the wrong man."

Joanna cringed. Her brother always found the precise words to unearth her worst fears.

Despite their closeness since his release from prison, she sensed Adrian still kept a dire secret. Did William know of it, or was this another hoax? The only way to be certain was to go with him. But not today.

"William, you know very well this is Corpus Christi day and I must help with the guild's play. They've spent weeks preparing. I was just about to leave."

"Of course I know what day this is, which is how I knew you'd be awake so early. You can't tell me that some play about Jesus destroying Hell is more important to you than your husband."

"If you truly know something about Adrian, it will keep until the morrow. This day is important to the entire town, not only the guilds. Find a spot at one of the stations to watch the plays and come back tomorrow."

"Tomorrow might be too late," he insisted. "Surely you can spare a few minutes?"

She bit her lip. Her brother had disappointed her so many times. Was being too gullible, too willing to trust one of her flaws?

"Where we need to go is close to Pageant Green. Don't the wagons still gather there?" he asked.

"I see you do remember something. Very well, I'll go, but let's hurry." If William had a nefarious purpose, better to be in a crowd than alone at her studio.

Joanna quashed a frisson of fear as she followed William. "Is Adrian in danger?"

"No. Not that. You'll see."

She barely noticed the doorways decorated with flowers as they wound their way through streets already crowded with people trying to secure a good vantage point to view the pageant wagons.

Each wagon presented one of the forty-eight Corpus Christi plays telling the story of the Bible from the Creation to the Last Judgment. The cycle began early in the morning and lasted well into the evening. At least William wouldn't dare try anything untoward with so many people around.

They ended up at a small house, which true to William's word was close to Pageant Green. She could see whatever he wanted her to see and still be on time to meet up with her guild.

Instead of going to the door, William squatted beneath the window. He tugged on her gown. "Get down. Be careful, so they don't see us."

"Why such secrecy?" She gathered her skirts and stooped beside her brother.

"You'll see." He poked his head slightly over the ledge and gasped. "Yes, I was right. Look, look at that!"

She raised her head. The window was grimy, the room beyond was dim. But she could make out two people embracing each other. Was one of them naked?

As she leaned forward to get a better view, the door opened.

"Why, Joanna, so kind of you to visit. And who have you brought with you?"

"Adrian?" What was he doing here, and how could he have gotten here before she did? She'd left him sleeping in their bed when she went to her studio, and hadn't spent much time there.

The sun hadn't yet climbed over the rooftops, leaving the street in shadow. She stood, and gasped. Before her stood not Adrian, but Andrew, wearing a thin robe. His voice and face so closely resembled her husband's, but there was no mistaking this man's shorter hair. Nor the eerie gleam in his blue eyes. William whispered behind her. "I told you so."

Joanna wanted to collapse with relief. Whatever was going on in this house was Andrew's doing, not Adrian's.

"I've seen enough. Goodbye, William." She turned.

"You can't leave now!" William and Andrew said in unison.

"William, you fool, this isn't Adrian. This man is Andrew, Adrian's twin brother." Slowly, she began to back away from them. "I too am a fool for coming here with you."

William's mouth dropped open. "But...but...," he sputtered. "They're so alike."

"Look closely. Andrew has shorter hair. His wrist bears no scars. And believe me, they're even more different on the inside."

"Sister-by-law, you wound me," Andrew said, putting his hand over his heart. "Now that you're here, now that you know, you must stay for a visit. See up close what you glimpsed through the window."

His tone sounded pleasant but Joanna detected an undercurrent of malice.

"I can't accept your invitation. I'm expected at Pageant Green." She wanted to run there, anything to get away from Adrian's sinister brother.

"But I insist," Andrew said. He grabbed her wrist and dragged her to the house.

Joanna tried to pull her arm free, but Andrew's strength far exceeded hers. With her free hand she grabbed the door frame. The uneven wood bit into her fingertips.

"William! Help me!" she cried.

William simply stood there, his mouth hanging open. Then he turned and fled.

Andrew tugged harder. She clung to the door for dear life, but she couldn't maintain her grip. She tried to kick Andrew, but he avoided her feet.

"No! Let me go!"

A couple dressed like Adam and Eve paused briefly, then hurried past.

"Help! Someone help me!" A fingernail tore as Andrew yanked her into the house. Burning pain consumed her.

He closed the door, barely missing her still-grasping fingers. He turned the key in the lock and hung the chain around his neck.

Joanna shivered as blood dripped onto the floor. She had to escape. Perhaps the house had a rear exit. At the moment, Andrew blocked her path.

"I'm sorry you've hurt yourself. Here." He tossed her a clean handkerchief. "I have something special to show you, Joanna. I hope you'll enjoy it. I know I will. Even more so with you here."

She caught the cloth and wrapped it around her bleeding finger. "Andrew, let me go. I must get to my guild's wagon. I didn't have time to see anything through the window. I have no idea what you do here. Nor do I care."

"Come, sit beside me," he ordered.

She didn't move.

"I said sit." He grabbed her wrist again and pulled until she sat on the worn velvet bench. His fingers were clammy and cold.

Her hand throbbed, her heart raced. How could she get out of here?

Andrew let her go and clapped his hands. A thin young man wearing only a frayed silk robe entered from another room. His hair was long, blond and curly. Like a woman's.

Joanna couldn't fathom what Andrew had in mind. Her nervousness and desperation increased. How had she let William lure her here? And how could he have abandoned her to Andrew?

"This is Henry, just like our true king." He walked over to Henry and took him into his arms. He turned to look at Joanna. "Watch us."

Andrew kissed Henry on the lips.

Joanna jumped and ran to the door, though she knew the key dangled from Andrew's neck. She faced the portal to freedom. She wouldn't turn around.

She'd heard that some men preferred men to women. For such a seemingly pious man as Andrew to commit what their religion considered such a sin....

"Joanna. I said you were to watch," Andrew called, his voice harsh.

Without turning, Joanna said, "Andrew, please open the door. I wish to leave."

"I wish you to stay. Sit down or I will tie you down. Mmm. I would like that. And don't close your eyes."

Reluctantly, Joanna returned to the bench. There was no way to escape. She should consider herself lucky they didn't want her to participate. The thought turned her stomach. Resolutely she opened her eyes, but concentrated on a distant point on the wall behind them so the men before her blurred.

Even with her unfocused vision, she could tell Andrew and Henry had shed their clothes. They kissed passionately.

Joanna bit her tongue to keep from crying. Why did they want her to watch? Somehow her presence must increase their enjoyment, for every few seconds one of them glanced in her direction to make certain she was still paying attention.

Maybe she could slip past them. She stood and dashed toward the back of the house.

Only a few more steps to freedom.

She jerked to a halt. Andrew had a hold on her skirts. She looked up at the ceiling to avoid his nakedness. "Unless you're coming to join us, sit back down. Or I will sit you down myself."

Her heart hammering, mouth dry, she returned to the bench and sat. What now? How much more would she have to take?

The front door crashed into the room. Adrian stalked in, sword in hand. William followed close behind. Face filled with fury, Adrian strode past Joanna, blocking her view of the two naked men.

He turned and scanned her up and down. "Are you all right?"

She nodded, overcome with a mixture of relief and joy. Adrian had come for her.

He turned back to Andrew, who'd backed away from Henry and hastily donned his robe.

"So, my brother. What have we here? A secret of your own,

as bad if not worse than mine. I'd say this cancels out the other, wouldn't you? I don't think you'll be turning me in or testifying against me. Ever. Or I'll be doing some testifying of my own," Adrian said. "Now I see why you've been so troubled of late. You weren't praying for an answer to what to do about me, you sought guidance for your sins. How conflicted you must be, struggling with your licentious thoughts. Succumbing to your weaknesses."

The blond man scurried away as Andrew clutched his robe closer.

"You can't intimidate me," he said. "When I turn you in to the Church, who will they believe? Me, the devout, or you, allied with the Devil? When I reveal what I know about you, if you try to tell them anything about me, they'll know you lie in a vain attempt to discredit your accuser. They'll laugh off your tales as will I," Andrew taunted.

Blessed Lord, what on Earth was Andrew talking about? What was Adrian's secret? The suspense was unbearable.

"Your supposed devotion mocks the true faith," Adrian said. "A man who has sex with other men is considered a sinner. You know the punishments and penance are severe. And it's against the law."

"Nothing has changed between us," Andrew said with a sneer. "Except now you may have to tell your lovely glass-painter wife the truth about your affliction. I'm sure she's been wondering what all the secrecy is about."

Wondering? She was dying to know. It was all she could do to stay quiet and not insist Adrian tell her immediately. But she wouldn't give Andrew or William the satisfaction of being present when she found out. And find out she would. What "affliction" could possibly be "as bad if not worse" than what she'd just seen?

Joanna forced the still-vivid events of the last few moments out of her head. Soon she'd learn what Adrian had kept from her. But why had they spoken of testifying? Had Adrian committed a crime? What had Andrew meant by "affiliated with the Devil?"

The room was so silent she could hear Adrian breathe. He hadn't moved; all she could see was his broad back. What was he thinking? Was he considering what to tell her or still absorbing the shock of discovering his twin with another man?

"Joanna, I should've known my brother wouldn't have the courage to tell you. So I will," Andrew said.

"Don't. Do not say another word. Or I'll make you regret it."

Joanna had never heard Adrian sound so harsh.

He turned to William, who still cowered by the door. "I never expected to offer you thanks for anything, but I must thank you for bringing me here and for exposing Andrew's crime."

"Don't thank him. William brought Joanna here in the first place. He thought you were me," Andrew said. "The only person in this room without a tainted past seems to be the fair Joanna."

"What do you mean?" Joanna asked.

"You obviously don't know what your brother has done," Andrew said with a sneer. "But I know that, too. Tell her, William, or I shall. You told on me, 'tis only fair I even the score."

William turned a strange shade of red. His eyes darted from side to side. "I don't know what you're talking about."

"Of course you do. Where were *you* the night Lady Anne was killed?"

"All right. I'll admit it. I was visiting the stews. As were you," he said to Andrew. "I saw you there. I thought I'd seen Adrian, but now I know it was you."

"And before that?" Andrew pressed, his voice low and encouraging. "What did you do before visiting your whore? Do tell."

"What difference does it make?"

"Your whereabouts will make a big difference to Adrian." He turned to face his brother. "I cannot atone for my sins, or convince you not to share what you now know. But please accept this small gift I give you." He glared at William. "Tell, or I will," he repeated.

"I've gambled enough to know when a man is bluffing," William retorted. "You've got nothing on me. And I've nothing to say."

"Ah, William. Another lie?" Andrew shook his head. "You saw me, but I heard you. Even I am surprised that you could gloat about such a thing."

"What the hell is going on?" Adrian hissed, echoing Joanna's thoughts. Tension radiated off him so clearly that Joanna sensed he was but a hair's breadth from striking both of their brothers.

William sucked in his breath. "Andrew. You really know?"

Andrew nodded slowly, a look of supreme satisfaction on his face.

"How? How?"

"Remember your friend the whore? The one you had following me? I know now she eventually succeeded in trailing me to what most consider an unsavory but I find highly enjoyable place. When I noticed her slithering behind me, I cut through a tavern and turned in the opposite direction. I happened upon you and heard you singing your tuneful little ditty. A drunken song of victory and murder." He smiled the most evil smile Joanna had ever seen. "Perhaps God will ease your punishment if you confess before Adrian beats the truth out of you," Andrew taunted. "You can see that he wants to."

William sank to the floor, clearly defeated. "I had no choice. It was her, or my fingers," he wailed, yanking off his black glove and waving his four-fingered hand. "Don't you see? They were going to cut off another if I didn't pay my debts. So when they asked me to kill the old lady in exchange for the money I owed, I did."

"You killed Lady Anne," Adrian said.

Joanna gasped. "And you let Adrian go to prison for your crime? You wanted him to."

William hung his head. Not from remorse, Joanna was sure, but because he'd been caught.

"Now I understand. With me in prison, you thought you could gain control of Joanna's workshop," Adrian said. "But you failed."

"Aye," William whispered. "One thing led to another. Each step along the way, I managed to convince myself I was doing what had to be done. Then there was no way out. Kill her or lose more fingers." He replaced his glove and looked at Adrian and Joanna, his gaze pleading for them to understand. "Have you never faced a difficult choice? What would you have done? I was trapped."

Her smooth-tongued brother sounded rather convincing. But her sympathy for him had vanished a long time ago.

Adrian grabbed a fistful of William's tunic and hauled him to his feet.

"As you will be for years to come. It's your turn to enjoy the Keeper's hospitality. You thought losing a finger was bad. Wait until you spend a night with the rats."

CHAPTER 24

lmost midnight. At last this endless day was over. Joanna dropped onto their bed, with Adrian right behind her.

Joanna kicked off her shoes, closed her burning eyes and flexed her sore feet. He took her hand. For a few moments, they remained silent in the dark, fingers entwined. She couldn't savor the fact that they were finally alone. Not until he'd bared all.

After the unspeakable scene at Andrew's house, she'd told Adrian she had to fulfill her obligation to the guild while Adrian handed William over to the sheriff. He'd apologized for his brother's actions, she'd apologized for hers. They'd not spoken of his "affliction." The timing hadn't been right.

She'd made her way to the pageant wagon, which had already begun its slow procession from Trinity Priory to Pavement, one of the market squares. She worked behind the scenes, ensuring that the actors were ready to make all of their entrances and hadn't forgotten any pieces of their elaborate costumes.

A few hours later, Adrian had poked his head behind the wagon's curtain to tell her William was in custody, and that he'd follow the wagon for the rest of the day. She was surprised he had the patience to watch the play again and again as the guild members performed it at each of the twelve stations. But then, given all that had happened, maybe he wanted to keep an eye on her. To make sure Andrew didn't pursue her, or that she didn't flee in fear of his secrets.

Now, though all she wanted to do was curl up in Adrian's arms and sleep, she gathered courage to ask him for the whole truth since he hadn't yet offered it. Their agreement be damned.

"Are you upset about William?" Adrian broke the silence.

"Not really. He brought this on himself. I am sad that my brother and yours could do so many awful things. That mine could even kill someone. And I didn't know how to help him."

"Gambling is a big part of it. It gets inside a person somehow, and makes them do things they wouldn't ordinarily do. Like a sickness. I learned that from my father."

"The only good thing to come out of this is that as a felon, William will be evicted from the guild. So he can't work as a glass painter. The studio is all mine by default, though I still plan to meet my father's requirements. I'll be glad when we can put this behind us," she said with a sigh.

"As will I. My brother had been acting strangely for some time, but I had no idea what he was up to." He slid closer to her. "An odd coincidence. Not only are both of our brothers misguided, their true natures were brought to light at the same time."

They fell silent again. The quiet became awkward, as if both realized the only subject left to discuss was one neither seemed to know how to broach.

Adrian's secret.

Joanna couldn't stand not knowing one minute longer. "Are you going to tell me?"

"No."

Her heart sank, though deep inside she'd known that would be his answer. Or he'd have initiated the conversation. Still, disappointment scorched her.

"I supported you, did all you requested while you were in prison. I prove my passion for you each night. Yet still you refuse to trust me with your past." *Or your heart.*

He squeezed her fingers, but the gesture didn't reassure her. They shared making love they shared these rooms. No point ever hoping for more. If he didn't trust her now, didn't think her worthy of knowing him, he never would.

She'd been a fool to believe otherwise.

She ached with misery. "I don't know if I can bear to live with you without knowing everything."

"You get what you want—your workshop—and of a sudden want to break our agreement?" Adrian sat up. "I'm sorry, Joanna. I didn't mean that. I know how difficult this must be for you, how Andrew's taunts must've heightened your curiosity. You must believe me. It's for your own good that I don't tell you. Can you do that?"

"I don't know, Adrian. I just don't know."

❧ ❧

Adrian heard Joanna undressing, then heard the ropes creak as she climbed back into bed. Instead of reaching for him as she usually did, Joanna turned away. He couldn't blame her, but he needed her touch. Not in a sexual way, but as comfort to his soul.

She breathed steadily, but he knew she wasn't asleep. The overwhelming relief he'd enjoyed all day after discovering Andrew's secret faded to nothingness in the face of Joanna's unhappiness.

At first, Adrian had thought he was free of the sword hanging over his head. By coming upon Andrew at that propitious but shocking moment, he'd eliminated the ever-present danger of his brother accusing him of sorcery or witchcraft. Andrew couldn't turn him in the authorities or call him heretic now. For what sheriff or church official would give credence to the words of a known sinner who fornicated with men?

But as the day went on, Adrian realized nothing had changed.

If he told, Joanna might believe him. She might even accept his "gift." Her understanding wouldn't change the dangerous position such knowledge could put her in if someone else saw him in the midst of a vision. Depending on the caprice of those in authority at the time, relatives and cohorts of the accused could also be taken into custody and punished. Her not knowing might be her only hope for freedom.

Even if it cost him the incredible closeness they'd shared since his return from prison. Just being with her would have to be enough.

But what would he do if she decided to leave him?

❧ ❧

The next day, Adrian and Joanna received a summons from the new king, Edward IV, to Baynard's Castle, the York family's London house by the Thames. No reason was given, so the preparations and the journey were fraught with unease. Adrian hadn't heard from Warwick and said he had no idea why the king had asked to see him.

Joanna chafed at yet more time away from her work when she was so close to obtaining her goal. But one couldn't say no to the king.

Margery, who didn't seem the least upset to be left behind to work with Thomas, begged Joanna to take notes of all she saw so she could share every detail.

Joanna barely spoke during the journey. There was only one topic she wanted to discuss, and he'd refused. What more was there to say? She'd have to find a way to endure the pain his silence sparked or find a way to live without him.

Far more nobles crowded the hall than when the king had visited York, and many more women. All were dressed in the most elaborate gowns and jewels Joanna had seen. Warwick's wife had loaned her a beautiful gown, so that instead of being out of fashion in Margery's finest, she felt like a queen herself in a high-waisted brocade gown with a collar and train trimmed in gold thread. She wore a tall headdress with embroidered edges and a sheer gauze veil, unlike her own rounder headdress with a folded fabric roll on the top.

She wanted to take in every detail as she'd promised Margery, but her thoughts were of Adrian. He too was resplendent in borrowed finery. Warwick had loaned him a long gown and a hat with a gold brooch.

Joanna noticed other women staring at him as if he were a sweetmeat. She didn't appreciate their interest in her husband. Though he might not be her husband for long. Even if she decided to stay, now that Adrian's need for an heir had lessened, her hold on him was fragile at best. He wouldn't disclose his secret, and she needed to know.

The king stood in the front of the assembly.

She'd thought Warwick imposing, but the king's grandeur exceeded his. Edward wore a flower-patterned black and gold tunic with wide velvet cuffs and a short black collar that stood up against his neck. Across his chest rested six strands of pearls, each with an oval gold pendant studded with a huge sapphire dangling from the center. A black felt hat with an angled brim partially covered his wide forehead. He had reddish-brown hair just past his chin and a long nose in a long face. Handsome, but with his narrow eyes and pinched lips, the new king looked calculating. As she supposed a king should.

Adrian rose from a deep bow.

"Sir Adrian Bedford, Knight of the Garter, your friend and mine the Earl of Warwick has eloquently pled your case," the king said. "He has told me of your contributions to my campaign and also what befell your father under Henry VI's reign. The irony is that by refusing to fight for Henry, your father indirectly aided me.

"I believe in recompense to those who are deserving, even as I work to unearth the rest of the Lancastrian rebels. I hereby grant you an official pardon. You may return to your ancestral home, Bedford Castle. It now belongs to you and your heirs."

He gestured to a clerk, who bowed as he handed Adrian a large piece of parchment with red wax seals dangling from the bottom.

Joanna's heart swelled with pride. Adrian's family name had been restored. His hard work had paid off. Now he'd move to Bedford Castle.

With or without her?

🙥 🙦

Absolute jubilation flowed through Adrian. If he hadn't been in the king's presence, he would've jumped for joy.

He'd done it. He had achieved his life's goal. He couldn't resist glancing at Joanna, who stood nearby with a group of women. Her face glowed with delight. His joy increased. Though he knew she remained upset with him for not telling her all, she'd set aside her anger and was happy for him. For them.

He went down on one knee at the king's feet and bowed his head. "Your Grace, I cannot thank you enough for your kindnesses to me and my family."

"You are most welcome, but I am not finished being kind yet."

Those close enough to hear the king's remark laughed.

"Rise, Lord Bedford, Baron of Haverly. For your past services to me and to secure your future aid, I ennoble you and restore you to the station of your birth. I also grant you additional lands. With the title comes three estates and their revenues."

Adrian couldn't believe his good fortune. "My most gracious thanks for your generosity, Your Grace."

"I wouldn't be on the throne if not for the assistance of men such as you," King Edward said. "And I won't remain here without your continued support. We shall meet again."

Never had Adrian been happier. He'd fulfilled his obligations to his mother and grandmother. Owing to the king's generosity, he'd be able to provide for Joanna and their children, as promised.

Adrian couldn't wait to transform Bedford Castle into their home. He'd purchase a big bed with the softest mattress and pillows he could find for Joanna's comfort. And garments that would enhance her beauty as did the gown she wore today. Now that he was a baron, he'd buy her jewels, too.

After bowing to the king, a group of well-wishers surrounded him. He barely heard their congratulations, for his thoughts were of Joanna and their strained relationship.

Since the eventful Corpus Christi day when she'd had the courage to ask him to reveal his secret and he'd refused to tell her, she'd spoken to him only when necessary. His lack of courage in the face of hers destroyed the closeness they'd shared. He'd faced enemies on the battlefield, where a stray crossbow could cost his life, but he couldn't summon the backbone to deal with his own wife.

Her indifference stung like a deep, open wound.

Once he'd thought he'd never need more than to restore his family name and return to his home. Now he had far more, but jubilant as he was, something was missing. He missed his wife. He wanted Joanna's friendship again, the happiness they'd enjoyed after his release from prison. He longed for Joanna more than he appreciated his new status.

His failure tarnished his success at court. How could he be so greedy as to want more from Joanna when he knew the circumstances keeping them apart were of his own making? Even with the bounty he'd received, he still couldn't tell his wife about his visions. If they were discovered, he could still end up back where he started.

Awash in treason. Or dead.

❧ ❧

After offering her congratulations, Joanna didn't say another word to him on their journey back to York. Because he wanted all traces of Lady Anne and her son's presence eradicated before moving to Bedford Castle, they'd returned to the rooms he'd once shared with Andrew. He couldn't wait to leave them behind and start their life anew in a home of their own making.

Joanna was folding some things she'd brought to London when he approached her.

"I plan to visit my new estates as soon as possible. But I can wait until the guild confirms that the workshop is yours. I hope you'll come with me so we can decide whether we want to live at Bedford Castle all the time."

She didn't look up. "It doesn't matter."

Only three words, but all she needed. He knew what she'd really said. Nothing except her work would matter to her until he disclosed the truth. He'd wanted an impersonal marriage of convenience and that's what he'd get.

He broached another topic. "Warwick and the king look forward to receiving the windows they want you to design for them."

"So they said." She bent to put something in the trunk.

This was sheer torture. But he deserved every minute of it. Even so, the loss of their closeness ate at him. He should've added a clause requiring that.

Though she still made love with him each night, their

coupling was mere sex now, and paled in comparison to the passion they'd shared. She didn't deny him, which would violate their agreement, but neither did she give of herself or even take from him. Sex seemed to be a mere item to check off on her list of daily tasks. Get up, break the fast, visit clients, paint windows, have supper, have sex.

Adrian felt worse than the night she'd awaited him spread-eagled on the bed. He sorely missed his wife.

"I must go to my shop." She left without looking at him.

He was alone. He rubbed his temples to alleviate a burgeoning headache. How could all he'd most wanted seem so unimportant now? Because Joanna barely spoke to him. Because she no longer shared any part of herself.

Which at this very moment was a good thing.

His head was a nail with a hammer pounding it. The fish he'd eaten threatened to leave his stomach.

Another vision.

Thank God Joanna had left. If he couldn't bring himself to tell her that he had visions, he certainly didn't want her to witness one. He dropped to the floor, strength draining from his muscles. Iced fog twisted around him, tentacles of smoky white clutching, drawing him under. He couldn't fight it.

A woman wearing a white gown strolled through the trees, red-gold hair shimmering in the moonlight. Joanna! His heart jumped into his throat. Her skin was translucent, her eyes vacant emeralds. She floated closer.

He held a large red flower in his hand. He wanted to give the blossom to her. Then he saw a sword protruding from her back. His sword.

He couldn't reach her. Red oozed down her white gown, making jagged stripes.

"No!" he cried. "No!"

Splash. Splash. Drops of blood fell to the ground.

"It is over," she murmured. "Over."

Joanna fell face first, her descent excruciatingly slow. She landed in a pile of colorful oak leaves, sending them into the air. The leaves floated down, burying her. Only the bloodied hilt of his sword remained.

He looked at his hand, which now held a crushed flower. The sticky remains stained his fingers brilliant red.

Adrian woke before he could see more, his heart pounding, his own cry resonating in his head. He'd never had a vision about Joanna before. What danger did his dream portend? If anything happened to her, he'd never forgive himself. How could he protect her without spending every minute by her side?

He sank back to the floor. He prayed his vision of her death wasn't literal, but represented some other peril. Maybe Andrew or John planned something. At least William was in prison. Maybe this was one of his rare figurative visions. His secrecy could represent the sword in her back and the flower her feelings for him. The vision might have revealed how he had killed their marriage and crushed her love by not telling her, no matter the ultimate cost to them both. So if he told her everything, would their marriage thrive? Or did the vision relate to the war between the Yorkists and Lancastrians?

He stayed flat on the floor, waiting for the room to stop spinning. Carefully he pushed himself to his feet. He wobbled a bit, then regained his balance.

Frustration. He could drown in it. How many times had he analyzed his visions, trying to discern their meaning before it was too late? And then spent more hours worrying, deciding if and how he could help. He slammed his fist into the wall, then swore at the pain.

He had to be calm, or he'd be of no use to anyone.

A sudden prickling at the back of his neck made him turn.

Joanna stood in the doorway, a look of horror on her face.

❧ ☙

"What a waste of time," Joanna muttered to herself as she hurried back to their quarters. How could she have forgotten to bring the vidimus she needed to show her new client?

She knew how. So focused was she on her disappointment in Adrian she'd left their rooms in a rush. At least Sir Darvon had been understanding and offered to wait while she returned to fetch it.

Though Adrian had encouraged the king and Warwick to order windows from her and had offered to commission windows for any of his estates to ensure that she earned enough to satisfy her father's wishes, she wanted to succeed on her own. She certainly didn't want to take much of anything from her husband right now. If she accepted Adrian's money for her windows, she'd feel as though he was purchasing her acceptance of his silence. Even though she didn't think that was his intent. Thus, she couldn't afford such carelessness as she exhibited today. Not when she was so close to proving herself.

But that's what came of letting thoughts of Adrian invade her working hours. Of loving him.

She was furious with him for refusing to trust her, but she couldn't stop caring. Not talking to him except when necessary, not succumbing to tempting desire probably caused her more grief than it did him. Love did make people into fools.

Gasping for breath, she opened the door.

"No, no!" Adrian shouted.

Joanna froze against the wall. He sounded scared. Panicked. She'd never heard fear in his voice before.

If he was in danger, could she help or would she make matters worse? She flew up the stairs and peeked into Adrian's room.

What she saw stopped her breath.

Adrian was alone, writhing on the floor. His face screwed up in agony, his hands opened and closed on nothing. She ached to help him, but feared if she moved closer that he'd strike her in the midst of his thrashing.

Was he having a nightmare? Some sort of fit?

"No!"

She clung to the door, unable to move. Should she run for the physician, or wait to see if she could help?

Of a sudden he lay still, quiet as death. His skin turned pale, a strange bluish hue. Only by staring could she see the slight rise and fall of his chest.

Sagging against the door in relief, she thanked God. The seizure, or whatever it was, hadn't killed him. She straightened, ready to go to him, but he climbed to his feet, his back to her. He stumbled away as though drunk, then righted himself. She watched as he punched the wall, sending plaster chips crackling to the floor. With his fist still in the dent he'd made, he turned to look at her.

She recoiled automatically, for he looked more like Andrew than himself. His eyes were icily vacant, yet glowed strangely.

Mystically. In the blink of an eye he returned to normal. She shook her head. What had she witnessed?

"Adrian, are you all right?"

He flexed his fingers, then rubbed his hand. "Yes," he rasped.

He walked to a chair and grabbed the back as if he needed its support to keep from falling.

Joanna poured him a cup of watered ale, watching him all the while out of the corner of her eye. He took the cup. Plaster dust whitened his knuckles. Silently he drank.

Never had there been such tension between them. The strain made the air heavy and thick.

Suddenly she understood. His seizure was part of his secret. He had epilepsy.

No wonder he was leery of discussing his sickness, his affliction, even with her. Most people believed epileptics were mentally ill, perhaps possessed by demons. Was he worried she'd pity him, or worse, fear him?

She had to ask. They couldn't go on as if nothing had happened. If he abandoned their marriage because she violated their agreement by broaching a personal subject, so be it. She had done her best to live by the tenets of their contract. But something snapped inside her, as though she were a piece of glass that could only sustain so much pressure before it cracked. As much as she needed Adrian for herself and for her work, she couldn't live under these constraints any longer.

Sudden panic gripped her. *Are you sure you want to know? What if he is mad, or possessed? Could you live with that? Yes,* she answered herself. Because she loved Adrian, she had to know. Because she loved him, she would accept him no matter his secret.

Now she knew. Acceptance was love's greatest power.

If he didn't tell her this minute, their marriage was over. No matter how much she loved him, no matter what cost she might pay, she'd reached the point where trust was paramount. She couldn't go back.

"Do you have epilepsy?"

"Epilepsy?" He gave a short bark of laughter. "No, not that."

Then what, she burned to ask. But she wouldn't tell him what was at stake if he refused to explain. She wouldn't demand it. The truth had to come of his free will.

Each beat of her heart marked the time he remained silent.

He drained the cup, then set it down. He walked to her, and took her hands. His were surprisingly cold.

Joanna held her breath. She prayed he would trust her at last. If he lied, would she be able to tell? The suspenseful silence tormented her. She wanted to say something, anything, to break the spell. But she gritted her teeth and waited.

Adrian swallowed. He cleared his throat.

"I wish I'd been brave enough to tell you on my own, instead of you having to find out this way. You may not believe me, but I'd finally decided I had to tell you. I just couldn't seem to choose a good time. Or, as painful as this is to admit, maybe I was afraid to.

"Only one person in the world knows what I am about to say. My brother Andrew." He looked at her, his eyes dark and unreadable. "I see the future."

Such a quiet, short admission after such a long wait.

"You see the future." She took a moment to absorb the words, almost understanding why he hadn't told her sooner. No one would freely admit to such a capability, because it was considered heresy, against the tenets of the Christian faith. "After all this time, after what Andrew had said, I'd feared something so much worse that this is almost a relief."

She reached out to embrace him. He pulled away.

"When we first married, you couldn't know you could trust me. I might think you a sorcerer as most people would," she said. "But what kept you from telling me after you got out of prison?"

"Plenty. What happened to my grandmother. What my father did to her and what has happened to others. What almost everyone else believes about those who claim to have the Sight. If I told you and you were like them, it would be too late for both of us. Either you'd want to accuse me to save yourself, or you'd be in danger if anything happened to me. As you are now. The authorities would torture you until you divulged what you knew. They'd make you talk against your will. I couldn't bear to have that happen to you." Adrian took her hands, his thumbs drawing gentle circles. Perhaps the soothing gesture helped ease the pain of his tale. "I believe having to confess that her mother had the Sight is part of what killed my mother. They forced her to betray her own mother's confidences. Then she had to watch her mother burn at the stake."

He let go of her hands and sank into the chair, as if releasing so much personal information had sapped his energy. Or as if doing so was an incredible relief.

"You're not appalled?" he asked. "Not going to flee in disgust?"

"No." Joanna sat on his lap to prove his secret wouldn't scare her away. She wanted to show him that the truth could make them stronger. He looked up at her with a tender smile as he put his arms around her waist.

"You are the way you are," Joanna said. "I can't imagine what it must be like to have such horrors haunting you. I do know that to live in fear is not to live at all. I'd rather enjoy whatever time we have, even if happens to be only a short while, trusting each other, than live a thousand years with secrets between us.

"Surely there aren't many cases of people being accused of witchcraft. You can't know that what happened to your grandmother will happen to you." She froze. "Or can you? Have you seen your future?"

※ ※

Adrian relished Joanna's nearness and the calm that flowed over him when she sat on his lap, as if cleansing his soul. Her familiar scent comforted him. Her support amazed him. "No. I've never had a vision about myself."

And only one about you.

"I want to know everything. What do you see? When? How? How often? Tell me," she said. "I want to understand."

He had no words to describe the relief he felt. His wife accepted him, flawed as he was.

"I can't control the visions, nor do I know when they'll come. I see a wide variety of things, but they all portend danger. Often what I see comes to pass, but not always exactly the same way. The hardest part is not being able to help those who'll soon face peril or death, because they'd wonder how I knew. I tried several times to pass on information but faced many questions and skepticism when I could offer no proof. On some occasions I managed to tweak the truth and so was able to help."

Joanna held him tight. "Most people are afraid of what they don't know and have no way to understand. They always will be. Andrew is loathsome for holding this over your head all of these years, for trying to control you. His 'secret' is worse than yours. Our brothers have betrayed us."

"Andrew felt it was his duty to tell the authorities," he said. "You're right, I lived in fear of what he might do. He could still be a threat. He's very convincing, and as he said it'd be his word against mine. Who can say what the authorities would believe? But I just can't turn him in."

"How did you know you could see the future?"

"Joanna…."

"Please. Tell me."

What difference would it make? Joanna might as well know everything. The secret was out. Revealing details couldn't make matters worse. She'd already seen him in the throes of a vision and hadn't fled in fear. She'd stood by him.

"When I was six, I started having detailed dreams. The first I remember was of a cat having six kittens, three mostly white and three mostly black. Shortly thereafter, the blacksmith's cat had six kittens, just like those in the dream. I had more dreams, or visions, that would come to pass."

"It must have been awful to know things but not be able to tell anyone."

Relief washed over him. How good he felt surprised him. Not only was he finally sharing his darkest secrets with Joanna, her feelings for him didn't seem to have changed for the worse. He saw no fear, no apprehension in her eyes. In fact, she seemed happier, more comfortable now that she knew.

"And after your grandmother's…death, there was no one else you could trust."

"Being different terrified me. But I refused to be weak and feeble like my grandmother. She had no money, no power with which to protect herself. I trained harder than the others to make myself strong I kept myself apart from other boys as much as possible, so they wouldn't learn my secret."

"Were you lonely?"

"Yes," he answered. With each confession he felt as if another brick was taken from the pile of his troubles. "But better to have no friends than to have them suspect me or think I was a lunatic. Or cursed."

"I don't believe in curses. If anything, you have a gift. Some people believe using herbs and medicines to cure the sick is witchcraft. But physicians want to help people, just as you would. I know you'd never use your visions to do harm."

"Not intentionally. One of the worst problems with some of my visions is not knowing whom to help. How do I know whether what I see is supposed to be changed or if that's what's supposed to happen?

"You need to know that if I'm accused now that I'm noble again, the punishment will be worse. Witchcraft is implied treason." He kissed her fingers, which made her smile. "That's another reason I wanted to spare you. I didn't want you to be accused along with me, and hoped your innocence would prevail. I still believe I'm putting you at risk."

He felt as though he could breathe freely for the first time in years. At last he had someone with whom to share all of his burdens. Even had he known how wonderful telling her would make him feel, he still would've kept quiet for her protection. Yet how could they have continued if she hadn't come upon him in the midst of a vision?

"You're right that at first I didn't tell you because I didn't know if I could trust you or if you would accept me as I am," he said. "But as we grew close, I realized you wouldn't fear something out of the ordinary. I know you'd never betray me. Yet telling you wasn't an option because of my concerns for your safety should the worst happen."

Would that risk, that fear ever go away?

"Will our children have visions?"

"I don't know. It seems to skip a generation. My mother was normal. And as you know, Andrew isn't afflicted. I'd hoped he'd be my heir so I could avoid dealing with this. But you see how he is. I've worked for years to undo my father's damage and couldn't let my efforts be for naught. Yet I could be subjecting our child to a lifetime of misery."

"Are you miserable?"

"No," he said, and meant it. "Not anymore. I have you."

She smiled again and ran her fingers through his hair. "We will love and care for our child however he or she is. We'll do our best to prepare him or her."

The determination in her voice soothed him. He'd worried about her safety before she knew the truth and he would worry now. But at least, and at last, there were no more secrets between them. He felt cleaner than he had after his post-prison bath.

"I love you, Adrian," she said.

CHAPTER 25

Joanna couldn't breathe. She'd been so caught up in the moment, her love for Adrian so strong, the confession had spilled out of her as though she were an overfilled pitcher. She'd wanted him to know her truth, as he had, however unwillingly, shared his. She wanted him to know that his seeing the future didn't change her feelings for him.

They'd been having a very personal conversation. But telling him of her love directly violated their agreement. She'd vowed to tear the thing up when he returned home, and now had done it figuratively.

What would he do? Surely he wouldn't have told her everything to abandon her now. Even if he did leave, she'd done the right thing. The agreement constrained her very existence, as though she were a window upon which the sun would never shine.

She felt naked. A chill coursed through her, making her skin prickle. As much as Adrian had revealed about himself, she'd gone farther. She'd opened her heart.

At what cost?

He hadn't moved. He looked as if the touch of a single finger would topple him off his chair. Silence stretched endlessly. His expression hadn't changed. No pity, no disgust flared in his eyes. But no welcoming warmth lingered there, either.

She jumped off of his lap and smoothed her skirts. She had to say something. "What I meant was, I love having you back at home. That's what I meant."

❧ ❧

Later that night, Adrian stood in the small yard behind the house, haunted by Joanna's confession. The air held a mixture of chill and warmth, spring trying to push aside the harshness of winter. No moon graced the sky. The stars hid behind drifting clouds gray against the blackness. The dark enveloped him, offering no distractions to sway him from his thoughts.

Joanna loved him. What a lout he was for not embracing her disclosure with grace at least, if not with matching warmth and enthusiasm. He'd been so stunned, so unresponsive, she'd tried to cover the astonishing news by saying how happy she was to have him back at home.

At home. That was how Adrian felt with Joanna. He'd never thought he could experience such comfort with another person.

Having Bedford Castle back thrilled him, but it no longer mattered if he lived there again. He just wanted to live with Joanna. To look forward to going home to her each day, to see her special smile, to hold her in his arms. That was what mattered.

His grandmother's last words all those years ago rushed back with stunning clarity. His blood ran cold as he heard her voice as clearly as if she stood next to him in the yard.

"Follow your heart."

His heart was Joanna. Wherever she was became his castle, even his drab little rooms.

How had his grandmother known? Had she seen so far into his future? Had she been trying to tell him, even then, that winning back Bedford Castle wasn't the important thing? At last, after years of trying to ferret out the meaning, he understood her message. The only way she could, she'd tried to tell him love was the answer. That only by truly loving someone could he forgive his past and live his own life instead of trying to salvage the remnants of his father's. Love was what made a person whole, not retribution.

Follow your heart. If he'd listened then, might he have saved himself years of heartache and struggle? Probably not, for he hadn't been ready to accept the truth. He would've scoffed, as certain he was too different to deserve love as he was convinced he was incapable of it. With her constant devotion even in the face of his strange behavior, Joanna had shown him another way. By trusting and accepting him as he was, though she knew he concealed so much from her.

By loving him.

Oh, God. Joanna loved him.

Understanding hit him like a punch to the gut. She wouldn't have dared tell him, for such a personal declaration would flout their agreement. He realized how she showed him, every day, with every smile and every touch. How he could've read it in her eyes, if only he'd looked. His trusting her with his most intimate disclosure must have convinced her she could trust him with her own. Or perhaps she'd reached her breaking point.

Because of his past, he hadn't wanted to think about what she felt for him, or what his constant thoughts of her meant. He'd never cared for or desired another woman as much as he did Joanna. He'd not known need could run so deep and true. His feelings for Joanna merged inside him just as her windows coalesced from colorful pieces into a unified composition.

He loved his wife.

Tears filled his eyes. He couldn't contain them. The last time he'd cried was nineteen years ago, when his grandmother burned. Yet the realization that he loved and was loved breached his fortified defenses.

He sank to his knees in the damp dirt and cried.

❧ ❧

"Lady Joanna, it is time to present the final tally of your earnings over the past year."

John Petty sat across from her at a long table in a meeting room at the Guildhall, his expression revealing nothing. Finally, the day she had been waiting for, the day she'd know for certain whether she had achieved her goal.

If she'd failed, what would happen to her workshop? William was in jail. No one she knew was capable of following in her footsteps, not even Thomas. She'd have to close her doors, and other glaziers would absorb her clients.

As she'd been at court for Adrian, so was he here for her now, seated beside her. She was glad he'd come, but wished they could be comfortable with each other again. He'd said nothing about her confession yesterday. Most unsettling. She didn't have the courage to raise the topic again.

"I am pleased to report that your tallies match mine. Your father's wishes have been met by a small margin. Congratulations." He handed her a document, but tears blurred her eyes so she couldn't read the words.

She'd done it. Though she'd felt a sense of accomplishment with each completed window, the satisfaction coursing through her now ran deeper.

Adrian opened his arms, and she received his hug. She wouldn't let anything spoil this moment. "Thank you, Master Petty, for keeping track of my revenues. I look forward to producing many more windows under the auspices of the guild."

As they walked out of the hall into the bright sunshine, Adrian said, "Now both of us have achieved our goals."

Joanna squinted, using her hand to block the sun as she looked at him. "Have we?"

When they arrived home, Adrian handed her a small silver box.

"Open it."

"Thank you. It's beautiful." Joanna put her papers on the table, then took the elaborately carved box. She stared at the raised, entwined flowers and leaves, knowing she'd have loved the box were it ugly and empty because it came from Adrian. This was his first gift to her and she wanted to savor the moment.

He shifted nervously from foot to foot, almost like an eager boy. A tentative smile tugged at his lips. "Well?"

The promise of what lay inside set her heart to racing. A wedding ring? Even a slim, plain band would do. She yearned for a symbol of their union.

Joanna raised the lid. The box contained torn pieces of parchment. The best gift of all. Adrian had shredded their agreement.

She burst into tears. No more rules, restrictions or secrets. Theirs would be a true marriage at last.

Sudden dread gripped her. What if his gift meant the opposite of what she most desired? What if he was setting her free, releasing her from their mutual obligations, instead of showing her that he cared for her?

Tears teetered on her eyelids as if uncertain whether they'd become tears of happiness or grief. She gripped the box so hard the metal foliage bit into her palms. Her throat went dry. She strained to swallow. "What does this mean?"

"It means I want to free us of the constraints we willingly agreed to. The contract was the right approach when we married. But things have changed."

Joanna clutched the box against her chest. What was he saying?

"I didn't think I'd come to care for you as I have, that I'd want to share myself with you. And that even more, I'd need you to care for me in return." He cleared his throat, then continued. "I never thought I deserved it. For who would love me as I am?

"You said you loved me. You covered your admission up admirably, and I know why. Because I said nothing in return. I'm so sorry, and want to make it up to you. As best I can, I want to make up for all the sorrow you've suffered because of me."

He dropped to one knee, and spread his arms. He looked like a chivalrous knight from a romantic tale sung by a troubadour, so handsome and sincere. "I am honored and amazed that you've stood by me, despite all I've put you through. That you could accept me knowing everything I am means more to me than you'll ever know." He took her hand. "I never thought I'd say these words, much less mean them. I love you, Joanna."

She dropped to her knees and threw herself into his arms, much as she had the day he returned from prison.

Adrian loved her. She'd never been happier.

He held her face in his hands as he said, "Being with you has shown me things about myself that at first I didn't want to accept. I thought I had to be without flaws to be loved. But I learned if you can give love, you are worthy of having it yourself.

"I spent so many years pursuing redemption for my family, restoring our family name and honor. Who can say what honor is? As many do, I once thought it was what others thought of you. How you fit into the world. Are you a noble or a peasant? I've learned if you can accept the things you can't change, you can live with honor.

"We shall keep this box always, to remind us of where we've been. From now on, I want us to be more than we thought we could be when we began. I want to be your lover and your friend. I want a true marriage. Do you?" he asked. "Tell me that you do."

Tears of relief and happiness spilled down her cheeks. "I do. With all my heart. I've wanted so to tell you how I felt, but between our agreement and not knowing whether you returned my feelings I—"

He smiled his incredible smile and bent toward her. "You showed me every day. It just took me a while to see."

Her heart filled with joy as he kissed her tenderly, then more deeply as desire took over. She felt the familiar tingling spread from her core.

How she loved him.

Moments later he broke the kiss, but held her close against the evidence of his passion. Despite the barrier of their clothes, her need awakened.

"This time we'll do things right. Margery and Thomas must attend, and we'll invite Warwick. And your clients and guild members, if you'd like." He fairly bubbled with enthusiasm.

"What are you talking about?"

He pulled her to her feet and swung her about in a circle. "I want to marry you all over again. In a true wedding, with feasting and dancing and merriment. I want to celebrate our love." He paused, a serious expression replacing his smile. His eyes glowed with the intensity that she loved. "Until that day arrives, I want you to know that I take you for my wife."

Joanna couldn't believe her ears. To many, just his speaking those words aloud, even without a priest or witnesses, created a valid marriage. He had just bound himself to her and pledged to do so yet again.

She'd only wanted to hear him say he loved her, but In true Adrian fashion he had taken her desires several steps further by taking action. The shredded agreement, his vow and plans for a second wedding showed her more than words alone ever could that he loved her.

"One thing more." Adrian reached into the purse on his belt and pulled out a gold band. He slid it onto her finger, then kissed it.

Only once before had she felt this complete: the first time they had made love. Her heart felt light, as if freed from chains. She could tell him now, without fear of recrimination or rejection. She'd say the words every day from this day forward, for herself and because he needed to hear them.

"I love you, Adrian. I take you as you are for my husband, now and forever. I will marry you all over again."

She sealed their vows with a lingering kiss. The desire she'd tamped down for weeks rushed back with full force.

"I have missed you," he said, trailing hot kisses down her neck.

"And I you," she answered. "We're so fortunate, to have so much."

"Yes," he whispered as he pulled her close. "We are fortunate, but have worked hard to get where we are. But there is still one thing we lack."

"That would be?" Maintaining coherent conversation grew increasingly difficult as his hands worked their magic on her. She wanted to stop talking and start kissing.

"Our heir," he said with a smile of delicious promise.

She returned his smile. "Ah, yes. I suggest we begin working on that right away."

And they did.

Epilogue

Joanna and Adrian stood under the vast, vaulted ceilings of York Minster. Multiple glorious stained glass windows attested to the creativity of glaziers over hundreds of years and to the generosity of their patrons. From the circular Rose Window to the elaborate grisaille of the Five Sisters lancet windows and the great west window with its heart-shaped tracery, Joanna never came here without feeling awe for the majesty and incredible beauty of the windows. Just as she knew she'd never stop appreciating the wonder of her life. She had so much to be thankful for, more than she ever dreamed.

"Which is your favorite?" Adrian asked.

Since the shredding of their agreement, he'd asked dozens of questions about her past and her interests, and she'd done the same. She enjoyed getting to know him as much as she enjoyed their physical closeness.

"The east window. It's the largest, but that isn't why I like it the most. Come this way," she said.

They walked hand in hand toward the pointed arched window. Each time she saw it, she was overcome by its width, height and complexity. "This window shows the history of the world from beginning to end. There are a hundred and forty-three saints, prophets and the like depicted. At the very top, it says '*Ego Sum Alpha et Omega*'. I am the Beginning and the End."

Adrian smiled at his wife. He'd been to the Minster dozens of times, but had never seen its true glory until he saw it through her eyes. Of course he'd admired the windows, but never really noticed their elaborate designs and myriad details until her enthusiasm made him appreciate their splendor. She'd opened his eyes to many things, and the companionship they shared made him love her all the more.

Here, in front of her favorite window, he had news to share.

"I have something to tell you," he said. "I wanted to be sure before I said anything. But I've suspected for few months."

"Suspected what?"

He looked around to make sure no one was close enough to hear. "I haven't had any more visions."

She looked at him in surprise. "Can visions simply go away?"

"Time will tell. The last one I had was just before I realized I loved you." That ghastly vision of Joanna with the sword in her back.

A shiver coursed through him, followed by an incredible sensation of serenity. He knew his grandmother was finally at peace. As he was.

And why his visions had stopped. Because he was in love.

Daylight streamed through the stained glass windows, bathing Joanna in multiple luminescent colors, reminding him of the first time he'd seen her. Lately, she looked even more like a Madonna from a painting than she had then. Every day, he thanked God for giving her to him.

She rested her hands on her rounded abdomen, as he'd noticed her doing often in recent weeks. Her eyes widened, and she drew in a long breath.

"Here," she said, taking his hand and placing it where hers had been.

Adrian felt their baby kick. He knew that a silly, proud smile lit his face as their child moved inside his wife, beneath his fingers.

He didn't know why he was so blessed, so fortunate. He had Joanna, his new estates, and would soon have the heir he so desired. If their child had the Sight, they'd find a way to make his or her life far easier than his had been. And he'd know what to tell him or her to make the visions stop.

He would tell his child, "Follow your heart."

Author's Note

Dear Reader,

Thank you for reading *Follow Your Heart*. I hope you enjoyed sharing Joanna's and Adrian's journey as much as I did writing it. I loved researching details about 15th century England glazenwrights, their studios and their designs. The Internet is an amazing resource, but many historical details I needed can only be found in books. Maybe Joanna's half-sister Margery needs her story told?

I did my best to be as historically accurate as possible and to reflect the views of people living in 15th century England, whether or not those views are shared today. Even in modern times, some people have difficulty accepting and/or respecting those with beliefs different from theirs.

I'd appreciate feedback on what you liked and even what you didn't. You can contact me at ruth@ruthkaufman.com and learn more about me and my writing at www.ruthkaufman.com. To learn about future books and important news, please sign up for my newsletter on my home page at www.ruthkaufman.com. If you'd like to follow me, I'm on Facebook at Ruth Kaufman Author & Actress and Twitter: @RuthKaufman.

If you're so inclined, I'd appreciate a review of *Follow Your Heart*. My Amazon author page is www.amazon.com/author/ruthkaufman. My Goodreads page is www.goodreads.com/ruth_kaufman.

ABOUT THE AUTHOR

Ruth Kaufman is a Chicago author, on-camera and voiceover talent and freelance editor and speaker with a J.D. and a Master's in Radio/TV. She loves peanut butter and chocolate milkshakes, singing in a symphony chorus and going to the theatre.

Writing accolades include Romance Writers of America® 2011 Golden Heart® winner and runner up in *RT Book* Reviews' national American Title II contest.

She's appeared in indie features, short films, web series and national and local TV commercials, and has voiced hundreds of explainer videos, e-learning courses, commercials and assorted characters.

Learn more about her at www.ruthkaufman.com and www.ruthtalks.com. Follow her on Twitter: @RuthKaufman or Facebook: Ruth Kaufman Author & Actress.